A STORM OF WRATH & RUIN

A STORM OF WRATH & RUIN

DAUGHTER OF ERABEL ~ BOOK THREE

KRISTIN WARD

ALSO BY KRISTIN WARD

Daughter of Erabel Series

The Girl of Dorcha Wood

Blood of the Lost Kingdom

A Storm of Wrath & Ruin

Legion of Shadows

Young Adult Dystopian Series

After the Green Withered

Burden of Truth

Young Adult Fantasy

Rise of Gaia

A Storm of Wrath & Ruin
Daughter of Erabel Series, Book 3
By Kristin Ward

Copyright © 2022 Kristin Ward

All rights reserved. No part of this book may be reproduced in any form or by any electronic or mechanical means, including information storage and retrieval systems, without written permission from the author.

Editing by David Taylor
Cover by JD, JDCoverDesigns

ISBN 978-1-7327923-7-1

Characters and events in this book are fictitious. Any similarity to persons, living or dead, is coincidental and not intended by the author.

Visit https://www.kristinwardauthor.com/

To the warrior in each of us.

PROLOGUE

*H*undreds of years ago, humanity worshipped Crom Cruach on bended knee. Fear and blood were their offerings, tears and screams their prayers. They sought to quell his appetite and protect their lands. But time and hardship eroded their devotion. They revolted, drove him out, destroyed his idols until he was nothing more than a relic.

An old god.

Consigned to the past.

Forgotten.

But some things should not be.

CHAPTER ONE

Fiadh wandered through the charred remains of Dorcha Wood. Ash floated through the air, stirred by her passing and the beating of Dasha's wings. So much needless destruction. So much pain. And for what?

Her eyes tracked the path the fire had taken. Moving from the scorched trees to the bodies of those animals who could not escape the flames or the arrows that had felled them. It was eerily quiet. Still. Lifeless. But Fiadh knew that beneath the ravaged soil, the heart of Dorcha Wood continued to beat. Bending down, she brushed away layers of soot from a sapling and pressed her fingers against its small trunk. Closing her eyes, she felt the fragile life within it, felt its struggle to survive. Whispering healing words, she imbued what would one day be a massive oak with energy. The scorched branches twitched, and tiny buds appeared along the limbs. A promise of growth. Life. Future.

Sitting back on her heels, she listened to the soft thump

of approaching footfalls. "You're angry with me, aren't you?"

Krulan stalked from a line of trees that had escaped the flames and grumbled. *Frustration is my keenest emotion. You are young and inexperienced.*

That may be true, but that doesn't mean I don't know my mind. No more fighting, Krulan. No more death.

He growled, teeth flashing in his muzzle. *Look around you, Fiadh. This is what man does!*

She gazed at the ruined landscape.

War is coming. We must choose when and where it is fought! he huffed. *If we do not, mankind surely will.*

I'm sorry, Krulan. I know I've disappointed you, but if you've come to change my mind, you're wasting your time.

Veren stepped from the shadows just then, white-blond hair shifting in the breeze as his violet gaze snagged hers. She met his stare and raised her chin. "You too?" She glanced at Krulan, who looked away. Shaking her head, she said, "I don't want to talk about it, Veren."

He stood watching her. "You can't run from it."

"I'm not running."

"Fiadh, we have to press our advantage." He came toward her, his sinewy body hardly making a sound. "The enemy is weak. They're scared. We must strike at their weakness and attack."

She rose and faced him. "Attack?"

"Aye."

Glaring at him, she said, "I think you mean kill."

His eyes grew hard. "Are you blind? Don't you see what

men have done? *They* killed! If we let them gather in strength and number, they'll return and finish us!"

Listen to him, Krulan said. *He knows of what he speaks.*

He doesn't know everything.

Fiadh cut her eyes to them and stalked away, stopping when the toe of her boot bumped into something soft. She looked down. All that was left was a mass of charred fur, layered in so much ash it was almost unrecognizable. Her gaze swept the landscape, blurring as she took in dozens of small mounds that dotted the ruined border of the forest.

Surveying the remains, she asked, "Hasn't there been enough killing?"

"Fiadh," Veren said, coming to her side. "You speak as though peace between our peoples is within your grasp. That you could forge such a thing by your will alone. But that is nothing more than a dream. And we can't live in dreams. We have to fight for the world we want. Not sit back and wait."

Her mouth turned down. "Why are you here, Veren?"

"What?"

"If what you seek is war with mankind," she said, craning her neck to look up at him, "why not stay with Rygeil? He would give you all the killing you want."

He recoiled and pressed his lips into a thin line.

She moved away from him, feet digging ruts in the thick ash. Dasha soared overhead, and Fiadh held out her arm, holding herself rigid under the weight of the raven as he landed. Stroking his feathers, she considered Veren's perspective. It was true that they couldn't afford to stand idly by and wait for Darragh to attack again. To burn the forest and all who called it home. She couldn't let that happen. But, seeing so much death ate at her.

Fiadh scanned the ruined landscape, chest tightening. Weakness, much like she had felt when traveling with Gideon, made her head feel fuzzy, detached. Dorcha Wood was in pain, writhing beneath the blackened dirt. She knew that retaliating, causing more suffering by attacking the people of Felmore, was wrong. It was not who she was.

Yet, all around, others were telling her how to lead. Everybody seemed to know what she should do. What she needed to do. Everybody, except her. But she didn't want to be a puppet leading vengeful armies just because Krulan or Veren or Kaelari told her she should. Danu chose her for a reason. She couldn't believe that reason was simply to be another Rygeil, fighting and battling and slaying mankind. She remembered Gideon saying something once about men praying to the Great Mother, too … praying to Danu. Mankind were Danu's children. Or they had been. They may have strayed from her, but so too had the elves—Rygeil and his hordes. Leading great armies to slay Danu's wayward children, hundreds of them, thousands. It couldn't be what the goddess wanted of her. It just couldn't be.

Pressing her lips to Dasha's beak, she whispered and launched him into the sky, where he sailed through the air against the low clouds. She watched him for a few moments, then looked at Veren. "By your logic, you're saying that Danu would wish for us to go to war. To kill for the sake of killing."

Veren muttered and paced. "It is not killing for the

killing's sake when we fight to defend our home and way of life! The Great Mother understands this."

"Does she?" Fiadh cocked her brow. "I feel her beneath my feet. In the air. Within every life-form in these woods. She suffers as we suffer. But nowhere in those feelings is a desire to harm. To take life."

"You're right."

Her mouth parted in surprise.

"But," he said, holding up a hand, "that doesn't mean she wishes for us to hide and wait for mankind to attack. And they will. I will not allow you to lead us like lambs to slaughter!"

Fiadh scowled.

"She gave you gifts, Fiadh. Powers beyond any I have seen." He stepped toward her and took her hands. "Do you think these were given lightly? Do you truly believe the Great Mother endowed you with these gifts if she didn't expect you to use them to fight for your people?"

She made a face and held her ground.

"Fiadh, we can't wait for Darragh's forces to return. You must stand with me, with all of those who came to Erabel. Together, we could breach their walls and finish this. A few may die, it's true. But they will die so others can live. You have to fight." His eyes pleaded with hers as he gripped her hands. "You have to."

"I will not wage war on mankind!"

He dropped his arms. "Then, you've doomed us."

"I don't believe that," she argued. "You and Kaelari see things only in terms of battle and steel, but you miss so much."

Veren mumbled and turned his back on her.

She pressed her palm between his shoulders, feeling his anger, fear, sorrow, and something else. Something he tried to hide from her. Though she was tempted to delve into his thoughts, she dropped her hand and walked around his rigid form to face him. "Do you think I won't protect my home? Do you believe I would stand aside and watch it all burn?"

"Nay," he said, hanging his head. "But you would let the enemy grow stronger, putting us all in danger."

"There is another way. There must be."

He shook his head and rubbed the back of his neck. "This is about him, isn't it?"

Her eyes narrowed.

"That's why you won't march on Darragh's keep. Why you wouldn't kill him after he slew one of your people." His throat bobbed. "You still love this Gideon of Belfirth and would risk our future for his sake."

"You're wrong."

He rested his hands on his hips. "Am I?"

Krulan growled.

She turned to the Cù-Sìth, seeing a flash of wickedly sharp teeth. *I'm sorry I had to use my power to stop you, Krulan. There was no other way. I… I couldn't let you kill him. I couldn't.*

You are too soft for this world.

You mistake mercy for weakness, she told him, but inside, where he couldn't hear, she doubted herself, wondering if she really were weak.

Veren's body was rigid when she looked back at him. She raised her hand, wanting to soothe him, then dropped it. "This isn't about Gideon, though I understand you find that difficult to believe." Fiadh turned away and paced in a small circle, shoulders sagging when she stopped before him. "I… I had to let him go. To kill him would kill a part of myself."

Veren mashed his lips together as a flash of pain marred his face. "What has he done to earn your love? He would've killed you like he did Tainsi! And you let him go!"

"Veren, please," she begged.

A wounded look crawled across his face before he masked it. "How can you love him after all he's done?"

"I told you I don't."

Veren scoffed. "You may tell yourself that, but your actions speak otherwise."

"It's not love. I don't know what it is." She shrugged. "In the end, it doesn't matter. I won't kill him. I won't become something I'm not."

He sighed. "If you refuse to raise arms against him and those he aligns with, then what is the path you would take? What would you have your people do?"

"Prepare for what's coming."

"By waiting?" He flung his arms out with an exasperated sound. "You expect us to watch a horde descend upon our home and do nothing?"

"Have you so little faith in me? So little trust in the Great Mother?"

He looked away sullenly.

"Veren, I have no intention of surrendering to our enemies. I will train, and we will protect our home from Darragh's forces when they return." She reached for him and paused, fingers curling. "But, I will not seek a fight. I will not wage war. Let them come, and we will see who is stronger."

"It's a mistake, but you leave me no choice. I cannot force you." He sighed. "I will abide by your wishes."

"Thank you. I know it's not what you want or what you feel is right, but I need to walk this path." Her face grew soft, and she added, "It means a great deal to me that you will be at my side."

His lips curved in a crooked smile. "Always."

Fiadh gave his hand a squeeze and, with Krulan at her side, continued to walk through the wounded forest while skirting the edge that led to the open killing grounds where the corpses of Darragh's men lay where they had fallen. She healed the trees and animals she could, and eased the passing of those who were beyond her aid. By the time the sun had reached its zenith, her back ached, and she felt drained.

Krulan tugged on the sleeve of her tunic. *I sense others coming. We must go.*

Fiadh whipped her head around, the action mirrored by Veren who had also felt it. She looked at him with wide eyes and shook her head as he reached for his sword. "Don't even think it."

His mouth pulled down, but he jerked his head in a curt nod.

Krulan knelt, and Fiadh climbed onto his back. Together, with Veren running at their side, they made their way back to the protection of Erabel. But all the while, she kept looking behind her, wondering if Gideon was there, if he'd returned, and what it would mean if he had.

CHAPTER TWO

Gideon stood in the meadow at the edge of the charred forest and looked at the carnage. The bodies of Lord Darragh's men lay where they had fallen, limbs contorted, faces masks of terror and pain. He had seen it many times before and knew he would see it again. The thought was a stone on his chest. He absently rubbed his torso to ease the heaviness, but it did not dull the ache. The weight of it was rooted too deep.

So much blood, so much death. The elves, and their monsters, had wreaked havoc on Darragh's soldiers. He had little doubt that soon enough they would sally out of their forest and attempt to lay waste to Felmore, slaughtering men, women, and children, just as they had done in the east and, if the rumors were true, in the north as well. The fiends had to be stopped, their power somehow broken before it was too late.

From the corner of his eye, he watched as townsfolk and

soldiers collected the dead, piling their ruined bodies into carts. He ignored them and came to the spot where Fiadh had materialized during the battle, staring at the ground where she had stood, her face a mask of shock and horror as he'd ripped his sword from the body of her comrade. He didn't think he'd ever forget that look. Reaching for his neck, he touched his throat, feeling the small puncture wounds from her elven beast's teeth. As his fingers ran along the raised lumps, his mind conjured images of that monster attacking the men who'd fought with him. They had been woefully unprepared, their fear of the bear-sized Cù-Sìth overriding years of training until they stood helpless. He must train them better. They needed discipline and stronger shields.

But, in those bloody moments, Fiadh had stopped the animal before it could tear his throat out as it had done to the others. It was the second time she had saved his life, and that knowledge made him uneasy, torn. Did she truly mean him no harm? Had she really felt something for him? Or was it all part of some evil plan, some attempt to manipulate him, cause him to hesitate at some vital moment to come? Elven witches were known for their treachery, beautiful enchantresses deceiving and manipulating men, from the common soldier to great lords and kings. Their trickery was a thing of legend. It was said that during the Great War, they walked among mankind, seducing and luring men to their doom, enthralling them until they were little more than puppets dancing on their strings.

She was one of them. Her accursed people had slaughtered his. He should feel rage, not this jumble of emotions that ran from hate to longing. The spirits of his family called to him, demanding vengeance.

But when it was done, what then?

Casting his eyes to the north, he thought of the Scarlet Mountains and the life he could carve out in those jagged peaks with Aishling, far away from war. He had written her often, hoping to one day receive a missive in reply. Was she content with her new life? Did she think of him? Bringing her face to mind, he shut his lids and let the innocence of her shy smile bleed into his thoughts, overriding the horror of what he'd see when he opened them again. But her image blurred, overlaid by the faces of his murdered family.

With a sigh, he let thoughts of her go and looked around. This was reality, not the far-off mountains of the north. Craning his neck, he stared back at the body of one of the soldiers the elven female had killed before he'd stopped her. He did not recall the man's name, but his youth was evident in the frozen grimace on his face. Gideon bent and grabbed hold of the soldier's stiff legs, dragging his body to a waiting cart. Too young. Unskilled and not ready for battle. But the enemy cared nothing for age and lack of experience. They would kill. They had always killed. It was their nature, and he was foolish to think one of their kind could ever truly be his future. His love.

Nay. He would not leave on the eve of battle. It would be cowardice to allow the soft looks of the enemy to sway his true purpose. Fiadh had chosen her side. He had, too.

Glancing into Dorcha Wood, he sucked air into his

lungs, hardening himself against what had made him weak. Dredging up the worst of the memories of his slain family, he turned his head and spat on the ground, watching the spittle settle into the scorched earth. Smiling grimly, Gideon closed his eyes and breathed new life into his hatred. Images of Fiadh grew distorted as anger flooded his mind. She became cruel and ugly as his thoughts were pummeled with wrathful righteousness. The burden pressing into his chest diminished as though it flew from his body, feeding off his anger and leaving him unshackled. He opened his eyes and stared balefully at the scarred tree line.

Striding forward, he pulled his sword from its sheath and entered the wood, ignoring the gasps and calls to retreat from the soldiers and villagers, who looked on with shock. He felt the moment the forest stirred, heard the creak of the trees and the rustle of branches. But it was weak, its efforts to dispel him from its borders useless in the face of the vicious swings of his blade. Gideon hacked at limbs, smiling grimly as sap oozed from the severed branches of oak and hazel, pine and ash. Grunts of exertion filled the muted landscape as he tore through the underbrush and entered a part of the forest that had escaped the flames. Bending over, he dropped his sword and gripped his knees, taking huge pulls of air.

"Tell her I'm coming," he muttered, then rose to his full height. "I know you hear me! Tell her. Tell her war is coming, and I will lead it!"

His roar hung in the air for a moment. Cocking his head, he listened. Wind whipped through the trees as they bent and groaned. Spinning in a slow circle, he held out his arms in challenge. "Is that it? Your blood magic is weak! I do not fear you! I will burn every tree in this wood until she comes out of hiding and faces me. Do you hear me?"

From a branch high in the bows of an oak came a loud caw. Gideon tracked the sound and spied a crow who launched itself into the sky, a black mass of wings and shrill cries of warning. He sneered. "Aye, go to your mistress, foul thing. She will learn that I am coming for her and all who stand with her."

Gideon stalked from Dorcha Wood, brushing aside those who ran to him, peppering him with questions about what he saw in that wretched forest. Whistling to Aridius, he marched into the open field and swung his body into the saddle, nudging his mount into a full gallop. The clatter of hooves filled the bailey as he pulled on the reins, bringing the horse to a halt before hopping to the ground. The stable boy jogged over, and Gideon headed into the keep.

Darragh sat at the high table, surrounded by platters of food. Pulling a greasy glob of meat from his mouth, he wiped his sleeve across his face and looked at Gideon, his uneaten food dropping onto his trencher with a splat. "The heir of Belfirth returns!"

Gideon bowed. "My lord."

Looking around, Darragh cocked an eye. "And, yet, I still see no Aos Sí witch in chains at your side."

"She hasn't shown herself since the battle."

Tsking, Darragh leaned back and folded his hands on his stomach. "Don't you mean since you let her escape?"

Someone must have seen the skirmish and witnessed him walking away from Fiadh, Gideon realized. Lifting his chin, he said coldly, "I give no quarter to elven scum."

"Hm. And, yet, I have heard otherwise."

"You were misinformed."

"Do you suggest my men would lie to me?" Darragh asked dangerously.

"I suggest they did not clearly see events unfold. None of your soldiers still lived when I was attacked and fended off the enemy."

Shrugging, Darragh picked a piece of lint off his tunic. "I will let it go. It is enough to know the witch hides in the depths of Dorcha Wood. She was lured from its safety once, and I have no doubt she will be again."

"Agreed. She has an affinity for the forest and the animals that dwell there."

A sly smile lifted Darragh's mouth. "She cares for the wild things, you say?"

Gideon nodded.

"Perhaps we can lure one of her creatures as bait."

"My lord?"

"I shall arrange a hunting party." Resuming his meal, he stuffed a hunk of bread in his mouth and chewed slowly, watching Gideon's every movement. Pocketing the food in his cheek, he said, "You will lead them."

Gideon stiffened and schooled his features before bowing and leaving the hall. It should matter little what beasts of the forest he killed, but part of him cringed as the image of Fiadh's animal companions filled his mind. He shook his head, angry at the wave of pity he felt for anything of hers. She would surely come to their aid if she knew his actions. It was a good plan. If he were lucky, a few of her elven beasts would fall under his sword before he captured her.

CHAPTER THREE

Tainsi's body was laid upon the ground just after dawn. She was shrouded in white linen decorated with delicate patterns of blue and green. Hidden under the layer of fabric was the mortal wound Gideon had inflected. The moment of her death was branded in Fiadh's mind. The startled yelp. The mask of pain. Her body falling to the ground, and then, the face of the one who had slain her.

She could feel the weight of stares at her back from those gathered. Did they blame her for not taking Gideon's life? Krulan shifted at her side, his massive body brushing against hers. Fiadh didn't need to wonder about his anger. It was a living thing—present in his every thought.

Kaelari's voice mixed with Veren's, filling the quiet with soft chanting. They spoke to the earth, and it trembled in response, releasing minerals and rock that wove around Tainsi, embracing her body. Flicking her eyes to the side, Fiadh glanced at Threa's tomb tucked next to her beloved Aeson. Hatred and greed had taken so many lives.

"Mother," she whispered, and was met with a gentle breeze. Dark wisps of hair blew around her face, and she closed her eyes, imagining she could hear Threa's voice in the wind.

Taking a deep breath, she stepped toward Tainsi's burial mound and laid her hand upon the stone. Fiadh muttered a prayer to Danu for the female she had barely known. The goddess whispered back to her as she often did now. Palpable sadness cast a pall on the gathering as the ground settled and the chanting drifted to silence. Though only one of thirty who had come to Erabel had been slain when Darragh's soldiers attacked Dorcha Wood, one felt like too many. The rustle of bodies separating and moving away indicated the end of the ceremony. There was no talking, only pained quiet as each of them faced the reality of what had occurred and what was to come. Even the pack of Cù-Sìth slipped back into the trees like wraiths, their greenish fur blending so completely they became one with the forest.

Dorcha Wood would heal. As she had seen and felt, new life stirred underground, and it would rise from the ashes like a phoenix. But the attack would not be the last. In many ways, it felt like a test.

Fiadh found a quiet spot and sat down mutely, her hand absently stroking Dasha as he perched on her knee. Looking into the trees, she wondered what had become of Gideon. Had he returned to Lord Darragh? And what had he said as he'd walked away? His words, like so many things, had been carried on the wind and… lost.

Meara, Veren's mount when he had arrived in Erabel, appeared from beneath the thick boughs of a tree, separating herself from the shadows like a wraith, the tip of her horn glowing in a shaft of light that struck it as she drifted toward her. She was one of a handful of unicorns who remained with the elves, most having fled to hidden breeding grounds following the Great War when their numbers had been decimated. Fiadh watched her come, marveling at the strength that emanated from the unicorn with each step. She had become a frequent visitor of late. Veren would say it was because she was bored, but Fiadh felt it was more than that. Maybe the unicorn sensed something coming. When Meara stood a few paces away, she folded her front legs, groaning as her body sank to the ground. Scooting toward her, Fiadh ran her hands along the base of Meara's horn and around her ears, lips curling in a smile as she watched the unicorn's eyes flutter closed. Dasha marched over, grumbling.

"You already had your scratches, greedy rascal," Fiadh scolded when the raven pecked her leg.

Low sounds of talking caught her attention, and she looked over to see Veren and Kaelari in deep discussion, heads bent toward each other. It didn't take any stretch of the imagination to guess what they were discussing. Fiadh studied Veren's face. Beneath the beauty of his features was a hardened warrior with firm resolve. She had no doubt the next time he crossed Gideon's path, the man would die. She hoped that day would never come but feared Veren would seek it out. For a moment, she wondered what he must have been like before war made him into what she saw now.

Her name floated in the air, and she cocked her head to better hear their words.

"She doesn't wish to fight," Veren told Kaelari.

"Then she must be made to," she snapped.

Rising slowly, Fiadh balled her hands into fists and walked toward them. Meara rose to her feet as well, shaking off dirt and tossing her head before following a few paces behind like a dark shadow.

"I am not your pawn!" she yelled at Kaelari. "Nor am I a child that you can order about!"

Kaelari's eyes sparked with anger. "You are acting like a child when you refuse to do what you must to keep your people safe!"

"Kaelari—" Fiadh started, then pinched the bridge of her nose and muttered, finally looking up to meet her hard stare. "You see things from a warrior's eyes, and I respect your experience and skill. But I won't wage war on man. I won't attack Darragh's holding and slaughter his soldiers."

Flinging an arm in the direction of Felmore, Kaelari shouted, "Right now, they're planning their next move! Every moment you give them to recoup and rethink their strategy is a risk. They'll return! And with greater numbers!" She paced away, then spun on her heel. "What will you do when Rygeil attacks? And he will if he continues to see his soldiers leave his ranks to join yours. Should we lay down your arms and let him kill us all?"

"Of course, no—"

"Do you think it's only those who stand with you who mark the moves you make for our people? The elf lords know of you now. They watch and wait. Oh, they offer fealty to Rygeil, but your grandfather is not well-loved. He has made enemies. If you show strength, show you are worthy of their loyalty, they will come over to you—as we have done. But if you do nothing. If you do not respond to this attack, all will believe you a weakling. A child. None will change allegiance from a strong king who promises victory to a naive girl who refuses to fight for her people." Kaelari paced. "Rygeil is no fool. He may be reluctant to attack now, fearing his soldiers may not follow him, maybe even rebel if he orders them against one of their own. But give him an opportunity, show such a sign of weakness, and he will not hesitate to exploit it." She paused and pinned Fiadh under her stare. "And there would be none to raise their blades in defense of one who will not raise her blade for them."

Fiadh flinched.

"We… *I* am ready to die for you, Fiadh! I believe in you that much, but you must see the world as it is, not as you wish it to be. Beyond our borders, it is unforgiving. And we must be too if there is any hope of a future."

Fiadh clenched her jaw and made a frustrated noise. "You are asking me to build a future on a foundation of blood, Kaelari. What kind of future is that? How can we live side-by-side with people we've needlessly killed?"

She looked coldly at Fiadh. "It's not needless when we're fighting for our place in this world. A place, I might add, that had been stolen from us by the very people you refuse to fight."

"I did not say I'd refuse to fight them. Should Darragh's army attack Dorcha Wood again, I will fight to protect it."

Kaelari raised her chin. "Will you?"

"Aye," she said. "But that doesn't mean I will march on

his people. I will not wage open war. If his soldiers threaten our home again, I will stand with you and fight."

Mashing her lips together in an unhappy but resigned frown, Kaelari nodded curtly. "I will hold you to it."

Fiadh gave her a weak smile and reached up to stroke Meara's muzzle, which now hung next to her head. Veren said something too softly for her to hear, and Kaelari walked away, finding her place among a small group of those who'd gathered along a stone wall.

"It's hard for her," Veren said. "She has the heart and mind of a soldier. As do I."

"Sometimes I wish I had that too," Fiadh said quietly. "It would make all of this simpler."

Meara nudged her shoulder, nearly knocking her over and eliciting a startled laugh. The sound cut through the tension that hung in the air. Butting her playfully, Meara forced Fiadh to let go of her angst, and she nuzzled the unicorn, giggling when Dasha let loose a string of complaints at having been left out.

"She has chosen her mistress," Veren said, looking wistfully at Meara.

Fiadh stroked the unicorn. "Has she?"

"Aye, she told me as much. It is a good thing. She's seen many battles and will keep you safe."

"I didn't mean to take her from you," Fiadh said, feeling guilty.

Veren shook his head and chuckled. "Meara has a mind of her own, and I think she waited many years for you, as we all have. She was always yours."

The unicorn bobbed her head, the translucent tip of her

horn flashing in the sunlight. "I hope I can live up to her expectations."

"You will."

"But not up to yours," she muttered.

He gave a crooked smile. "You've already surpassed mine. All that matters is I live up to yours. Let's get away for a spell," he said, jerking his head toward the unicorn.

She nodded and reached for Maera's mane, bending low and jumping so she could hop onto her back. Veren gave her a boost as her leg hung awkwardly, then vaulted up behind her, wrapping his arms about her waist. She felt his chest against her back, the thrum of his heart and the warmth of his body. Pressing into him, she tapped her heels into Meara's sides and let the unicorn go where she wished. As they made their way through the forest, Veren chatted softly in her ear, telling her interesting tidbits about the many species that lived within Erabel. He interspersed each telling with stories from his childhood. It reminded her of the tales Gideon had told, and she took comfort in the similarities between such different people.

An hour later, Veren swung off Meara's back and lifted his arms to help Fiadh down. Her body slid down his and hung suspended against his chest for a moment, the tips of her toes barely touching the ground. Her heart beat wildly, and she took a breath as she met his eyes. Clenching his jaw, he released her and stepped away. She felt flustered and busied herself rubbing Meara with a handful of dried grasses. Giving the unicorn a pat to send her on her way, Fiadh strolled through the trees, touching leaves and branches, feeling the Great Mother.

A powerful current snagged her attention, and she walked toward its source, stopping when she reached the barrier surrounding Erabel. Fiadh considered it, tilting her head to catch the light, allowing her to see the subtle shimmer of energy that coursed through it.

Flicking her gaze to Dorcha Wood beyond and back to Erabel's barrier, she asked, "Is there a way to create a barrier large enough to encompass all of Dorcha Wood?"

Veren stepped forward and ran his hand over the nearly imperceptible filmy substance. His brow furrowed as though he hadn't considered the possibility before. "It would require power far greater than yours or mine to extend it beyond our border. It was created centuries ago to protect Erabel and the creatures who call this place home. Beyond it lies the realm of men, though Dorcha Wood still holds power and magic of her own."

She frowned, recalling the memories Danu had shown her when Carmun attacked Erabel. The terror and anguish as those protections failed, Fiadh craned her neck toward Veren. "If we can't protect all of Dorcha Wood, at least we could fortify this barrier. Teach me how to do it."

CHAPTER FOUR

"Barriers are born of magic," Veren told Fiadh. "The same power you use to call the wind or water weaves into words, molded by your will until the words have substance."

She thought back when she had shaped the earth or caused the air to stir. Within those experiences were softly spoken things that came from somewhere inside her, unknown until they spilled from her lips. Their origins and how she had known them were a mystery, but they were there, hidden within until she called them forth. One vivid memory flashed in her mind. The attack on Dorcha Wood and Krulan with a man helpless in his massive jaw. It was a word that had halted him before he tore open Gideon's throat. No, not a word. A *Word*—imbued with power and magic.

"How is it I'm able to wield magic I wasn't taught?"

"Magic is in our blood, passed from generation to gener-ation." Confusion crept across her face, and he chuckled.

"Think of it like a spider, Fiadh. A spider isn't taught how to build its web. It just knows."

"Hm. Why is it I never experienced magic until I was here? If it's always been inside me, wouldn't I have used it before now?"

"Are you so sure you didn't?" He watched her mull that over. "I'd wager you've been using magic all your life. With the animals that came to your hand and in the moments when you spoke to the forest."

Her eyes widened. "I never thought of that as magic."

"But you feel the truth of it now." Taking her hands, he pressed them against his—palm to palm. "The magic in our blood comes from Danu. It is her gift to us. Her legacy. Listen to the words I speak. Feel their power and echo it."

Veren chanted, his voice tugging at her until the world and all within it faded. There was just him. Him and the spell he cast that caused her muscles to tremor. Words crawled out of her throat, joining with his. In the infinitesimal spaces between their palms, she felt heat bloom and particles coalesce, pressing against her flesh as they grew into a tangible film. Forcing her eyes open, she stared at what she felt but could not see. There was nothing visible, and, yet, something had grown between them, something that bent and twitched as her hand flexed.

Digging a finger into the substance, she felt the barrier stretch and hug her skin. Fiadh wiggled the other digits and finally saw a faint shimmer beneath the pads of her fingers as the barrier vibrated with the disturbance. Rounded eyes found Veren's, and he smiled. She answered it, her mouth parting in a grin that spilled into laughter as she pushed hard against the barrier and saw him take an involuntary step back.

"How long will it last?" she asked, tucking her elbows closer to her chest.

Muttering a handful of words that were spoken so quickly she caught only snippets, he lowered his hands, and it was gone. She looked at her palms, rubbing her fingers along her skin where the echo of the barrier lingered in every nerve.

He reached over and slowly drew a spiral in the center of her palm with the tip of his finger. "There is a wealth of power in you, Fiadh. I can feel it beneath your skin."

His touch was like a brand. Tingling awareness spread up her arm before traveling to the pit of her stomach. Darting her eyes to his, she saw the shadow of emotions he tried to hide. A blush stained her cheeks, and she looked away.

Veren released her hand and took a step back. "A barrier is only as strong as the will behind it. The spell itself is born of the one who speaks it and, as you experienced, can be strengthened by another. The stronger a person's connection with Danu, the more influence over the barriers they can have, from simply passing through them without difficulty to imbuing them with something akin to a will. When done right, they are nearly indestructible."

Nearly, she thought. Her mind took her back to a memory Danu had shared when Carmun, and the mages who stood with her, had breached the barrier protecting Erabel.

"It's like a living thing," he continued. "Once created, it

will stand for all time—fed and nurtured with the power of the Great Mother." He paused and shook his head. "At least, that was how it had always been… until Rygeil stole her power—stabbed the oak that sheltered her essence. These are perilous times. Danu grows weak." He looked pained. "I fear for you. For all our people."

"Then our best chance of survival is protecting Erabel from attack." She reached for his hand. "The barriers must hold. Let's begin."

Nodding, he worked with her into the long hours of the afternoon. Kaelari, Arel, and two others came upon them, having searched when neither had returned. Their presence made Fiadh feel clumsy at first, but there was no judgment, and she soon relaxed her body and focused on their suggestions. It was strange to be surrounded by so many individuals. It was what she'd always wanted as she and Riona lived apart in Dorcha Wood. As a child, she had always been alone with only the animals of the forest to keep her company. But the hum of their voices and the weight of their observation eventually took their toll. She begged leave to stop, weariness dragging her shoulders down.

Veren nodded, studying the barrier they'd poured energy into. "You've done well. I can feel a subtle strengthening."

She watched his hand stroke the invisible field, lips curving in a proud smile. When a soft round of applause drifted toward her, her face flamed, and she ducked her head, avoiding the faces of her elven audience, and trudged to a fallen tree where Krulan lay sprawled in the dirt. She sat on the mossy surface and silently observed the others as they chatted. Dasha flew down and landed at her feet by a small twig. Fiadh eyed the piece of wood and picked it up, drawing in the dirt. The beginnings of Gideon's face looked back at her, and she rubbed it out, quickly drawing spirals and whirls over the patch of ground. Dasha croaked and cocked his head, then hopped over and tried to grab it from her. She snatched it away. "Get your own, thief!"

He squawked and pigeon-walked toward a bush where he spent a solid minute yanking a twig from a branch, crowing with triumph as it broke free. Sauntering toward her, he tilted his head and dragged the end of the stick through the dirt, effectively erasing the spiraling pattern she'd sketched. "Hey!"

He flapped, causing dirt to cloud around him. Dropping his stick, he lurched away and sneezed.

Fiadh laughed. "Serves you right."

Grumbling, he picked up his stick again and continued to draw. Her attention wandered, and she found herself once again watching Veren and Kaelari in quiet conversation. Focusing, she soon realized of whom they spoke and curled her lip in distaste.

"She should have begun her training years ago," Kaelari complained.

"And had she been born in our lands, Rygeil would have drained her, as he has Calum, and she would be nothing but a shell of what she is. It had to be this way," Veren said.

Kaelari paced, her feet brushing along the ground in hushed movements. "I still say the girl is naive. She does not have the wisdom and experience to lead. Better we do as we must and unleash her when we have to, rather than wait for her command."

"She is young. She will learn, and her power is growing fast."

"She's a fool!"

Veren's face flushed with anger. "Fool or no, she forbids us to march on Darragh's fortress, and I have sworn myself to her."

"As you swore yourself to Rygeil?"

He scowled.

"We should attack Darragh's forces rather than hiding behind that barrier," she complained, flinging her arm out. "She doesn't understand war. She's not a fighter, Veren. I don't know if she'll be ready for what's coming."

"When it comes, she will be."

"Even against Rygeil?" She looked at him and frowned. "He is strong. Even now, with all that has been taken, he wields great power. I fear for her… for us. If she falters…"

"So do I," Veren said quietly. "But I sense something in her, something untapped. I believe when the time comes, she will surprise us all."

"I hope you're right," she sighed, "for if you're not, all who stand with her will be nothing more than ash."

"We must have faith, Kaelari. Danu chose her. Are you so quick to question the will of our Great Mother?"

"Danu hasn't always made the best choices," she grumbled.

Fiadh rose and turned away, lacking the energy to argue for what she knew was right and not wishing to hear any more. "Come, Dasha." He dropped his stick, taking one last look at his masterpiece, and flew onto her shoulder.

Krulan lifted his head. *Where are you going?*

For a swim. I need time to think.

His yellow eyes bore into her, but after a moment, he lay his head on his paws and let her go.

As they walked, Dasha tried to coax her into a game, but she shooed him away and leaned over to pick out a rock that had somehow made it into her boot. Tossing it aside, she looked at her hands. They were coated in layers of grime. Along the edge of her palm was a slash of black soot, remnants of the fire and the lives it had taken. It wouldn't come to that again, she promised herself. Veren and Kaelari thought she was too weak and unprepared for this world. They assumed she would stand aside and let the unthinkable happen. They didn't understand her fierce need to protect her home and all who dwelled within it. When the time came, she would be ready. She had to be.

CHAPTER FIVE

*D*asha flew from tree to tree, calling to her in his strange language. From her periphery, an obscured shape tracked her movements. Fiadh paused and stared into the undergrowth until a Cù-Sìth stepped from the shadows.

"Rivya, have you come to join me for a swim?" she asked.

The Cù-Sìth snorted. *I think not. Krulan sent me to keep you out of trouble. You should not travel alone, even in this protected place.*

I'm sure you have better things to do than follow me. Besides, I'm not alone, Fiadh countered. *Dasha is with me.*

She gave a throaty grumble. *That bird could do nothing but squawk should you need aid.*

I am sure he could pluck out the eyes of an attacker at the very least!

Rivya growled, and Fiadh smirked, continuing her trek with her protector at her side. Their pace was slow, by Cù-Sìth's standards, and she often cast glances at her charge.

Fiadh felt them and waited for a thought to follow, but nothing came. It struck her as odd that Rivya joined her so frequently, as though Krulan had bestowed the role of nursemaid. Fiadh chafed at the idea he may see her as little more than a wayward child. *I'm not a child who needs tending, you know. You needn't look after me as though I'm helpless.*

Rivya's eyes widened, and she huffed. *My mate does not see you as a babe, though he worries about your safety and thinks you are reckless.*

Muttering about showing Krulan reckless if he thought her behavior now fit into that mold, Fiadh picked up her pace. Rivya's strides easily matched hers.

Don't be angry, young Fiadh. I meant no offense.

I'm not angry with you, but I resent being treated like I'm an ignorant child in need of a warden.

I am not your warden. Rivya stopped, and Fiadh swung around to look at her. *I am your friend.*

Sighing, Fiadh hung her head. *You are my friend. I'm sorry, Rivya, my words were not meant that way.*

Forgiven. They continued on in silence before Rivya said, *But you do need looking after.*

Fiadh swatted at the Cù-Sìth, who leaped away barking laughter. Giving chase, the two ran through the woods. Not to be left out, Dasha joined them, dive-bombing the Cù-Sìth with shrill caws and ready talons. Rivya stumbled, rolling in a cloud of dirt and snarls, while Fiadh took the lead. Breaking through the last of the foliage, she pumped her arms and spun around to watch Rivya gambol toward her, teeth snapping at the raven when he plucked a chunk of fur from her scruff.

"Ha! I win!"

You had help, Rivya grumbled, shooting daggers at Dasha as she plucked a thorn from her paw. The raven cawed, taunting her and staying just beyond the reach of her massive jaws.

"That matters not. Winning is winning."

The Cù-Sìth flicked her ears and settled under a bush, watching Fiadh as a mother watches over her young. Bristling at Rivya's reluctance to let her bathe alone, she stomped to a rock and sat, pulling off her boots. "They treat me like I'm a babe," she muttered.

Rivya sighed. *I'm not your nursemaid.*

Well, you're settling in over there like I need looking after when I bathe! she said, throwing up her hands. *Can't I have any privacy?*

You don't complain when Eradar visits you.

She rubbed her forehead. *That's different. He doesn't look at me like I'm helpless.*

Her left paw curled, claws digging into the dirt. *If my presence bothers you so much, I could leave.* She rose and shook her massive body free of debris.

Frowning at the water for a few moments, she mulled over her feelings. Fiadh knew Rivya meant well, but she was never alone, not even for the simplest things. They were always watching, always cataloging everything she did. At least, that's how it felt.

But along with those thoughts came pangs of regret for how she'd snapped at her friend. "Rivya, I'm sorry. I didn —" Fiadh started to say, pausing when she craned her neck and found nothing but disturbed earth where the Cù-Sìth had lain. "I shouldn't have snapped at her," she grumbled.

Sighing, Fiadh tried to put the Cù-Sìth from her mind. She looked at the pool that glistened in the waning light. Eradar, a guardian of the Merrow, was absent. Not unusual, as he rarely joined her until after she entered the water. Peeling off her tunic and leggings, Fiadh tossed them onto the rock and made her way to the water's edge, hugging her thin shift to her body. Her reflection stared back at her on the glassy surface, and she cocked her head, realizing the face upon the water looked changed. Older. She touched her cheek, watching the image do the same, and grimaced when a streak of dirt was left behind. Dipping a toe into the still pool, she jumped in.

The water felt delicious—warm and smooth—hugging every inch of her as she stretched her arms and dove into its depths. Fish of every color scattered at the intrusion, hiding among the softly waving arms of water plants or in crevices between jagged rocks. As Fiadh swam, a sense of peace passed through her, the same feeling she had whenever she visited these waters. It took away the grief, numbing her to the aching loss of Riona, Gideon, and Tainsi. The looming threat beyond the borders of Erabel faded. All the worries that had plagued her mind until she couldn't sleep became little more than a gentle buzzing, so she could pretend, for a little while, that they didn't exist. It wouldn't last. She knew this, but, for now, it felt decadent, and Fiadh relished the freedom.

Eradar eventually joined her, swishing his tail through the water in mesmerizing green, blue, and yellow undulations. Fiadh swam to the edge and slung her arm onto the rocky lip as she waited for him to surface. Moments later, he launched himself out of the water to perch on the edge and greeted her.

She gave a passing glance to the gills that sealed themselves as his body acclimated to the air and focused on his striking face, unmarred by years of living and devoid of any expression, hiding the thoughts that prowled beneath his stare.

Smiling, Fiadh said, "Good day, Eradar."

He arched a brow. "From the look on your face, I'd say it hasn't been."

Fiadh chuckled and let out a sigh. "You're not wrong. It's been a long day."

"Hm. I sense there is more to it than the length of the hours."

A long pause followed as Eradar waited her out, knowing she'd speak when ready. He was a good listener.

"We buried Tainsi today."

"Ah. It is difficult to say goodbye to those we lose." Cocking his head, he looked at her so long and hard she squirmed. "But there is more than the passing of the elf," he said softly.

She looked down and sifted her hand distractedly through the water. "I argued with Veren and Kaelari."

"Oh?"

"They wish to go to war, to attack Lord Darragh's holding."

"And you disagreed?"

"Hasn't there been enough killing?"

"I didn't know there was such a thing as a quota when it comes to death."

Fiadh shook her head and grumbled under her breath.

"You worry about what's coming," he said flatly.

"They expect so much of me," she complained, staring off into the trees. "I don't know if I'll live up to it. Maybe I can't. I'm not a fighter like they are. I won't seek the slaughter of armies of men. What I've seen over the last few weeks… the awful things I've seen…" She shook her head. "Mother kept me from such things… and I… I don't… what if they're right and I'm not ready for this world? Or what's coming."

"None of us is ready for war," he mumbled.

"So, you think there'll be one?"

"There is already war. The only question is how long until it comes to Erabel? It is much the same, the—" He stopped and pursed his lips. "How to describe it?" Swinging his gaze to her, he continued. "It's palpable. This energy of things to come. Before the Great War, I felt it, almost oppressive as the time grew nearer, like hands pressing down on you. Smothering. That's how it feels now. It's coming and there's no way to truly prepare. You will simply face it because you must."

"Did you fight in the Great War?"

Pain flashed across his face, marring his perfect mask of stoicism. "They came for all of us, trapping so many in watery realms and poisoning the waters. Those who tried to escape to the surface found men with spears waiting. They had no chance. Even the young were slain. This," he said, sweeping his hand across the pool's surface, "may very well be the last kingdom of my people in the whole of the world. In my youth, I would travel from one domain to another using underground rivers, but the poison men loosed into our kingdoms did not know the boundaries of our realms. It traveled, as men surely knew it would. We sealed off all passages leading here once our queen, Ithraen, was safely within. Not all of my people made it before it was sealed. I can only assume they are dead."

"I'm sorry, Eradar," Fiadh said softly, reaching out a comforting hand.

He took it, tilting her wrist so that her palm faced up. Tracing the tiny lines in her skin, he said, "I can see her within you."

"Danu?"

Eradar shook his head. "Your mother. Threa."

"You knew her?"

His touch sent tremors down her arm, tiny pulses of power that made her muscles spasm. "She would come to this pool as a child. We were both children. Many days were spent together and as we grew older, I thought myself in love with her. But her heart belonged to another," he said with a shrug.

"My father."

He nodded and grew pensive, idly running the tip of his finger along the deepest crease in her palm. "You are much like her."

"I wish I knew her," Fiadh whispered. "Though I loved my mother—the woman who raised me—deeply and would not trade the years we had together for anything, I wish I had met Threa, known her."

"Aye." He dropped her hand. "I think she would be proud of you."

Fiadh made a face. "I've done nothing to make anyone proud. All I've done, my whole life, is just…" she waved her hand limply, drops of water falling from it, "just lived. Until recently, I roamed the forest without a care in the world. And now… now everything is so different. I suppose I am too." She looked at Eradar and smiled. "You know, I used to dream of having a big family. I would sneak to the border of the village and watch children playing, wishing I could join them. Here, in this place, I have more people around me than I've ever known. They all know me, all are kind and nice and smile when I approach, but even so, I am not really one of them. And, yet, I have no idea how to be. *Who* to be."

"You wish to be someone else?"

Fiadh snorted. "In truth, I envy Kaelari. Her skill. Her passion. She has such determination."

"Kaelari is strong," Eradar agreed. "She is a warrior. She thinks with her blade. Countless years shaped her into a female with deadly skill. However, she does not have your perspective, and it is that which I see as infinitely more valuable."

"How do you mean?"

"You were raised among mankind, part of their society. You understand them, and that is important."

Fiadh shook her head. "Nay, Eradar. I was wholly separate. I never entered the village or played with other children. It wasn't until recently that I understood why."

"Your mother, Riona, is the link I speak of."

"But she was just one person among so many. What am

I to understand?" She frowned. "Mankind rejected her. They would've rejected me too."

Eradar shrugged. "You have been witness to their cruelty. You have seen how their minds work and that insight is a boon as we near a dark time in our history. I believe you will be instrumental in our fight against such people."

"I don't hate them. I can't," Fiadh said quietly, darting a glance at Eradar.

He cocked an eye. "Who is there to love?"

Fiadh looked away and reluctantly thought of Gideon. Those wounds were still raw, as though the hurt was unfinished. "I thought I loved someone once, but… he showed me what he truly was." She made a strangled sound. "It doesn't matter what happened between him and me."

"I beg to differ. I believe it matters greatly."

She studied him, looking for some hint of his deeper thoughts. But he gave away nothing.

"Did this man you speak of cast you aside rather than welcome the love you offered?" he asked. She winced, but said nothing. "If that is so, it is clear to me that his hate for our kind was more powerful than any other emotion. And that is the hallmark of the children of men. Their hate will always conquer their love."

"I don't forgive those who killed my mother and—" She swallowed hard. "I do not forgive Gideon's unreasoning hatred. But I cannot condemn an entire race for the acts of a few, Eradar."

"I think your love for Riona, an exception, an outcast as

you say, clouds your judgement. For one Riona, how many Gideons? How many Lord Darraghs can be counted among them? I'd wager you could walk a thousand miles through the kingdoms of men and not find another of her kind. I can assure you, men will give you no quarter in the battles to come."

"So be it. I will do what I must, but I do not see this world as whole without all of its people—mankind included."

He eyed her, and she held his stare until he looked away and said, "Threa thought as you did once. It did naught but get her killed. It would grieve me to see you follow her fate."

"I do not wish to cause you grief, but I must follow my heart. To kill for the sake of killing is wrong."

"Bah!" He dove into the water with an angry splash.

Fiadh frowned at the disturbance he left in his wake and let go of the ledge, paddling to the center of the pool. She dipped her head beneath the surface, aching for its healing power to wash away her anger.

Life bloomed everywhere she looked in the watery realm. She focused on it, smiling as a small creature, no larger than the length of her palm, drifted toward her, its face like an open flower with two iridescent eyes staring back at her. It extended its tiny fin, a leafy fern-like arm, and brushed it across her cheek before darting away to others of its kind.

Surfacing, she turned to Eradar as he swam toward her. "I don't know what hate or love lies in the hearts of mankind. I only know what I've seen and felt. There is ugliness and beauty." He opened his mouth, but she stopped him. "Can we talk of something else? Something simple?"

He chuckled. "As you wish. Of what should we speak?"

"Tell me of your childhood. Did you cause trouble?"

Eradar gave her a wry grin. "I was a most obedient son."

Fiadh snorted. "Why do I find that hard to believe?"

"You think me a rebel?"

She laughed. "I think you are and were too curious for your own good."

"Ah, well. There may be truth in that. Though I suppose it takes one who bears those traits to see them in others."

Fiadh made a face. "I may have been an inquisitive child."

"Ha! Come then, oh curious one, and let me show you my kingdom, for you are well-favored in my eyes."

She blushed, taken aback by his trust and acceptance. "Thank you, Eradar."

Slipping off the edge, he took her hand and studied her, looking so deeply she could feel him in her mind. "If you are to rule Erabel, you must know all its peoples. It is an honor to show you mine, though I should warn you there are some who may see you as dangerous. They fear the past, the bloodshed between mankind and Aos Sí that led to the destruction of so many of my people."

"I understand."

His lips curled in a small smile, at odds with his placid features. "Know that without a guide, my kingdom is unassailable. Many wards were placed to protect us after the Great War."

Fiadh gazed at the water, trying to plumb its depths but

unable to see more than shadows playing in the light. "I cannot hold my breath for long."

"You will have no need. Merrow have long held magic that we can pass along to those we welcome… or steal."

Her eyes widened. "Steal?"

"We have, shall we say, an interesting history."

"You'll have to tell me of it."

"Another time, young Fiadh. Come," he said, tugging her, "let me show you a world unlike any other."

She let him pull her along, heart racing as she glanced at the deepness of the pool. Filling her lungs, Fiadh ducked beneath the surface.

CHAPTER SIX

*D*onal greeted Gideon as he left the great hall. "A small contingent of soldiers arrived this morning from Lord Mulligan."

Raising his brows, Gideon asked, "Is there a problem with the men?"

"Men?" Donal scoffed. "The old fool sent us boys. Untrained, the lot of them."

Gideon frowned.

"They'll make a fine distraction, though," Donal mused. "Perhaps, next time we attack, I'll send them in first to divert the elves from our real fighting force."

"But… won't they be slaughtered?"

The commander shrugged. "Well, you're welcome to turn them into the finest soldiers the kingdom has ever known if it bothers you so. Take them, train them, die with them. I care not."

"Where are they?"

"Watching real men fight," Donal said, jerking his head toward the field.

They strode onto the training grounds, boots sinking into the mud with squelches. A group of soldiers trained with swords and shields in the center of the field, grunts and the clash of metal filling the cold air. Along one side stood a dozen young men who watched the skirmish with wide eyes.

Gideon stood with his leg bent, arms folded, and looked them over. As the commander had warned him, they were young, most with only a few whiskers on their chins. *Barely out of boyhood,* Gideon thought. Those who had armor wore relics that had seen better days. A few of them carried crude weapons. A farmer's scythe, a rough-looking bow, and a woodsman's axe. Not a sword to be seen amongst them. To a man, they were in awe of the soldiers they watched, making clear they'd seen nothing of battle. At his signal, they trotted over with gangly legs, the sparse ill-fitting armor bouncing off narrow shoulders. They came to a halt and stood awkwardly before Gideon and Donal.

Studying their faces, Gideon marked each one. "I'll take them," he said, preferring the youths learn from him rather than spending their days as sport for experienced fighters.

"You've got your work cut out for you," Donal said, slapping him on the back.

Leading the group to a drier section of the field, he introduced himself and got their names before going from one to the other, tugging at the armor of those who wore it, and sizing them up. Though eager to learn, they could do little more than clumsily swing sticks, half of them losing their footing and falling in the mud as they sparred. "It's going to be a long day," Gideon muttered, watching two of the men bat their sticks at each other like children.

As the day wore on, he struggled to be patient and was rewarded when a couple showed progress. It was minimal, but he'd take it.

"Brody and Quinn," he shouted, drawing them from the rest of the group, who continued to practice the simple patterns he'd taught them.

He stood with his hands folded behind his back, legs spread apart. "Unlike the others, you lads have had some training. I will choose one of you to be my second in command."

Chests puffed, and backs straightened.

"Do not assume the appointment of second in command will be reached easily. To attain that position, you must prove yourself," he paused and looked each of them in the eye, "to me."

They nodded in unison and he smiled as he noted Quinn mirroring his stance. The young soldier's dark eyes stood out against his bright red hair and freckled face.

Calling the rest of his troop over, he announced, "You have earned a hearty meal and a good rest." Smiles mixed with pride filled every face. He noted their sweat-plastered hair. "I suggest you all find a bath as well."

Laughter followed, and Gideon watched them shove each other playfully as they left the field. Their banter reminded him of Doran. He and his brother had often wrestled and laughed after a day of trying to best each other. Wiping mud splatters from his sword, Gideon called up a memory of Doran's laughter. It was bittersweet.

He went straight to the blacksmith. The lads would need short swords—there was no time to teach them how to wield a great sword. Besides, in the confines of Dorcha Wood, a short, one-handed blade would serve them best. And while Darragh's main forces wore heavy plate, leather armor would give them speed and agility while still offering protection. He'd have to measure them and bring the figures to the tanner. Once done, he'd toss the relics a few of them wore into the refuse.

"I'm busy," the blacksmith grumbled when Gideon arrived. He was a hulking man with bulging muscles beneath layers of sweat from the fires. "His lordship has me working day and night to outfit his men. I don't have time or materials to waste on untrained rabble."

"Might some coin make it worth your while?" Gideon asked, handing him a small bag.

The blacksmith took it and dumped gold coins into his grimy palm. He picked one up and bit it, glancing at the imprint left by his teeth. "The swords will be ready in two days."

Gideon thanked him and left.

He found his men in the barracks—nothing more than rows of tents—after the evening meal. They sat around a fire swapping stories of female conquests none of them had likely ever had. He paused in the shadows and listened.

"Oh, aye?" Brody challenged. "Kate took me to her bed long before you, Roland!"

"You only wish she did. Kate wouldn't give you the time of day. You're too green to know what to do with someone that fine. Besides, she deserves a man who can pleasure her, not some boy with naught but a twig in his britches!"

Guffaws rang out, and Gideon heard the rustle of someone hastily standing.

"Do you want to say that again?" Brody yelled.

He was about to step from the darkness and break up the squabble when he heard Quinn's voice.

"Stand down, Brody! Roland is just funning and, like a child, you're letting him rile you."

"He's right, Brody," Roland said. "I was just funning."

Gideon paused to give the young man time to lower his fists and rejoin the group before he came into the light of the fire.

Aidan spied him first. "Lord Gideon!" He sprang up, knocking over his mug of ale.

The others rose quickly, but he noticed how Roland and Brody didn't meet his eyes. Pretending not to have heard the exchange and near scuffle, he spoke to each of them, commending their hard work and wishing them a good rest as their real training would begin at dawn. As he left, he heard Quinn say, "Lord Gideon slew an Aos Sí warrior in Dorcha Wood."

Gasps of awe and doubt followed the pronouncement, and it tempted him to listen, but he turned away, letting the darkness swallow him.

Alice, a maidservant, gave him a missive when he arrived at the keep. He looked at the parchment, and his heart caught at the sight of the clumsy letters scrawled across the paper. Tucking it into his tunic, he grabbed a trencher and mug of ale, scarfing the meal down with little more than a few grunts to those who spoke to him. As soon as he'd finished, he found his tent, tossed his weapons and armor aside, and sat on his pallet with a candle.

His hands shook as he broke the seal and unfolded the letter. There were two sheets of parchment, the first containing a short, poorly written message from Marion, the farmer's wife, telling him Aishling was well and had begun to learn her letters. *Aishling's spelling will be atrocious if Marion's doing the teaching*, he thought after he read the note. Setting it aside, he read the message his little foundling had penned. His eyes blurred as he imagined her painstakingly drawing each letter with quill and ink.

I MIS YU. MARION AN OWEN AR NISE. THAY TEECHET ME LEDDERS. THAY GOT A HORS AN HE LET ME PET HIM. I MIS YU. WEN AR YU COMING BAK? I LUV YU.

Gideon ran his finger along every line. Picking up a new sheet of parchment, he bent his head and wrote back, telling her that Aridius missed her and hoped she would save some of her pets for his horse, how proud he was that she was learning her letters and that he hoped she was being a good girl and listening to Owen and Marion. He finished with how much he missed her and that he'd come for her when it was safe. Pressing his ring into the wax, he sealed the letter and set it next to his pallet.

Dousing the candle, he stretched out on the lumpy bed

and stared at nothing. There was a lump in his throat that wouldn't go away, no matter how many times he swallowed. Aishling was better off where she was, far from the battles, away from cities and villages that could become targets of marauding Aos Sí. But he missed her. He missed her sweet smile and her tiny hand in his.

CHAPTER SEVEN

*E*radar's watery realm filled Fiadh's vision, distracting her from tickling sensations on her sides that were growing more intense. She winced as the flesh on either side of her ribcage flared with knifelike pain that ripped through muscle, traveling into her chest until it punctured her lungs. Fiadh yelped and struggled to free herself from Eradar's viselike grip, but he held her fast.

Panicking, Fiadh shook her head when he said, "Breathe."

Taking her hand, he lifted her shift that ballooned from her body and pressed her fingers to her side, just under the outer curve of her breast. She flinched when she felt three deep gashes. Craning her neck and twisting, she stared at what could only be described as gills. Fiadh's mouth gaped, and she realized with a shock that her body had sucked in water and, rather than filling her lungs and suffocating her, it had passed through them and out a bony protrusion just above the uppermost gill.

"Remember when I told you my people have magic of our own?" Eradar asked, his voice deeper, richer, than when on the surface.

She nodded, hair flowing in black curtains around her face.

"Behold one of our gifts."

Heedless of her state of undress, she ran both her hands along her sides, gently tracing gills that pulsed with each pull of water. Each gill felt like the petals of a flower—soft and pliable. It was both unnerving and fascinating. Eradar chuckled, the sound passing over her in strange waves.

Catching her eye, he smiled and relaxed his hands. "Ready?"

Fiadh jerked her head with a quick nod, the motion causing her dark hair to fan out around her face.

"Try speaking. Just as you would above the surface." Eradar grinned at her look of uncertainty. "Go on. Say my name."

"Er… Eradar." Her eyes went wide as her own voice echoed in her ears, having that same crisp quality as her guide.

Clasping her hand, he tugged at her, angling toward the deepest part of the pool. All manner of creatures darted in and out of her field of vision. She wanted to look at them all, to watch their colorful bodies glint in the light that pierced the water, but Eradar's strength was relentless as his body propelled them toward a large jut of rock from which she had seen him emerge many times. Kicking her legs in half-hearted strokes, she slipped into a world that had no place in mankind's legends. A secret realm.

It was dim as they passed under the submerged ledge, illuminated by plants and aquatic life whose forms gave off softly glowing light in hues of purple, red, and green. One such being darted toward her, its body undulating just beyond her face. Eradar stopped his progress and let her admire its horse-like upper body, tapering into that of an eel.

"She is an each-uisce and a young one at that," Eradar said as Fiadh extended a finger toward the curious being. "Like my people, they abandoned their homes and came here for refuge. Ithraen, our queen, took them under her protection and we have lived side-by-side since those dark days. You will see others of her kind, full-grown and powerful, as we venture deeper into my kingdom. They are formidable guardians of our realm."

Fiadh glanced at him as the small each-uisce inspected her finger with quick nibbles and flicks of its gritty tongue. "Does she speak?"

"Aye, as they grow older. But this one will be many years before she masters speech. Like your people, each-uisce have few offspring, but they grow slowly, much more so than you and I. It is why they came here. Had they not, the last of their kind would have been slain in the Great War, and we would have lost them forever."

"Has she a mother?"

"Aye, though their young are curious at times, leading them beyond the watchful eyes of their dams." Leaning forward, Eradar stroked the small creature, then said, "Come, her mother will no doubt be along soon."

Stretching her arms and kicking her legs, Fiadh

followed, mindful of the myriad of life that trailed in their wake. The passage they traveled was long and twisting, following the flow of the earth. Eventually, the dimness began to fade, and she found herself in a giant cavern that stretched so far she could not see where it ended. Illuminating the expanse were huge orbs of light fixed into the rock in massive, bulbous clusters that arced across the dome of the cavern, creating false light that was so bright it felt like day. Everywhere she looked teemed with life of so many varieties and colors that after a few moments, her eyes blurred, unable to take it all in. Within the vibrant world were structures unlike any she could imagine. Spiraling towers with spires of coral, domed edifices intricately carved with ornamental whirls and arched openings, and among it all were masses of plant life waving gently in the current that flowed throughout.

"It's beautiful."

"Aye, it is. There is no other realm that could match its splendor. Come, I will take you to the seat of my people."

Fiadh relaxed her limbs and let Eradar pull her through the water, her body feeling heavier with each stroke, pulled toward the rocky soil so that her feet were merely hovering above the ground. Eradar read her face and chuckled.

"It is not so different from your world."

She looked up, mouth gaping. "How am I not floating up there?" she asked, pointing.

"The magic of Abadon anchors you to the earth from which her power springs."

"Like Danu's power in Erabel," Fiadh remarked.

Eradar considered that. "I suppose, though it is not the same."

Fiadh wanted to ask more about that, but the flash of a colorful body caught her eye and her train of thought fled. Everywhere her gaze fell was something new. Something wonderful. It soon reached her awareness that many of the life-forms in this submerged kingdom had gathered, following their progress. And many of them did so with less than friendly expressions. The most intimidating came from a giant each-uisce. Its upper body was a strange blend of horse and fish with its eel-like lower half whipping through the water in angry swipes. She stared, growing uncomfortable under its stony expression, gaping when the creature's form shifted, changing from its natural horse-like head to one so like Eradar that he could have been his twin. Sensing her distraction, Eradar turned and found the object of her attention. Uttering a guttural threat, he lunged at the each-uisce, sending it off in a blur of shifting features and warning snarls.

"I am sorry, young one. As I mentioned, there are some who hold on to the ugliness of the past and lay blame on those who came after." He eyed her strangely, a shadow passing over his face.

"I shouldn't be here," Fiadh said, ducking her head to escape the stares of the many beings who crowded closer.

"Never say it! You are most welcome."

Grabbing onto his arm with both hands, she gave herself into his care and passed under the archway of what appeared to be a massive underwater keep. The halls were magnificent, making the seat of Erabel look drab. Sculptures and engravings covered everything, telling their own stories that she tried to see as she was tugged along. Too soon, Eradar stopped in a room off the main hall. She righted her body, bobbing in the water, and took in the scenery, her eyes falling on two Merrow who watched her.

He lifted a hand toward her. "Behold, Fiadh, heiress of Erabel."

"My lady," one of them said, bending at the waist. "Welcome to Abadon."

A look passed between Eradar and the male who had spoken, but Fiadh couldn't discern it. She realized, in that moment, that if she wanted to leave this place and return to the surface, she would be unable to without Eradar's aid. She was trapped, should he wish to hold her. Looking at him, she tried to gauge his intent, but, as always, his features held no expression, making him impossible to read.

Nudging her arm, Eradar said, "My lady, may I introduce you to Cyraeneus, Ithraen's heir."

Her eyes widened, and she felt flustered, clutching at her shift as it moved in the water, threatening to reveal more than she would ever wish to show. "My lord."

Cyraeneus laughed and flapped his hand. "There is no need for such formality. Please, call me Cyraeneus." Motioning to the figure at his side, he added, "And this is Tulaer, my most trusted advisor."

She nodded to each of them. "Thank you for welcoming me into your kingdom."

"And what think you of my realm, young Fiadh?" the queen's son asked.

Eradar backed away from her. She felt a flare of alarm

and craned her neck, watching him move toward the doorway, but her attention was brought back to Cyraeneus when he softly cleared his throat. Recalling his question, she said, "It… it's truly beautiful."

The prince smiled, though it didn't reach his eyes. "There is none to equal it."

She nodded and darted a glance at Tulaer, who had moved to her side, then swung her eyes back to him. "I hope your welcome signals that our people will be united should the war come to Erabel."

He smirked. "You waste no time, do you? But speaking of such things before we know you better is not the way of my people."

"I apologize." Heat crawled across her face, and she wished her dark hair would drift in front of it to hide her embarrassment.

"You are forgiven," he told her. "I understand you have not reigned over Erabel long. Is that correct?"

Eradar must have told the prince about me, she thought. "Aye, that's true. I lived in Dorcha Wood with my mother until recently."

"Among humans, they say." He glanced at Tulaer. "Unusual, isn't she?"

"A rare prize."

Fiadh's brow furrowed. Prize?

"Tell me, Fiadh," the prince said, "what was it like living among the children of men?"

"I… I wouldn't know, to be honest. Mother and I lived alone in the forest. I didn't speak to anyone else."

"Hm. That's not entirely true, is it?" Cyraeneus gave her a calculated look.

Had Eradar told him of Gideon? The idea of her friend sharing something so personal with someone she didn't know stung. "There was one other, but he's gone now," she said softly.

"Did you lie with him?"

Fiadh scowled. "What?"

"Did you mate with the human, or are you unspoiled?"

Clenching her fists, Fiadh said coldly, "I believe it's time for me to go."

The prince chuckled and cocked his head. "I can see that you are uncomfortable speaking of such things. I apologize for the intrusion. Shall we speak of other things?"

Her eyes flashed, but she nodded. Better to play the part of a polite guest than gain the ire of a prince. They spent the next few minutes chatting about the remarkable things she'd seen in Erabel and Abadon. They were safe topics and Fiadh relaxed. Eventually, the conversation hit a lull. They stared at each other for many moments; the silence stretching into an uncomfortable minute. Eradar was nowhere to be seen, and she had no concept of how much time had passed since she'd arrived. It was time to go.

"I thank you again for inviting me to Abadon. Perhaps we can discuss our future another time," she said. "I should return to the surface."

"So soon? I thought you were here to speak of an alliance."

She pursed her lips. "Are you offering one?"

"Being air breathers, you have an advantage in a war

with mankind. Will you be marching your forces into their kingdoms?"

"I have no plans to attack them, but I'll defend my realm with all I am."

He looked at Tulaer. "It is as we heard, then. She will not unite with us against them." He shook his head. "She leaves us no choice."

Fiadh watched the exchange, growing anxious. "My people wait for me."

"Do they?" he asked slyly.

She smiled to hide the fear that slithered down her spine. "Aye, they keep a close eye on me. Is Eradar able to take me back to the surface?"

"Your guide has other duties to attend to," Cyraeneus said. "For now, you are here and I will decide when you shall leave."

"I don't understand."

"Don't you?" He drifted toward her, and she backed up, arms pumping in the water. "Did you think you were granted entry into my kingdom to simply see its magnificence and be on your way?"

She shook her head, yelping as her back bumped against Tulaer.

"Seize her."

CHAPTER EIGHT

Claw-like hands gripped her arm, digging into her flesh so deeply drops of blood drifted into the water like wisps of smoke. She screamed and threw her body against Tulaer.

"You draw blood, Tulaer." The prince tsked. "Loosen your hold, my friend." Cyraeneus closed the distance between them and gently took her chin in his hand. "I'm afraid you have become a pawn, my dear. The elves seek to use you to increase their power, but I fear your realm will see dark days should the armies of men come to Erabel. I would be a liar if I said did not wish to see that day come, when Aos Sí arrogance is crushed."

Her eyes grew hard.

"Ah, but I do not hate your people. Truly, I don't wish to see them fall, though I have every reason to." A look of confusion crossed her face, and he cocked his head. "Did you know that Rygeil and the rulers of the other kingdoms tried to goad us into fighting alongside them in the Great

War? To leave the safety of the waters and use our magic to alter our forms and fight in their ranks?"

She shook her head, hating the feel of his finger sliding along her cheek.

"Rygeil sought vengeance on those who refused to fight."

She paled.

"You didn't know? I'm not surprised. It is likely not an act your people are proud of, though I would wager Rygeil will seek us out again should the tides of war turn against him."

Fiadh turned away from his touch, and he dropped his hand. "You told me you don't hate my people," she said, "or wish to see them fall, but you've stolen me from them. How does this not hurt them? If the war comes to Erabel and I can't protect my home, Darragh's armies could kill us all. Is that what you want? You want mankind, who killed so many Merrow in the Great War, to win?"

"They may win in a battle against your people, but they will never defeat my kingdom."

"We're part of the same world! If you're working against us, you're helping destroy what's left of your people, too."

"They cannot breach our borders, Fiadh. We have become stronger in our exile."

"That's a fool's dream! If Erabel falls, so shall you!"

He looked at Tulaer. "She's not how I imagined."

"Nor I," he said.

"You know, it is a favor I do, keeping you here. You will remain safe and beyond the reach of mankind." The prince rubbed his finger along a puncture wound from Tulaer's nails and frowned. She watched as red stained the water, turning pink before disappearing completely. "Perhaps, when your people learn humility, I will release you. Until then…"

Cyraeneus jerked his head and Tulaer hauled her from the room, covering her mouth as she made to scream. He flew through the water and those who saw stopped and stared. Before she was thrust into a dark corridor, she caught sight of Eradar. For once, emotion filled his face before he masked it. Stricken, he turned away as Tulaer took her into the depths. Fiadh fought the Merrow's restraining grip, twisting and bucking, calling on the water surrounding her. The earth. Its creatures. But nothing responded.

"Your spells do not work in Abadon," Tulaer snarled, thrusting her into a cell.

Her foot scraped against the rough rock that lined the small space, tearing the skin. Tulaer looked at the thin line of blood floating up from the wound. "Frail being."

"Why are you doing this?" she snapped, clutching her appendage. "Our people have lived side-by-side for centuries. We share this world!"

He raised an eyebrow. "The Aos Sí abandoned us at Rygeil's command. They turned their back as my people were slaughtered!"

"Abandoned you? How can you even say that? They lost thousands, Tulaer! It was war!"

"A war of their own making," he said darkly.

She shook her head and turned away, listening to the thunk as he locked the cell door.

"Do not think to escape. Many have tried. None have succeeded."

Ignoring his threat, she waited in silence for him to leave. Drifting to a jut of rock that made a wide ledge, she sat and looked at her foot, grimacing at the flap of skin that bobbed in the water.

How could Eradar do this to her?

How would anyone even find her? Save her?

She let out a sigh, made strange by the sensation of water pouring from her gills. Grumbling, she took in her bleak surroundings. The walls were rough stone, abrasive to the touch. Two rounded openings and the door were the only sources of light and embedded into each of these were jagged bars of some type of shell, so thick they appeared unbreakable if one could get beyond the sharp points that surround their curvature. Toward the base of one wall was a mounted basin of some kind. Fiadh's lip curled in distaste as she realized it was meant for waste. How it worked would remain a mystery until her body decided it was necessary.

Hours went by, though they felt like days as Fiadh circled her prison, glancing out of the openings with every pass. No one came. Her stomach snarled. Placing her hand on her belly, she wondered how and what she was supposed to eat. Thirst clearly wasn't a problem, but food could be. *My thoughts must have summoning powers,* she mused, as the sound of someone approaching came to her ears. Fiadh went to the door and looked through the bars, watching as a young Merrow woman came toward her with a platter in her hands. She was frighteningly beautiful, her pale, dispassionate eyes marking Fiadh's movements as she floated toward the cell door.

Backing away, Fiadh watched the female wave her hand through the water just beyond the jagged opening. It was as though the jaws of her cell stretched, creating a space just wide enough for the platter to slip through and into her waiting hands. Fiadh hovered awkwardly, gripping the edge of the plate, and looked at the intricate etching on the silver lid while her brain scrambled for something to say, some plea to utter. When she looked up, she was gone and in her place was Eradar.

Her mouth filled with curses, the taste of them metallic on her tongue. Curling her lip, she sneered. "Have you come to gloat?"

He sighed. "I had no choice."

Setting the platter on the ledge, she spun around and met his face, eyes flashing. "No choice? How can you say that to me? We all have choices, and it's clear you've made yours." She glared balefully at him. "With this act, you have doomed my people should war come to our borders."

"They were doomed the moment talk of war spilled from their lips!"

"Liar!"

"You know nothing of war, young Fiadh. You have not watched men come for your people. You haven't seen them slay the young and old for the pleasure of it!" She turned away, and he yelled, "Hear me! You've never heard your mate plead for the life in her belly while you held her hand and *lied*, telling her all would be well even as you watched her life bleed out of her from the poison men spilled into our sacred waters." He sobbed. "You have not held your tiny son in your arms as her body expelled it in the vain hope of survival."

"Eradar," she whispered, aching at the image his words conjured.

"You don't know what it feels like when your allies lift their magical protections out of spite and flee when you cannot. You don't know what it's like when the ugliness of war comes for you and yours!"

Tears mixed with the water, blending with the soft currents. "You're right. I have not seen those things… I didn't know and my heart breaks for you." She drifted toward the cell door and snagged his pained gaze. "But taking me does nothing to honor those you've lost."

"I do not seek to honor them. I seek to wield your people as my sword of vengeance. It was Darragh's ancestor, Magnar, who convinced other lords to poison our waters, nearly wiping us out. Killing my mate and child." He made to leave, his strong back rippling in the dimness. Just beyond the passageway leading to the upper levels, he craned his neck, his profile barely visible in the shadows. "If your people think Darragh took you, they'll slaughter everyone in Felmore and my family will be avenged."

Pain and hopelessness filled Fiadh's face as he disappeared. She stayed there, suspended, staring at the spot where he had been before her body grew weary. What now? How would she escape this place and find her way home if they were just going to keep her locked up in here?

Closing her eyes, she let thoughts of Veren fill her mind. Her heart caught as she imagined the panic he would feel when he learned she was missing. The fear and rage if he thought Darragh had captured her. It was in those moments Fiadh acknowledged that deeper feelings for the warrior had grown over the time they had spent training and talking. There was something there. Something more than friendship.

Gideon's face suddenly invaded her mind—the look of anger mixed with longing as they had stared at each other from across the burning field. Why was it so hard to let him go?

Shaking her head, she fixed her attention back to Veren and reached for him with her mind, visualizing her thought traveling through the waters of Abadon and the forest of Erabel—to him. Over and over, she reached out, often shifting from Dasha and Veren to Krulan and Rivya. Whether any of them caught her thoughts, she couldn't say, but it gave her purpose as the hours passed.

Hunger finally drove her to the platter, and she lifted the lid, finding an assortment of water plants and a blob of something that ended up tasting like sour, pasty bread. It sat in her stomach like a stone, making her wish she hadn't eaten it. Beyond the cell window, the false light dimmed and with it, the magical landscape became something ominous, shadowy and strange. Fiadh retreated, her body feeling unnaturally heavy. Movement was so different here. She felt both weightless and grounded at the same time. Muttering, she stretched out on the stone outcropping and cradled her head on her arm. Sleep came, though it was fitful, riddled with nightmares. Veren was calling to her, his voice growing ragged and desperate. She couldn't reach him, couldn't find him in the dark.

Cyraeneus came for her the next morning, unlocking the cell door and entering the small space.

She faced him, not bothering to hide the hatred burning in her stare.

He chuckled. "It is good to see fire in you, young one." She backed away as he reached for her arm. He smirked. "Resisting me when you have no hope of winning is a waste of energy. You must learn to choose your battles."

"So, you are giving me advice? Let me give you some." She paused as he lifted his chin, waiting. "Let me go before you find yourself at my mercy."

Barking laughter, he pulled her toward him. "Mother will enjoy your spirit!"

Fiadh let him haul her from the cell, shock turning into a grim smile as she focused on the warmth of his skin against hers. Through the contact, she felt his power, the magic Eradar had spoken of many times. It was like a tiny vibration in his flesh. And it called to her, waiting for her to come and claim it.

CHAPTER NINE

ygeil watched as Crom Cruach was led into the hall by a rope around his neck, hands bound behind his back in a mockery of submissiveness. A lithe female warrior yanked on the fibers, eliciting a wet chuckle from the monster who could snap the length of hemp with little effort should he choose to. It was a game, and Rygeil was tired of games.

A handsome elf stood at the king's side, the wings of his dark eyebrows contrasting with his piercing green stare. Hair as black as his grandfather's hung past his shoulders, shifting slightly as he cocked his head. Calum, Fiadh's twin brother, studied the old god, noting the wicked glint of his eyes beneath the nubs of his fleshy forehead. His mouth turned down as Crom Cruach was forced to his knees at the king's feet with a sweep of the female's leg. The harsh smack of old bones on hard stone hung in the air for a moment, swallowed by the sound of cackling as he craned his neck and winked at the elf.

Calum watched her face as she gave the demon a withering look. *Ah, Riani. What a fierce fighter you are,* he mused. *Quick to anger and lethal.*

"Enough, Riani," Rygeil said with calm authority, taking the medallion she held out to him while the Cù-Sìth at the king's side pinned the demon in her yellow stare. "Why is he bound?"

"He attacked one of his guards, and I thought it best he be restrained before meeting with you."

Crom Cruach twisted his head to look up at her and whispered a Word. The rope exploded in a burst of heat, ash falling to the floor in tiny drifts.

"She-elves did not have permission to hide their skin when I first walked this earth." The demon fingered the hem of her tunic, licking his lips and ripping it to reveal her midriff.

Rage flooded her face. "Vile wretch," she spat, using her arm to cover her exposed skin.

"Leave us." Rygeil's voice cut through her anger.

Shooting Crom Cruach a look of loathing, she stalked from the room.

Rygeil leaned back in his chair, the slender fingers of one hand drumming on the polished wood while he traced the sigil on the medallion with his thumb. "You attack one of my soldiers and humiliate another in my very court?"

Crom Cruach shrugged and eyed the powerful disc. "It was a bit of fun, nothing more."

Should he have truly wanted to harm the guard, it would have taken little effort, even with the magic imbued in the medallion to control him. Rygeil knew this. He also knew that the ancient one would turn on him if he did not allow such diversions. He tossed the charm to Calum, who caught it with a flick of his hand, and watched his grandson study it before flicking his eyes back to the demon. A thin smile curled Rygeil's lips as he saw the effect the presence of the medallion had.

"You can control him with that," Rygeil told Calum, ignoring the hiss that pronouncement elicited. "But know that it is bound to this."

He slipped his hand into his tunic, drawing out a small figure that hung from braided sinew and turning it so Calum could see the symbol etched into its surface. "You will note the sigils are the same, and that is what binds them, though it is this one that holds the true power, and I will not part with it. You will wear the medallion and use it when he's less than—" he paused and looked at Crom Cruach, whose glare held the promise of pain. "Shall we say, agreeable to your wishes. I will teach you how to wield it."

"I look forward to those lessons," Calum said.

Rygeil held the demon in his stare and fingered the only remaining relic from Crom Cruach's reign—a miniature idol of the god himself, inscribed with a powerful sigil to hold him under his control. He had no desire to test the strength of the mark, fearing its limits and unwilling to show the old god any weakening in control.

"I suggest you temper your games, Crom, and seek sport among our enemies in the future." He reached for a sweetmeat on a silver tray and popped it in his mouth, then reached out to stroke the massive head of the Cù-Sìth who growled low in her chest.

The demon ignored the king and his protector, marking the moment Calum placed the medallion around his neck and acknowledging the need for patience, restraining his compulsion to snatch it from the elf's neck and crush it beneath his boot. "As you wish, oh splendid one," he said distractedly.

Calum heard the slight and stepped forward. Years of brutal training to protect and serve his grandfather flooded his mind. The whisper of his blade accompanied his movements as he held the tip to the demon's throat.

Putting a restraining hand on him, Rygeil said, "Sheath your weapon, Calum. He toys with you. Do not flatter him with your ire."

Stowing his sword, Calum gave a curt nod and retreated to his former post at the king's side. Crom Cruach watched the exchange but said nothing, though it was impossible to miss the calculating gleam in his eyes.

Rygeil reached for another candied nut, chewing thoughtfully. "It is time to collect a debt."

"Debt?" Crom Cruach asked, darting his tongue along his bulbous bottom lip. "What an interesting term you use."

Rygeil leaned forward. "It is my power that binds you to me. I bought your allegiance when I set you free. Even a god can understand a debt that is owed, is that not so?"

Crom Cruach grunted.

"Do not forget that I can cast you back into that prison should you fail to fulfill the price of your freedom."

His malformed lips twitched. "I am your humble servant," he said, bending low at the waist and letting out a loud fart.

Calum cursed in disgust.

"Childish theatrics. Would you prefer to return to your cell?" Rygeil asked.

The demon shrugged. "I am content to be where you have need of me. If that is in my cell, then so be it."

Rygeil shifted in his chair and wiped his mouth with a lacy cloth, letting moments pass before he said, "I have a task for you. Are you ready to serve me, demon?"

Crom Cruach straightened, the bones along his spine cracking, and delved into Rygeil's mind. "You wish me to lure your granddaughter from Danu's womb."

Alarm flared at the intrusion, and Rygeil threw up mental walls, shutting him out. He smiled, as if unconcerned, but felt sure the demon sensed his fear. The ease with which the old god's tentacles had penetrated his mind was… disconcerting. "You value yourself too highly. Calum will be the lure," Rygeil said, resting his arms on the chair. "You are naught but a means to aid him and keep those who fight alongside Fiadh from coming to her defense."

"You put much faith in her twin, Rygeil. Are you certain he has the strength to pull her out?"

At a nod from his grandfather, Calum raised his arms and whispered. The air stirred, shifting the rushes strewn upon the stone floor. He whipped his hands in the air and they churned, becoming a funnel of herbs and straw. Calum's eyes glowed as he called on a darker spell. One of many Rygeil had shared over countless years of training. Sparks flickered in the roiling mass, tiny currents of energy like miniature bolts of lightning, though they glowed red with a toxic promise to any who felt their fire. He looked beyond the mass and found Crom Cruach studying him, his distorted face a mask of indifference.

Debris fell to the floor with a mutter, leaving a small cloud of dust and a metallic scent of electricity in the air.

"Very impressive, little master. I see your grandfather has trained you in many forms of magic. But do you think it's enough to face your sister?"

"She will come to me," Calum said quietly.

"We shall see. And if she doesn't?" the demon asked, turning to Rygeil.

The king sipped from a jewel-encrusted goblet, considering. "Your primary task is to protect Calum and keep those who have betrayed me from harming him. Convince her to come to my side, to bring her powers to the battle. So together, united, we can rid the world of mankind once and for all. Should additional aid be needed, you shall do what Calum asks and only that. Do not forget that my blood runs in his veins."

Calum glanced at his grandfather, seeing an older version of himself sitting in the chair. One day, he too would have hosts of artisans composing ballads and crafting paintings of him to adorn the halls. Rygeil sought to turn Fiadh, bring her to Oadsera and merge their powers with his, becoming the most powerful elves the world had ever seen. But that would mean continuing to kneel at his grandfather's feet. Perhaps there was another way. These dark days would pass and, with his sister at his side, he could take the throne for himself.

Crom Cruach looked between the two. "As you wish."

With an order to a guard, Rygeil sent the demon from

the room. He left, feet shuffling in an awkward gait. At the threshold, Crom Cruach looked back at the king and his grandson, lips curling in a grotesque smile. He would abide by Rygeil's wishes so long as it amused him, but he would never again suffer centuries in the dank cell to which he had been confined. In that, the king had made a fatal error. Even now, he could feel his power swelling, fed by the fear that radiated from the Aos Sí soldiers as they avoided his dark gaze. He would reclaim his heritage, and, once again, mankind would worship him. And, perhaps, the elves would learn to bend the knee lest he shatter their skulls upon the rocky surface of his idols.

CHAPTER TEN

aegna rocked on the stool before her scrying bowl, muttering spells she had not known until they spilled from her mouth in ugly waves. They were not her words or had not been until the darkness spoke to her from the depths of the water that even now undulated in small currents beneath her breath. It did not matter that she was a tool, wielded by a being whose power reached beyond the iron prison in which he was confined. Her mind was bent on securing her son's position, thereby ensuring her own. When he became king of the western fold, she would have an unnaturally long life. Gifts would be brought to her from faraway lands in the form of the blood of youths whose throats would spill their precious lifeblood into her waiting chalice.

She muttered, spinning spellcraft that clouded the mind and crawled across the land, slipping through a weakened barrier. Haegna searched for the young queen of the Aos Sí using a seeking spell, frowning when she could not be found.

It would be more challenging to get this work done if she did not know where the elf was.

Her lips moved, showing flashes of stained teeth, as she sought one who Fiadh was attached to, feeling for a bond. She would target the one whose loss would be the hook she'd cast to bring the elf from her protective borders. Like a poisonous fog, the spell snaked through Erabel, searching for the guardian who rarely left Fiadh's side. But its powerful mind repelled the dark magic. The ancient Cù-Sìth knew better than to keep his thoughts unguarded. Drifting away from that one, she found another. Younger, open, and without the mental wards to keep her out. When she was certain Fiadh was nowhere to be found, she cast a powerful spell.

Ears twitched and rotated at the sound that came to them through Haegna's magic. The bait of Fiadh's voice. A plea that muffled everything but its cry for aid. A false summons. A lie. But the beast would not understand until it was too late.

Images danced upon the surface of the water, though to an onlooker, it would appear black and still. Haegna watched as the Cù-Sìth breached the barrier protecting Erabel, running through Dorcha Wood. Its mind was trapped so completely it could reach out to none of its kind. Nor be found by any who called to it.

"Let us see how well she fares without a watchdog at her heels," Haegna said into the stillness.

Rising slowly, she stretched her muscles, the bones along her spine protesting at the movement. Age—unforgiving and relentless—had crept into her body despite the lengths she had gone to stop it. Gnarled hands and graying hair were the hallmarks of its harshness. That time could mark her, steal her future, had long been a source of terror and rage.

She scowled as flares of pain shot through her legs and shoulders. Muttering, Haegna hobbled to the pot hanging above a weak fire and spooned mulled wine into a cup. The folds of her neck bobbed slowly as she took a long pull of the warm liquid—reminding her of blood as it slithered down her throat to warm her belly. Thin trails of red wine leaked from the corners of her mouth, staining her pale, thin skin and giving her the look of the Abhartach—a blood drinker of ancient legends. Swiping her hand across her mouth, she considered her plight.

The darkness had first spoken to her as she sat before her scrying bowl, head bent as she delved for power beyond her own. It had watched her for some time before that first connection, of that she was certain, having felt its presence before it made itself known. Promises of power, rivers of power, that would flow from her tongue in waves were given as she slowly let down her guard and opened her mind to Carmun's son. Her brother by blood. Thus far, Dothur had kept his promises… to a point.

But what she had been given had not stopped time from wearing her down, draining her very essence. Too soon, she would be nothing but an empty husk if a way to slow its progress was not found.

Haegna glanced at the scrying bowl. Even now, it pulsed with knowledge and power, calling to her. What if she slipped her hand into those dark waters? If she gave the drops of blood it begged for?

Dothur was something she was both drawn to and repelled by, the latter strong enough to keep her from plunging into its depths, giving him all he wanted. He was ancient. Powerful. Filled with wrath. She recognized the violence cloaked in his darkness. It was her own.

Sipping from her cup, she pondered her plight. To see her desires come to fruition, she needed the girl. Rygeil's daughter was her salvation, of that Dothur had been certain and she had sensed no deception in his claim. Taking one of the beasts that protected her was the first step. But what if that wasn't enough? Dothur had warned her of the girl's power. It had grown since she had returned to Erabel. Even Haegna could feel it. She needed to be drawn out, away from those who would protect her. Lured.

Who would be the bait?

The girl's hatred for Darragh was a given, but risking her son's life to coax the elven witch from her forest was too high a cost. Already, she felt drained from the spells she had just cast. What if she weakened further and the elves grew in strength? She would be unable to intervene and all would be lost. Darragh would fall, and she with him.

If only the mage were still imprisoned. With the aid of Dothur, she could use his power, merge it with her own. But Xander was gone, having toyed with Darragh before escaping. Nay, it was up to her, and she was tiring.

Lord Belfirth's brat had known Fiadh, spent time with her. Fallen in love with her, as his mind had reluctantly revealed under a mental assault. Haegna rocked and considered how best to use Lord Ross' son. She did not trust his hatred for the girl, having felt softness beneath it. But his thirst for vengeance was a powerful tool. It may be enough to bring Fiadh under this roof. After that, she would have no need of him.

Rubbing her stomach absently, she wished for sustenance to ease her cravings. But there was nothing but day-old stew. Growling in frustration, she slumped in her rocking chair and stared into the small flames of the fire. She had been left starving, consigned to this cell with naught but wine to slake her thirst. Darragh had threatened to refuse to bring her another fresh-faced youth if her attempt to lure Fiadh from Erabel failed. *How dare he!* He would do well to remember that without her, he would be nothing.

The scrape of worn shoes on cold rock drifted from beneath the door. She cocked her head, smiling as her maid-servant, Emer, shuffled inside.

"Fetch my son," Haegna barked.

Setting a basket of food on the small table, Emer straightened her dress, tugging at the fabric that strained against her soft stomach. Tucking graying strands of matted hair behind her ear, she looked at her mistress. "The lord has guests."

Haegna raised a brow. "Guests? Who?"

Emer shrugged and set about tidying the room.

"Have his men returned from their hunt?"

"I know not."

Haegna glowered. "Find out!"

With a huff, Emer left, her uneven gait echoing through the bowels of the castle.

As Haegna sat waiting, a voice she had come to know drifted to her ears. Eying her scrying bowl, she cocked her head and listened. Dothur called to her, the liquid rippling. His words tugged at her mind, though she sat rooted in her chair. He did not know her limits, nor did he care, and she would not tell him of her fatigue, knowing he may abandon her for one whose strength and youth were better vessels for his power. Hissing under her breath, she told him to be patient, grimacing as anger leaped from the gently vibrating surface and into the air.

Let him remain in his prison until he had served his purpose.

CHAPTER ELEVEN

Gideon crouched in a shadowy recess of Dorcha Wood, the thick rope of a net in his fist. The trees creaked, making the hair on the back of his neck bristle. At his side were Quinn and Brody. He'd drilled his men relentlessly day and night since they'd come under his command. They were battered and bruised and still rough as hell, but they had learned to follow simple orders and could coordinate together in at least a few basic maneuvers. He glanced at the lads' new swords. They were wickedly sharp, glinting in the shafts of light that pierced the canopy. And, while Donal and his men had crashed and banged, struggling in the undergrowth as they came through the forest, it had pleased Gideon to see Quinn and Brody darting silently and effortlessly through the foliage. Others could say what they would about its lord, but Felmore's craftsmen knew their business.

He heard the rapid breathing of the youths at his side—fear of the forest mixing with excitement for the hunt. A short distance away waited a group of Darragh's seasoned warriors, led by Donal. The bulk of the lord's fighting force remained in Felmore.

"I've never seen a Cù-Sìth. I thought they were a fairy tale," Quinn whispered.

"They're no fairy tale. They're monsters."

Quinn paled and darted a glance at Gideon.

He flashed a grin at the lad. "Don't worry. I won't let it eat you."

Gripping the netting as though it were a shield, Quinn nodded.

He's too young for this work, Gideon thought, remembering his argument with Donal when Darragh's commander had told him to select two from his troop. Quinn and Brody were the best among the dozen he'd taken under his wing, but they were nowhere near ready. How Donal had even known to set a trap for the Cù-Sìth was a mystery, though Gideon had been reluctant to ask, sensing he may not like the response. There were dark forces hanging over Felmore.

The crack of a branch brought Gideon's head up, and he focused on the clusters of trees in front of him. "Get ready," he told the two young men. "Remember what I told you. No noise. Wait for my signal."

Glancing at Donal's soldiers, he saw flashes of fear, though beneath that emotion was something much darker. Bloodlust. He caught the commander staring at him. It was no secret Donal sought to use him and his boys as bait. He'd said as much as they'd argued about the two lads taking part in the hunt.

Lifting his hand, Donal signaled his fighters. They

quickly filled the woods with raucous bellows and swords clanking against shields. Gideon frowned. Such noise was sure to be an enticing lure for the ferocious beast.

The massive Cù-Sìth hurtled through the forest, its paws digging ruts in the soft earth, drawn to the noises of Donal's men. Birds flew out of the trees and small animals scurried away, adding to the din of the approaching beast. Quinn muttered a prayer to the Great Mother. Gideon heard it and clenched his jaw.

Donal raised his arm, and Gideon's muscles grew taut, eyes fixed on the noises growing nearer. "Now!" the commander yelled.

Quinn and Brody yelped as a bear-sized wolfish creature with green and black fur burst through the trees. Gideon pressed his fingers to his lips and grabbed their heads, holding them down. The animal charged Donal's group, fangs snapping, ravaging those who stabbed at it.

Gideon motioned to Quinn and Brody, and they sprang in unison, launching themselves in a wide arc to encompass the creature within the folds of the huge net. The Cù-Sìth writhed in clouds of dirt, snarling and flipping its body. Quinn, frozen, watched in terror as a nightmare came to life slashing at the netting, furious yellow eyes pinning him to the ground. Brody worked with Gideon as more nets and ropes were tossed and pegged, tightening around the beast until it was trapped. The soldiers yelled in triumph.

Leaning over and clasping his legs, Gideon panted, body shuddering in the throes of adrenaline as the Cù-Sìth's movements grew still. Quinn laughed nervously when

Gideon slapped him on the back before he turned to Brody, giving the youth a nod of approval. The whisper of swords drew his attention. Soldiers fanned out to surround the creature as it lay prone, frozen in something far more sinister than fear.

Donal barked an order to Quinn and Brody. "Unsheathe your blades!"

The young soldiers looked at Gideon—their faces pale masks of dread.

"Leave them out of this," Gideon said. "I mean these two to be soldiers, not butchers."

"Are they too weak to do their lord's bidding?" Donal cuffed Brody, who stumbled. "I said unsheathe your sword," he hissed.

Brody's hand shook as he pulled out his blade. The muscles in Gideon's jaw ticked. "Do not touch my soldiers, Donal."

The commander looked balefully at Gideon. "They are only yours because Lord Darragh gifted them to you. Perhaps he did this in error and they should fall under my command."

The stark panic on Brody's face prodded at Gideon.

"That won't be necessary," Gideon said. "Quinn, draw your blade."

Quinn stood motionless as though he'd heard nothing. His eyes locked on the Cù-Sìth's, giving the impression that the animal somehow held him frozen.

Prodding him with his elbow, Gideon got the young man's attention. "Draw your sword."

The heavy breathing of the Cù-Sìth filled the quiet as Quinn fumbled for his weapon. It wavered in his grasp when he held it above the incapacitated animal. Gideon knew what was coming. He knew it, but nothing could prepare him for the savagery.

At Donal's signal, the soldiers plunged their blades into Rivya. Stabbing so deep, the tips ripped through her body and into the ground beneath. Gideon stood motionless, sword hanging untainted in midair. His mind fractured as the Cù-Sìth's yellow eyes swept to his, locked onto him, until they finally dimmed amidst the sounds of butchery. Like the dowsing of a candle, Rivya's mind was snuffed, her final moments—desperate thoughts—trapped within Haegna's powerful spell where, in the bowels of Felmore Castle, the witch savored their terror before letting them go as if they were nothing more than wisps of air. The ragged beating of Rivya's heart slowed, then stopped with a final shudder.

Roars of triumph filled the forest, silencing every living thing as if they had all born witness. Quinn stumbled away and vomited. Gideon let him purge himself in privacy and found Brody next to him, the soldier's sword dripping with blood, and winced at the shattered innocence he saw in the youth's face.

His stomach clenched with regret and horror, his gaze drifting over the bloody remains. This was vengeance. Retribution. It was what the spirits of his family had called for, was it not?

But as he watched blood seep into the soil, it felt like murder.

Donal's voice cut through his mind, severing his fixed

stare and bringing him back to the men who slapped each other on the back and bragged of trophies that would take from the cooling corpse. Robotically, he took hold of the corner of the net, folding it over the body, and helped drag it from the darkness of the woods, toward Felmore Castle. Brody had moved beside him with Quinn. Gideon felt the looks they shot him but said nothing. He would speak to them later when Donal was out of earshot.

It was taxing work, the dead weight of the Cù-Sìth sapping Gideon's strength as it snagged on exposed roots and shards of jutting rock, as though the forest itself didn't want to let it go. Breaking through the trees, Donal whistled for a waiting cart and they loaded the creature into it.

Gideon stepped back and studied the paw that hung limply from the wooden bed, noting a drop of blood that hung from the sharp tip of a nail before falling to the earth. He stared at it as the cart lurched forward, pulled by a pair of oxen. A couple of Darragh's men strolled by, bragging, wiping blood from their blades. One of them tugged at his tunic, then slung an arm around his shoulder, pulling him along. Gideon went, though his thoughts were dark and confused. He thought of little Aishling. What would she think if she had witnessed this? Would she be proud? Or would she be horrified? And he thought of Fiadh.

When the group reached the outer bailey, he sent Quinn and Brody to the nearby lake to clean up, knowing they'd find the rest of their troop to tell them what happened. He could only hope they would still see him as a worthy leader after news of this day's work was shared.

Envoys of King Stephan were exiting the great hall when Gideon and a handful of soldiers, led by Donal, strode toward Darragh's dais. They each had short beards and fine tunics embroidered with a golden eagle on the chest piece—the king's regalia. The five men glanced at Gideon, nodding briefly when their eyes flicked to the stag on his breastplate, the emblem of Belfirth. Without a word, the entourage swept past, and he wondered what they'd think when they came upon the gruesome corpse just outside the doors of the keep.

"It is done," Donal announced when they had reached the foot of the dais.

Darragh smiled and rose. "Take me to it."

Following at a distance, Gideon walked to the inner bailey where the oxen stood waiting, heads drooping as they remained tethered to the cart. King Stephan's men stood, mouths agape, a short distance from the body, the reins of their mounts hanging loosely in their fists.

Darragh circled the conveyance slowly, stopping when he came to the spot where the Cù-Sìth's head lay at an awkward angle against the wood. Reaching through a gap in the netting, he grabbed a hunk of greenish fur and lifted the massive head, peeling back an eyelid to stare into its yellow depths. Gideon watched with distaste as the lord chuckled, the sound growing into a full-blown guffaw. The crowd joined him.

"So, they can be killed after all," Darragh said, spinning in a slow circle as his eyes swept those assembled.

Looking on coldly, Gideon watched as Darragh drew a dagger from his belt and dug into the beast's socket, plucking its eye out and into his waiting hand. Gently closing his fingers, he glanced at the castle, then stepped back, jerking his head toward the corpse.

"Cut off its head and put it on a pike. Ensure all within that accursed wood know what happens when they stand against me."

"Aye, my lord," Donal said, motioning for soldiers to lead the wagon beyond the gates.

Gideon watched its progress, then turned on his heel, striding to catch up with Darragh.

"My lord," he called out.

Darragh turned, glancing at the eyeball that sat in his palm. "Not now, young lord. I have business to attend to."

Ignoring his words, Gideon forged ahead. "Now that we have killed the beast, should we not press our advantage and march on Erabel?"

Darragh turned slowly on his heel. "Are you so eager to spill more blood?"

"I am eager to rid the world of the Aos Sí, as you should be."

Lip curling, Darragh took a step toward Gideon, stopping when their noses were but a fingers-length apart. "What are you saying, boy?"

Holding his ground, Gideon said, "Naught, but what you hear. We should make our move now."

"You seek to advise me? You, who have no army or people to speak of? You who are worth no more than the clothes on your back?"

Gideon ground his teeth and lifted his chin. "I may have no wealth to speak of, but I know when to march and when to retreat. You squander our advantage by waiting."

"Wisdom learned at your father's knee, was it? Pray, how did such knowledge serve him?"

"Do not speak of my father."

Shaking his head, Darragh turned away. "Oh, little lordling, did you not see who has just left my hall?" He put up his hand before Gideon could reply. "Those were envoys of the king himself, come to seek my counsel as word travels of Rygeil's armies attacking strongholds in the east and north. The king wishes to know if I need aid should elves set their sights on the western reaches." He looked triumphantly at Gideon. "They come to see me! *Me!* Not you, landless whelp. Why spend my own armies when the king will lend me his?"

"He is sending a contingent of men?"

"Aye." He puffed his chest. "The king knows I rule the western fold and if we fall, so too will all of mankind. If you're a good lad, mayhap I will let you march with the king's men."

Gideon bit down on his retort and nodded his head, heading toward the door before he let fly with his true thoughts.

"Oh, Lord Belfirth?"

He stopped at the threshold and turned his head slightly. "Aye?"

"You would do well to curry favor with those who will live beyond these dark days."

Gideon's eyes narrowed. "I remember where my loyalties lie." He stalked from the hall, the sound of Darragh's laughter at his back.

CHAPTER TWELVE

*C*yraeneus pulled Fiadh through the winding halls of Abadon. She let him, curiosity for an audience with the queen outweighing her desire to steal his power and try to escape. His webbed fingers held her fast, though he kept his sharp nails from puncturing her flesh. As they made their way through decadent halls, she focused on her surroundings, marking each turn and doorway, committing them to memory so she would know the way out.

Eventually, they came to a massive entry blocked by ornately carved doors. In the center of the two panels was a huge carving etched into the material. Fiadh stared at it as Cyraeneus let go of her arm and knocked. It was an image of the queen. She was sure of it. Her icy beauty looked out from jeweled eyes, while beneath her magnificent tail, the Merrow swam, their gazes fixed on her in rapture. It was a vulgar display of fealty to Fiadh's eyes, and she looked away.

The doors opened dramatically, as though choreographed to draw a sigh of awe from those standing without them. She struggled not to sneer as the prince bowed low, his tail swishing in slow undulations. Fiadh kept her neck stiff and her eyes locked on the floor until Ithraen's rich voice broke the silence.

"Leave us, my son."

Cyraeneus looked at Fiadh and tilted his chin before taking his leave. The closing of the heavy doors behind her felt ominous. Straightening her shrinking form, Fiadh glided toward the throne on which the queen perched—a massive seat of power with giant shells of every color jutting from its sides like a huge fan. When Fiadh reached the base of the platform, she stopped and looked into the palest eyes she had ever seen.

"You wonder why you are here," Ithraen said matter-of-factly.

"Nay, I know why you have taken me prisoner."

Ithraen's brow arched, making a point so sharp that it was almost comical. "Oh? And why is that?"

"You wish to use me as a pawn in your quest for revenge."

The queen glanced at the doorway, then back at Fiadh. "My son has many faults. One of which is presuming he knows my mind."

A look of confusion crossed Fiadh's face.

"I do not seek revenge, young one," Ithraen said softly. "Though it would be my right to claim it."

"I… I don't understand. Why am I here?"

The queen rose, her body unfurling in a flow of fins and colors. She held out her hand. "Come."

Fiadh looked at it, uncertain, but sensing no ill will. She

grasped the queen's warm fingers and was pulled toward a balcony that overlooked the kingdom.

"During the Great War, the many realms of the Merrow across this world fell. When we refused to join the Aos Sí, the wards protecting our realms were sundered. We were abandoned. Poisoned. Slaughtered."

Fiadh opened her mouth, but Ithraen pressed a finger to her lips.

"Aye, our realms were laid bare, and we were abandoned while your people fought a war they could not win. But I do not place all the blame on the Aos Sí. It was not for them to keep humanity from our waters. That should have fallen to us." Ithraen sighed. "Those who survived fled here. Every channel that would lead to this place was sealed, dooming those who could not escape. That is my burden to bear, for I am the one who commanded it."

Sweeping her arm in a wide arc to encompass the landscape beyond the opening in the wall, she said, "This is all that remains of my kingdom. Many who call these waters home did not live here until those dark days. Now, they can never return to their true home. They will never know if loved ones yet live. Those ways are shut, and I would not see them opened."

"I'm sorry for your people, truly." Fiadh folded her hands and looked down. "But holding me here will not change the past."

Ithraen smiled sadly. "Even if it were in my power, I would change nothing."

The comment, said so plainly, startled Fiadh.

The queen cocked her head. "You think me heartless?"

"I—"

"To change the past would mean changing who we have become," she interrupted, gliding to her throne. Her body settled into it, the motion stirring the delicate strands of her hair, distracting Fiadh for a moment as they caught the light. "You see, it is only through the hardships of the upheaval that I believe we truly found ourselves—as a people. We have become strong. Much stronger than we were all those years ago. Our survival depended on it. I do not wish to return to what we were before... to devolve, so to speak."

"I don't understand."

Ithraen studied her, making Fiadh squirm. "You have felt the magic in our blood. When you touched my son's skin, it pulsed beneath your fingertips." It was impossible to keep the shock from her face, which only made the queen chuckle. "Our magic sings to you, does it not?"

Fiadh bit the inside of her cheek, suddenly feeling like a deer in the sharp eye of a huntsman.

"Of course, you may choose to keep silent, but it does not change what I know."

The door opened softly and Fiadh turned, finding Eradar. She glanced at the window, the only other escape, and bolted, legs thrashing in the water, arms outstretched, reaching for the lip of the window frame. The tips of her fingers had just reached the edge when she was yanked back and into Eradar's chest. His arms were a vise, trapping her against his body as she watched the queen float toward them.

"There is no escape," Eradar whispered harshly.

Fiadh snarled and gripped his arm, opening her mind to

the magic she had felt when she touched Cyraeneus' skin, but there was nothing. Nothing but the smooth texture of a strange fabric.

"You may hold your tongue, young one. It matters not." Ithraen looked at her slyly, eyes darting to the hand that struggled to find a gap in the material that appeared to cover Eradar's entire upper body. She reached for Fiadh's face and ran the point of her nail along the tender skin below her eye. "I have but to look to see the truth of what I say in your eyes. That is the magic I have honed since the Great War. Your father wishes to plumb the depths of your strength, your bond with Danu, and use you to increase his power. Foolish. He was always vain." Cupping her cheek like Riona had done countless times, Ithraen said, "There is no path that leads to the Aos Sí winning a war against the children of men. There never was. Even with your magic, you will lose. Even if Rygeil slays a thousand times a thousand of them, and he may, there will ever be more. If we continue on this path, in the end, it is men who will inherit all the world. You know this in your heart. You have felt it."

Fiadh opened her mouth to argue that inevitability, snapping it closed at the look the queen gave her.

"I do not hold you here to avenge my people. If not for those dark days, we would not be ready to do what our ancestors could not. Your power, daughter of Erabel, is wasted with your people. You will remain in Abadon. You will help me bring forth Caoránach, the mother of the Oilliphéist."

"The what?"

The queen smiled. "I forget you know so little of the world. The Oilliphéist are the true rulers of the earth."

Confusion flooded Fiadh's face.

"Hm, how to explain? Mankind may have called them dragons, but they are not the winged beasts of those myths. They once lived in every body of water, but they disappeared, becoming nothing more than legends, even among our kind. But, my oracle has seen that the essence of Caoránach yet lives. It sleeps, and you will help me birth it."

"I will not help you release a monster into the world!"

"Monster? There is so much of humanity in you," Ithraen said with pity.

Fiadh couldn't deny it. She had loved her mother, Riona, and if that made her more human, so be it.

"The children of men fear the things they cannot explain, and, in that fear, they kill. The Oilliphéist are not monsters. They are the rightful rulers of this world, and they will bring balance."

"Bring balance? How?"

"Oilliphéist are harbingers of rebirth. They will purify all the lands above, consuming those who corrupt it. Peace will finally be restored. Forever. Surely you can see the beauty in that."

"You're mad," Fiadh whispered.

Ithraen shrugged. "Those with great vision are often called mad by the small-minded. I will see this done."

Fiadh writhed in Eradar's grasp. "You cannot do this! You must let me go!"

"You are my guest, young Fiadh." Motioning with her webbed hand, she added, "Deliver her to a room that befits her station." She paused, adding, "And if I hear she is put in a cell again, you will answer for it."

Eradar nodded and pulled Fiadh along. She fought, winning little ground with her small contortions as he increased the pressure around her middle until black spots formed in her vision. He sensed her distress and relaxed his muscles. Throwing her head back, Fiadh struck his nose, and he lost his grip. She shoved against him, planting her foot in his stomach to propel her body, and charged again to the window.

"Cease," Ithraen commanded, the word laced with dark power.

Fiadh's body froze, locked mid-stroke. She looked with fear as the queen came toward her, shaking her head. "Fighting will gain you nothing." With a wave of her hand, she released Fiadh.

"You doom my people!" she cried, finding her strength and will again. "They will be slaughtered if I cannot protect them!"

"They are already doomed!" Ithraen shouted. "The Aos Sí do not wield their weapons! They do not have their numbers! They cannot win!" She visibly reined in her anger. "Taking you changes nothing. The outcome has already been written."

Fiadh sobbed and tried to fall to her knees, but Eradar grasped her roughly, holding her upright. "Please. You have to let me go."

"Your destiny lies with us now."

CHAPTER THIRTEEN

The room they consigned her to was opulent, garish, filling Fiadh with loathing. Everywhere she looked were paintings and sculptures in hues of gold and silver. Even the molding along the walls and windows bore accents of the metallic colors. She felt like an interloper. But what had her feeling truly morose was that she knew the fault of her predicament lay with herself. How often had she heard that she was too naïve, too trusting? Krulan, Veren, and Kaelari had said it many times. Even Gideon had told her as much.

And now she was here. The bars were gone, but it was still a prison.

Fiadh circled the room. Ornate furniture sat about the space just as it would if she were above ground, on land. Everything was so different here and yet, so much the same. Things didn't float around like unanchored boats. They remained in place, mostly. She never felt her body rising toward the surface as she would if she were swimming in the forest. In fact, it was a fight to rise above the floor, legs and arms pumping in the water until her muscles protested.

Flopping onto an oversized chaise, Fiadh sifted through her meeting with the queen. Ithraen was intimidating, her power a tangible thing. She made a frightening adversary. Fiadh knew that if it came to a confrontation, she would lose. Therefore, it couldn't come to that.

She flung her hand over her eyes. Her life had become surreal. Only yesterday—had it only been a day?—she was with Veren, learning how to protect Erabel with magical barriers. Now, she was the captive of a mad queen who wanted to awaken a monster from Merrow legends. For what? To bring some kind of balance? If such a creature existed and had been dormant all this time, why risk everyone's life and revive it? It made no sense. She was living in a nightmare.

A quick knock sounded at the door. She turned and saw two massive each-uisce enter, both carrying wickedly hooked spears. They glowered at her from their horse-like heads and motioned for her to follow. For a moment, she considered refusing, but their weapons practically gleamed with promises of pain, and their expressions begged her to resist. She huffed, sending a small current in front of her face, and went to them.

At the threshold, they stood aside, waiting for her to pass before following so closely she imagined she could almost feel the points of their spears at her back. "Where are you taking me?"

The creature on her right answered, though he kept his

gaze fixed ahead. "Our queen has given you leave to tour the grounds."

"Oh? And that requires spears?"

He craned his neck to look down at her, pinning her to the floor with an odious expression. "We are your guard, tasked with preventing you from escaping and keeping you safe from those who would see you dead."

She took a step away from his malice, bumping up against the other each-uisce who shoved her away.

"You do not have leave to touch me!" a deep, feminine voice snapped.

Fiadh turned her head and looked at the one who had spoken, flicking her eyes to its torso where, sure enough, there were two small, rounded breasts between a belt that crisscrossed her chest. Face flaming, she stammered an apology and shifted her body away.

No more words were spoken as they led her through hallways and into a courtyard of sorts, where water plants grew in chaotic profusion. To distract herself from her menacing guards, she plunged her hands into bunches of flowers, stroking their petals and leaves, while surreptitiously feeling beyond those soft tendrils. Sinking to the ground, she pressed her palms to the sandy soil and reached out to Danu, but all she felt was a faint brush of the Great Mother's awareness. The connection felt muffled, as though she was reaching through layers of wool, and no matter how much she focused, the link didn't become clearer. With a grimace, Fiadh let go and gave her guards a sidelong glance.

They watched her every move, eyes tracking her hands as she brushed the head of a bulbous flower. Not once did they look away, which meant she would have to find other opportunities to seek an escape. With her two sentries at her back, she wandered, taking stock of surrounding structures and halls, hoping to piece together a mental map of sorts. When her legs grew weary of the constant friction of the water and the odd weighted feel of her body that kept her from bobbing to the doomed ceiling of this underwater kingdom, she begged leave to return to her room. They were only too willing to oblige. As they turned the lock, she pressed her ear to the door, listening for their movements, wondering if they stood guard. A faint noise of departure made her smile. *Well, that is one less thing to worry about,* she mused.

A meal arrived midday, brought by Eradar, who stood stoically as she picked at the food.

"What do you want?" She scowled. "Am I to be watched as I eat now?"

He made a face. The expression turned his surreal beauty into something almost human. "Your people search for you."

"Aye, I imagine they do. Perhaps you should set me free before they invade these waters."

"They could not invade our realm even if they thought to look here, which they won't."

Her brow creased.

"They believe you left Erabel."

She looked up sharply. "Why would they think I left?"

He shrugged. "I may have left a false path for them to follow."

Fiadh rose slowly. "Why would you do that? I don't even know you anymore."

Eradar looked abashed but quickly hid the emotion. "It harms nothing to lead them on a merry chase. When they tire of looking for you, they'll move on, assuming you have, too."

She came at him then. "Why would you do this to me? To them! I thought you were my friend!" Her hands turned into claws as righteous anger spread through her body. Sobbing and flailing at him, it didn't register when her power flared, flooding her body. Eradar stepped back, alarm on his face. She snarled when she saw it and launched into him, knocking him back and into a chair. It toppled so slowly it would have been comical if the situation wasn't so tense.

Righting himself, Eradar shoved her back. "Enough!"

Her leg caught on the table, and she went down, staring fiercely up at him. A Word—imbued with the magic of his people—slipped from his lips, had her helpless on her back.

Fiadh panted, the feeling strange and almost suffocating as her body pulled air from the water. "I trusted you!"

A flash of pain crossed his face, masked so quickly she wondered if it was merely a shadow of flickering light from the window. "I know."

"If you truly loved my mother, how could you do this to her daughter? I think you didn't. I think it was all a lie."

"I did love her," he said, reaching out a hand that she batted away.

"You don't know the meaning of the word." Pulling

herself onto the chaise, she sat with her face in her hands, forcing her temper to cool. "Get out."

"Very well, but know that you will be summoned this evening to be examined by our oracle."

She gave him a hooded glare. "Leave."

Not bothering to watch him go, she curled onto her side, back to the door. Dasha, Veren, Kaelari, Krulan, and Rivya. Her people. Her family. For that is what they had become. They could be searching for her if what Eradar said was true. If he'd somehow made them think she had left. She hated him for that. But within that hate was also pity for what he had lost, and what he had become. Krulan would call that a weakness, no doubt. She shook her head. Maybe he would be right to.

The day wore on. Fiadh nibbled at her food, paced, looked out the window, and paced some more. Eradar returned, joined by her two guards from the morning, as the light faded into evening. He stood at the threshold, daring her to refuse to get up. She wouldn't give him the pleasure of a struggle and rose, stopping when she could feel the flow of water from the movements of his tail fins.

"I am glad to see you have accepted your fate."

"Is that what you think I'm doing?" She shook her head. "I'm merely curious to meet whoever seems to think I'm the key to unleashing a monster into the world."

"Caoránach is no monster! She is the rightful ruler!"

Fiadh cocked an eyebrow at his outburst.

He looked flustered for a moment, his pale face reddening as the guards at his sides stared at him. "You bait me, and, fool that I am, I have taken it." Tilting his head to consider her, he said, "Bind her arms."

She could have fought them but forced her body to remain still as she was flung around and her arms wrenched back painfully. They meant for it to be painful, and she clenched her teeth, refusing to show them any emotion.

They led Fiadh to a rounded room with a floor made from the pearl-like lining of hundreds of shells. The walls were dark, speckled with shards of something metallic, so they glittered like stars. Along the ceiling were swollen protrusions of light, like blisters in the rock. At the center was a Merrow woman, her pale form glowing as her tail swept back and forth. Her only adornment was a large, shell-like object that hung from a thong between her small breasts. Unlike all the other Merrow she had seen, the oracle was pure white. Even her eyes were colorless, aside from the dark pupils at their center.

Fiadh paused, her body fighting primal urges to flee as she was pinned in a stare that saw into her, cutting through the thoughts churning in her mind, into that secret place where she had always known who and what she was. The part of her that had hidden beneath a veil of humanity for years until it was set free when she crossed into Erabel. Balking at the intrusion, Fiadh threw up mental shields, but they were useless, breaking under the power of the oracle.

"Welcome, Fiadh, Daughter of Erabel. I am Aelrah." The oracle's mesmerizing gaze shifted to Eradar. "Release her and leave us."

"She is dangerous."

Aelrah tilted her head and stared at Fiadh. "Not to me."

Fiadh's arms sagged as the bindings were removed. She rubbed her wrists, flexing her fingers as tingles replaced the numbness that had grown there.

The oracle held out her hand. "Come, young one. Yours is not a different fate."

CHAPTER FOURTEEN

Aelrah cupped Fiadh's face, her webbed fingers curving around the line of her jaw. It was a gentle touch, but its softness belied the strength pouring from the oracle as she chanted in a language Fiadh had never heard. Images bloomed in her mind as the words circled the room in a vortex of water that lifted her hair and flung it into the current in a riotous mass of black tendrils.

Arms anchored to her sides as though bound by an iron will, Fiadh stood while her mind was flayed open, memories ripped from it, each one a brilliant flash before it was set aside for another. Tears spilled from her eyes as Riona's face and voice filled her vision, held for many moments as Aelrah considered them. Deeper she went, to the walls of her core where she finally stopped, having found the heart of Fiadh's power.

Circling it like a predator, Aelrah mentally jabbed at it, making Fiadh flinch, as she hunted for a way to penetrate Fiadh's heart of strength and use her for her own purpose.

Biting the insides of her cheeks at the invasion, Fiadh felt blood pool on her tongue. The tanginess triggered an involuntary response, as though a fundamental part of her sensed a threat and flared to life in violent anger. Her well of power swelled and opened, loosing itself on the only other living thing in the room.

The oracle yelped, eyes going wide, as she was repelled. Lips curled, lifting into a smile that revealed the sharp points of her teeth. "She bites back," Aelrah chuckled.

Fiadh seethed, hands balling into fists. She clawed at her power, dragging it free before it crawled back into her body under the weight of the Abadon's spells. Her mind grabbed it, tugging it free, so it flowed through her like the blood running through her veins. She called upon the water, felt its resistance, and punched through it, wrestling it to her will.

Lifting arms that were suddenly freed, she threw the full force of the current at Aelrah. The oracle saw it coming and deflected, sending it back at Fiadh twice as strongly. It knocked her to the floor, then lifted her, spinning around her body so quickly that Aelrah became an indistinguishable blur.

"You are strong, young one, but lack skill." Her voice echoed through the room, bouncing off the walls and cutting through the water. "Cease your struggles and submit, or I will cut through your mind like a blade and hollow you out and leave nothing but an empty husk."

Fiadh wanted to keep fighting but felt hopeless. Gritting her teeth, Fiadh reined in her power, feeling it slither into her. Eyes flashing, she sealed it in a protective shell where the oracle couldn't reach it and twist it to her will.

The waters slowed, then stopped, leaving only the movement of her hair floating about her face. Aelrah glided toward her, tail swishing in practiced undulations that caught Fiadh's eyes and held them transfixed. Fiadh stared blankly as the oracle's hands moved in a series of graceful motions before the talisman resting against her chest. The object pulsed with power, the surrounding water vibrating subtly. Its blue surface glowed with an inner light, and with the glow came a humming that started low and quiet, becoming louder until it pounded against Fiadh's ears. She tried to cover them, but her arms were useless lumps of flesh. The talisman shook against Aelrah's chest and opened, its face revealed slowly, like the moon from the clouds. Blue light spilled into the room, pulsing, growing brighter, mixing with the chanting. The spells smothering Fiadh's power fell away in the glow of magic, but she remained paralyzed. Her head felt fuzzy, eyes fixed open as she was washed in brightness that swallowed her completely.

She cried out, though no sound came from her lips, as a tendril of something followed the light and found its way to her. It pressed against her lips as she gritted her teeth, trying to find a way in. She tried to turn away, but her body was not her own and she watched in horror as a wormlike creature grew and found another way in. She felt like she was drowning as it plunged into her nostril, forcing its way down her throat and into her gut, twisting sickeningly for a few awful moments. Her stomach heaved violently, bile crawling up her neck, burning the lining of her throat. She choked, struggling to swallow it down as it pierced her body with knifelike pain, entering her airway. Heat bloomed in her chest. Her heart beat in a crazy tempo, mind screaming.

It was killing her.

Aelrah's voice found her in the darkness of her mind. It called to her, called her back from wherever she had been heading. She tried to block it out, fatigue draining her to the point of surrendering to the black chasm that had opened before her, but it persisted, snagging her in a web of spells. Fiadh wanted to weep, but her body could do little more than twitch where it lay prone on the floor. She fought the voice, the words that harangued her with a litany of commands. As she did, Fiadh felt a presence fluttering just beyond her tortured mind. Fixing her inner eye on it, she followed the sensation, so like that of butterfly wings, and found Danu.

The Great Mother embraced her, filling her body with warmth, making her whole. Fiadh kept still, letting Danu's being sing through her until she came fully back from that dark place she had been driven into. When she opened her eyes, it was to the feel of cool hands pressed against the sides of her head.

"You had gone from this place," Aelrah said.

Fiadh winced as the oracle's mind tried to delve into her memories to see what she had experienced. Danu rebuffed her attempts, shielding Fiadh as the elf rolled to her side. Batting Aelrah's hand away, she slowly got to her feet.

"Get away from me," Fiadh said, then clutched her throat. It felt raw, her voice a scratchy thing in the empty room. "What did you do to me?"

A smile teased the corners of Aelrah's lips. "I opened

you to Caoránach so she could sip your power and ready herself to be reborn."

The name of the Oilliphéist sent a tremor through her body, as though a piece of it still lingered within her. Her mind shied away from the memory of the wormlike creature, but she forced it to recall what it felt like, what it wanted. It was the latter where her memories drew a blank. Beyond the horror and pain of the invasion, there was nothing, as though she had been wiped clean of anything more than the feel of it in her body. Fiadh called to Danu, sensing her lingering near, despite the spells that had made that connection weak. Something had happened when Caoránach entered her body, something had been freed, and Fiadh feared it was more than her powers.

"I felt… something…" she said, eyes darting to the talisman dangling from Aelrah's neck. "Was that *it*?"

"A part of her, aye. It was the beginning. You will open yourself again, and when you and Ithraen combine your powers—Merrow and Aos Sí—Caoránach will be birthed into the world where she will take her rightful place."

Fiadh looked at her with disdain and considered drawing her strength into a weapon and battering the oracle with it. She had felt the moment the spells obscuring her power had fallen away as that *thing* invaded her body. But she must be patient. It was not the time to reveal them. Let Aelrah think she was a helpless pawn.

"I will not do so willingly," Fiadh said.

"I do not need your willingness." Aelrah went to the door and opened it, motioning for the two guards to enter. "You will do what I require because it is my will that you do so." Turning to the female each-uisce, she said, "Saesan, take her to her room, then fetch her a meal. I do not want her to weaken."

Saesan reached for Fiadh, twisting her arm and forcing her to the door.

"And, Saesan?" the oracle called.

"Aye?"

"Ensure that she eats what she is given."

A cruel smile lit the each-uisce's face, animating her horse-like mouth with a sinister expression. "I will see it done."

Fiadh let herself be led to her quarters while her mind raced. She would not be a part of what Aelrah and Ithraen had planned. It was enough that she had already been an unwilling participant, and she had no desire to feel that thing crawling around inside her again. Let them think they'd broken her. She would play upon the sad remains of Eradar's empathy and find her way to freedom.

CHAPTER FIFTEEN

Calum shut the door to his room and leaned against the smooth wood. In the morning, he and a contingent of his finest fighters would leave for Dorcha Wood. They would have the demon, Crom Cruach, with them. Thinking of the foul being, he drew the medallion from his neck and held it out, studying the disc as it spun slowly in the air. His grandfather believed he could control such a being, but Calum wondered if there was any magic strong enough to bend such a creature to another's will.

Setting the charm on a table, he walked to the window and looked out at a sea of yellow and orange lights—candles and fires burning in hearths—dotting the landscape of Oadsera. He barely remembered arriving in the kingdom as a child. The journey from Felmore to this realm was nothing more than hazy memories awash in confusion and grief at the loss of his sister and parents.

Rygeil had seemed like a cold giant as he'd looked down at young Calum. Those bright green eyes, so like his own, had pinned him to the ground, softening when the king's lips curved into a warm smile.

"Calum," he'd said, kneeling and taking his small hand. "Welcome home."

Of course, it hadn't been his home, not the home of his memories, and he'd backed away from his grandfather, begging for his mother and sister. Even now, he recalled the flash of surprise on Rygeil's face when he'd heard Fiadh's name. It was only as he'd grown older that he'd learned Rygeil had tried to capture Fiadh and failed.

At first, Rygeil had been a patient teacher and a warm, though not affectionate, grandfather, gently calling forth and honing Calum's power. But that had changed as Calum's abilities grew. He cringed as his mind conjured a dark memory of a round room with symbols covering the walls and floor. In that place, Rygeil had coaxed him to open his mind.

Thinking on it, Calum recalled a vague feeling of concern, a reluctance. But the king had smiled and taken his hand. All the while saying, "Trust me, young one. Trust me."

And he had. He'd opened his mind for his grandfather, never realizing the danger of such a thing until it was too late. Calum had collapsed under a barrage of spells, his body prone in the center of the room as Rygeil leaned over him and sipped his power like stolen breath, sucking it out with whispered spells. Mind flayed, Calum was helpless under Rygeil's second assault.

Rygeil had kissed his forehead, saying, "I'm sorry, my

boy. One day, you will understand that these powers will better serve our people in my hands."

His grandfather had ripped through his mind, distorting memories of Fiadh and his human parents until he'd learned to hate them. To crave the power his twin held. To want to crush the human society that had kept him from his true place in the world.

He shut the old memories from his mind and gripped the stone molding around the window, leaning his head against a pane of glass. "Fiadh," he whispered.

To know that, in a matter of days, he would face his twin after such a long absence was a heady thing. Of late, Rygeil had taught him how to use seeking spells to find her and mentalism to pummel her mind until it broke. His grandfather had even returned some small taste of the powers that had once been his.

"To aid you in your quest," he'd said. "Soon, you will have them all again."

When Calum had asked, "When?"

The king had smiled. "When you are ready, my boy. When you are ready." Calum did not reply to that, and Rygeil leaned forward, smiling again. "Trust me," he'd whispered. "Trust me."

"I do," Calum had heard himself say.

Wincing, he recalled the awful sensation when his grandfather had clawed his way into his mind, beating him down when he reached for the pale memory of familial connection. He'd learned to hide those feelings while welcoming the gifts Rygeil offered. He learned the skills he'd need to call his sister forth.

After hours of grueling practice, he had little doubt he'd be able to break through any mental protections she may have. Unlike him, Fiadh hadn't spent years practicing magic and training to fight. She was soft, and the world trampled soft things into dust.

Rygeil, with a Cù-Sìth at his side, met Calum in the great hall the next morning and passed him a goblet of mead. Lifting his own chalice, he held it up and looked around the room, marking every face, before returning his attention to his grandson. "Today, you leave to find your long-lost sister. May the hand of Danu guide you and bring you both home!"

Calum lifted his goblet among the cheers of those gathered for the send-off. "Blessed be the children of Danu." He drank deeply, eyes pinned to Rygeil's, watching the elder's throat bob and hearing the words he didn't utter aloud.

Do not fail me.

I won't. She will be at my side when I return.

Nodding subtly, Rygeil shouted a hurrah and slapped Calum on the back. Leaning in close, he whispered, "Do you wear the medallion?"

"Aye. It will not leave my neck."

"Good. Watch him. He is powerful, even with the strength of the sigil. Use him only in need and don't let him into your mind."

At Calum's nod, Rygeil called for the old god to be brought from a warded cell in the lower level of the keep. Not wishing to wait, Calum strode outside, slinging a satchel and bedroll over his shoulder. The group would not take horses, though the journey would be quicker if they could. They would be too visible on mounts, less able to hide among the trees that sustained their power, should men spot them and try to hunt them down.

Shuffling feet announced Crom Cruach's presence as he made his way to the waiting party. Pausing a few steps from Rygeil, who stood at the top of the steps leading to the courtyard below, he breathed deeply and said, "I do wonder if I shall ever see this place again. As a prisoner, that is."

"Is that a threat?" Calum asked.

He chuckled wetly. "Threats are for those who lack the will to act."

"I assure you Calum has a will to match my own," Rygeil said in a low voice. "Guard your tongue, Crom. Lest he gags you."

Casting Rygeil a sideways glance, the demon shrugged and said, "Just idle thoughts."

Riani strode up the steps then, stopping before the king. "Shall I take him?"

"Take me?" Crom Cruach asked. "Oh sweetling, you may take me anywhere." He puckered his bulbous lips and blew her a kiss.

Her mouth twisted in disgust.

Calum, watching the exchange, grasped the demon's arm, forcing himself not to shudder at the spongy feel of his limb. With a tug, they made their way toward the courtyard below.

Craning his neck when he was at the base of the steps, the ancient one looked back to see Rygeil staring down at him. *Soon,* he thought, *I will look down on you as you cower at my feet.* With a grotesque smile, Crom Cruach said, "Farewell, my king."

Rygeil lifted his chin, saying nothing, and watched them go.

CHAPTER SIXTEEN

Fiadh ground her teeth in frustration when Saesan and her counterpart opened the door with breakfast and an offer to stretch her legs. It would be harder to get away from them than if Eradar had taken on the task. Their suspicion and dislike were blatant, and she would be hard-pressed to get more than a few steps from their sharp spears. Requesting to return to the gardens, Fiadh drifted among the plants. As she did, her mind traveled into them, to the earth itself.

Suppressing a sigh of relief when she felt a response, Fiadh bit her lip and focused her energy on rebuilding her connection with the Great Mother. It was hard, but not impossible, and the more energy she poured into the effort, the stronger the link became until it was as though she were above ground, in the forest of Erabel. Fiadh fought the urge to sag with relief, keeping herself rigid under the scrutiny of her guards. She thought she could escape now, though leaving Abadon would require more than her magic. Their wards were too strong, made of spells that felt foreign, darker, more powerful. She needed something more, but from whom?

It was as she was passing by an especially thick cluster of plants and rocks, that a body launched itself from the watery foliage, the small dagger in his grip aimed at Fiadh's heart. Power burst from her in a violent wave, knocking her assailant back, but in the confusion, the each-uisce didn't notice. They were too focused on subduing her attacker. Saesan called for help, her deep voice traveling in strong vibrations across the landscape, as sound does through water.

Fiadh's heart hammered in her chest as she looked into the snarling face of the Merrow male who'd tried to kill her. He was pinned, but fought, tail thrashing, and screamed at her, "Elven witch!"

The words hit her like a cudgel, bringing her back to the day she watched Riona burn as a chorus of voices shouted the same curse. She wanted to slink away from the hate burning in her attacker's eyes. Digging her heels into the sandy soil, she scooted from him, flinching with every rage-filled shout.

Saesan's mouth curled cruelly when she looked over and saw Fiadh's fear. "You don't belong here, air breather," she hissed.

Cringing from the malice she saw, Fiadh got to her knees and crawled toward the keep. Sobs punctuated each movement as she struggled to get away from the baleful stares that marked her progress.

"Fiadh!" Eradar shouted, tail slashing as he raced toward her.

She crumpled into a ball when he touched her.

"Fiadh? Are you hurt?" Patting her back, he looked at her guards. "What happened?"

"She was attacked," Saesan told him.

Eradar's face grew hard. "How could you let this happen?"

The female's mouth turned down. "She was unhurt."

"She was lucky." Eradar looked at the struggling form in the grip of the each-uisce. "Put him in a cell. I will interrogate him later."

Without waiting to see that his command was obeyed, he went to Fiadh and picked her up, cradling her against his chest. "I'm sorry, young one."

"He tried to kill me," she whispered.

Eradar sighed. "My people… there are many who hold grudges. It won't happen again. I promise."

She nodded, her head bouncing against the bottom of his chin.

"I'll take you to your room."

"Please, don't make me go back," she cried, clinging to his neck. "Someone could find me… they could… don't make me go. Not yet."

Patting her back awkwardly, he said, "Very well. I suppose I could take you to Ruby Cay. It is quite beautiful."

She tucked her head against his chest, hand splayed on the smooth planes, and let him carry her away. It was many minutes before she realized that beneath her palm was nothing but his pale skin. And the magic within his blood.

They traveled quickly as he pulled her through the city to its outskirts. As the distance from the scene of the attack grew, Fiadh's racing heart slowed, and her body relaxed. Loosening her arms from around his neck, she noted red streaks on his skin where she'd clung too tightly and mumbled an apology. Eradar shushed her and pointed to a massive ridge that jutted from the earth in an immense wall of rock. She gaped as they rounded the bend. A reef of coral and plants in a riotous collection of reddish hues spread out before them. Creatures of all sorts darted among the rocks and plants so quickly they were little more than a blur.

Eradar laughed and set her on her feet. "I imagine that was the look I had when first I saw it. It's quite breathtaking."

She could only nod, truly stunned by the scene.

"Feeling better?"

"Much," she said, looking back toward the city though she couldn't see it from the cay. "I've never been so scared."

"You're lucky. There isn't a family in Abadon untouched by the violence of war. We've all felt the fear of death."

Fiadh drifted toward a particularly beautiful plant with leaves like the fronds of a fern. She stroked the edge of one, pulling her hand away when it curled on itself. "To hate someone, a stranger, so deeply you want to kill them just because... because they live..." She folded her arms against her chest and turned to him. "I've never understood it. It's no different here."

"Why would it be?" he asked. "Hate is hate. It doesn't

reason. It doesn't regret. It feeds off itself until it becomes something monstrous."

"So, you are a monster?" she asked quietly.

He shrank from her.

Fiadh shook her head. "Don't you see, Eradar? The hate of one who tried to kill me is no different from the hate that allowed you to imprison me. And I can't let hate win." Reaching out her hand, she touched his arm and said, "Forgive me."

He looked at her in shock when she ripped through his mind as Aelrah had ripped through hers, forcing her way into his being to claim the magic that lived there. Her body went rigid as she took it in and melded it with her own. In her mind, she could see it weaving with hers like the fibers of a loom, only stronger. So much stronger. Eradar's face went blank. He paled, a thing she had not realized he could do with skin so white, then fell at her feet.

Pressing her hand to his chest, she felt the slow rise and fall of his body, the dull rhythm of his heart. Hanging her head in relief, she said a prayer to Danu. He would live. She was not a killer. Eradar stared at her as he lay frozen.

Fiadh leaned forward and whispered in his ear. "I have stolen only what I must. But I am not my grandfather. I will not forsake your people as you feel the Aos Sí did in the past. Tell Ithraen I will keep your people safe. It is an oath."

Rising slowly and getting her bearings, she spotted the massive cavern that would lead the way out of Abadon. On either side of it were guards with sharp spears. What she couldn't see, but sensed, was a barrier, much like the one protecting Erabel. She would have only one chance to break free. Drawing on her power and the magic she'd stolen from Eradar, she called to the water. It came to her as it never had before, humming with energy and tinged with darkness. Fiadh commanded it to lift her up and take her.

As she hung above his prone form, with currents spinning all around her, she turned and said, "Farewell, Eradar."

The water held her in its fist, punching through magical wards and escaping into the cavern that had taken her to this hidden kingdom. She rode the current, barely seeing the life-forms that watched her race past, the looks of shock and fear. Some tried to follow, but none could catch her as she hurtled toward the surface. Light filled her vision when she came out from the rocky outcropping that hid the entrance to the kingdom of the Merrow. Power sang through her as she reached for it and launched herself into the open air.

Landing with a thud on the bank, she heaved, lungs seizing. Clamping a hand on her sides where her gills pulsed, panic consumed her. Mind racing, she reached within herself and drew upon her stolen powers, wielding them with knowledge she should not possess. Her lungs ached. Pain flared, hot as a metal rod from a fire, and wrapped around her chest. From beyond her haze of pain, she heard the shrill cawing of Dasha, felt him barrel toward her from the sky. Crawling to her knees, she doubled over and vomited gushes of water, body shaking with the force of it. Her lungs burned as she gasped for air, spasming in her chest before they remembered how to function. Dasha hopped in panicked circles, pulling at her hair, but all she could do was focus on breathing.

Fits of coughing expelled the last of the water and she

sagged to the ground, hand shaking as she reached for the raven. He shoved his head into her fingers, seeking comfort. Wiggling them weakly to rub the itchy spots between his feathers, she gave up one final cough and flopped onto her back, letting her hand drop to the dirt. Dasha tapped at it with his beak, croaking.

"I'm alright," she wheezed. It hurt to speak.

Not a moment later, Krulan burst through the underbrush. She rolled her head toward him, grimacing as he stirred up a cloud of dust.

Where have you been? his voice thundered in her head.

Thankful she didn't have to speak aloud when her throat felt as though a rusty lance had been thrust into it, she replied, *Eradar imprisoned me in Abadon. At the queen's request.*

Teeth flashed in his muzzle when his yellow eyes bore into the depths of the water.

Taking a grip on her chemise, he tugged her away from the edge of the pool. The fabric, having been waterlogged for so long, ripped. *Hey! This was my last one!*

I care not. He kept pulling, ignoring the huge rent that grew with every tug, until she was well away from the water. *We thought you had fled Erabel. We saw tracks.*

That was Eradar's doing. She sat up, patting Dasha, who refused to be farther than a hands-length from her side. *I tried to escape earlier, but I couldn't.*

Rivya is gone, Krulan said, the statement riddled with worry. *I have reached for her, but it is as though she has disappeared. I had thought perhaps she had gone with you.*

Fiadh paled. *She's gone?*

He paced, tail lashing. *The same day you disappeared. I have reached for her but felt nothing.*

It's my fault. I sent her away.

Krulan rose to his full height and towered over her. *Explain.*

She lifted her arms and let them drop to the ground, looking at the disturbed earth where Rivya had lain before she'd sent her away. *I was irritated. Someone's always watching me like I'm a child. I asked her to leave. To give me privacy.*

Growling, Krulan dug a furrow into the dirt.

I'm sorry, Krulan. I thought she'd return to the keep or find you or… I'm so sorry. She wouldn't have gone far. We'll find her.

Are you certain Rivya was not taken? he asked, looking toward the pool.

I'm sorry, Krulan. I don't know where she is.

He stared at the water, unmoving, finally tearing himself away and facing her. *We must go. Your people have been searching for you and need to be told of what happened.*

Krulan bowed his body, giving her leverage as she clung to his fur and righted herself. Her legs shook violently, unused to the sensation of standing on firm ground. *I don't think I can walk.*

Then, I will carry you.

CHAPTER SEVENTEEN

Calum eyed Crom Cruach as the demon sat against a log, sharpening a shard of bone he had picked up along their travels. He had no desire to find out where it had come from. The contingent of elves who traveled with them kept their distance from the old god, but Riani, a strong fighter, was always watching, marking his movements. Calum knew if the demon pushed her too far, she would lash out, and she hadn't the skill or strength to win a battle with that one.

They were taking a circuitous route to Dorcha Wood to avoid the bands of soldiers who patrolled the land. Only a fortnight ago, Rygeil had sent warriors through the primary route between the east and west, cutting through armies and encampments like a scythe. Yet, like wheat, they returned, growing in number. His grandfather had grown too bold, and men were flocking to the banner of their king and to Lord Darragh. The latter could become an inconvenience should his men be watching the borders of the forest.

A shrill whistle rent the air, and Calum rose, gaze fixed on Faraen.

The warrior stopped and bowed. "There is a small village ahead with little forest land surrounding it. If we bypass to the south, there are copses of woods where we can recoup and arrive at Dorcha Wood by nightfall."

Scowling, Calum glanced at the position of the sun. He was impatient to finish this journey, having waited years to fetch his wayward sister. "And if we press on?"

"We will be on open land should we attempt to maintain our course." Faraen said, glancing at Crom Cruach, who had stopped fiddling with the bone in his fist.

"I have no wish to lose time," Calum said.

The demon gave a wet laugh and awkwardly got to his feet. "Have no fear, little lord. I will protect you."

"I need no protection from the likes of you."

"You think not?" he asked, hobbling toward Calum.

Riani stepped forward and blocked his path with her sword. "That's far enough."

He tsked. "I do so enjoy your spirit, young *Ani*, but do you still believe a blade of steel frightens me?" With a wave of his hand, her sword grew hot, its blade and haft glowing like an ember. She yelped and dropped her weapon, staring at her blistered palm. Crom Cruach hissed and she looked up, giving him a hard smile when he scowled at his reddened hand.

"Did you not see the sigil carved into the shaft?"

The demon's mouth turned down as his eyes flashed to the sword, finding the mark etched into the metal. The spell in the sigil was simple enough, one that would bounce back and strike any who cast against the owner of the blade.

Tucking her hand in the sleeve of her tunic, she bent and picked up the cooling sword. "You are not the only one with power."

He cocked an eyebrow. "Impressive."

She lifted her chin.

"How is the guard I played with? He was a friend of yours, was he not? Does he have nightmares still?" he said, watching as his barbs hit their target. "Does he soil himself when he recalls the feel of my will crawling around in his mind?"

Growling, Riani called upon the earth and hurtled a shower of rocks at him, only to see them turn into a flurry of leaves that fell harmlessly to the ground. She ground her teeth and raised her hands, stopping when Calum sent a thin bolt of lightning into the ground just beyond Crom Cruach's feet. The current singed the demon's ragged tunic, though he remained unmoved by the show of force.

"You fight a battle you cannot win," Calum told Riani, placing a hand on her shoulder.

Turning his attention to the old god, he said, "Do not toy with my people, Crom. Save it for the humans." He slipped his hand into his tunic and pulled out the medallion. Running his thumb along the sigil carved into it, he added, "I have given you free rein, but we both know I could choose otherwise."

With a grunt, Crom Cruach spat on the ground and limped away.

Calum watched him, keeping his hand on Riani. Her body trembled with anger. "Do not let him goad you."

She wrenched her shoulder from his grasp and glared balefully at Crom Cruach's retreating form. Her hand ached with the burn, the heat of it traveling to her heart where it bloomed in hatred. Riani stalked to the healer who had accompanied the group, casting dark looks at the demon as spells of healing worked their magic.

Calum continued their march on their current heading, a choice that made the demon lick his bloated lips. They came to a span of open land at midday. A patchwork of farms with a small hamlet sat in a valley devoid of trees, as though they had been wrenched from the earth as punishment. Calum knew that without their strength, his would wane, but the desire to reach Dorcha Wood outweighed the inconvenience of weakness. His skill with a sword would be advantage enough against the remote and undefended community should it come to a skirmish. And, if not, he need only unleash Crom.

He frowned. The thought of releasing such a monster in the community didn't sit well with him. Since Rygeil had told him to fetch his sister, he'd been plagued by vague memories of his human mother. Her voice. The touch of her hand. Songs she'd sung in his cradle days. Calum had tried to shut them away, dredging up those times when his grandfather had ripped through his mind to sever links to his human-like past. But he couldn't rid himself of the memories. They had become like seeds in fertile ground.

Shaking his head, he motioned for the party to take a path through the thickest grasses well beyond the borders of the village. They made their way, crouching low and blending with the waving stalks. Holding up a hand, Calum called a halt and motioned to a small hill. Four soldiers on horseback were just coming over the crest. Darting his eyes to the demon, he jerked his head to one of his fighters, who sidled closer to the old god. Peering over the blades of meadow grass, Calum watched the horseman enter the village and stop at a squat building. *Likely stopping for ale*, he thought, as he noted a wooden sign just outside the doorway flapping in the breeze.

Taking advantage of the soldier's respite, the elves continued on, slithering along the ground when the stalks grew too short to hide them. It took the better part of an hour to go a quarter of the distance they had before. As Calum neared bushes surrounding a cluster of rocks, a flock of birds burst from the foliage. He twisted onto his back and reached out to them, commanding them to land lest they call anyone's attention to the elves' location. Black wings swooped over the group, circling in a mass of feathers before finally returning to the thicket. Letting out a long breath, Calum got to his knees and looked toward the village.

"We need to get to the trees," he whispered to Riani, who'd crept close to him.

"Aye."

Waving his hand to his warriors, he faced west and ran, keeping his body as low as possible. A warbling call stopped him after a few minutes, and he ducked, flattening his body to the ground and looking for the source of the call.

One of his fighters crawled toward him, eyes wild. "Crom Cruach is gone."

He got to his knees and scanned every face, grimacing when he saw the creature was indeed missing. "When?"

"I don't know. He had been but a few paces behind me until the birds came."

Crouching, Calum cursed. He had a good idea where the demon went. Gripping the medallion in his fist, Calum muttered a spell, but he was weak so far from the trees, and it faltered, the power of the sigil unable to seek far enough from where they hid. Growling in frustration, he cast about, searching the open landscape, then tried again, calling on Danu to give him strength. The disc throbbed in his hand, growing warm. He clutched it tighter and muttered the spells Rygeil had taught him. He felt the connection with the idol his grandfather kept in Oadsera and tapped at it, focusing on the magic imbued in the sigil. Pain flared in his palm as the medallion grew hotter. He flung the power of the medallion outward, aiming for the faint touch of Crom Cruach's mind. But Calum was depleted, and the spell rebounded, anchoring itself in the sigil.

Moments later, the first scream found its way to where the Aos Sí waited. They sprang to their feet and raced to the village, their lithe bodies blending with the grasses so that they looked like wraiths.

Crom Cruach stood in a meadow on the perimeter of a fallow field, the bodies of farmers strewn about him. Beneath his feet, grasses withered, the ends of the blades curling and turning black. The echoes of screams still rang in the air. This was but a taste. There would be more to come, more to feast upon. He wiped his hand across his crooked mouth, angling the appendage to better see the clotted blood that clung to his skin. Pressing it to his mouth, he sucked the remnants of life from his flesh, eyes closing in blissful surrender.

He remembered.

The flesh. The sacrifice. The squalling of infants as they were dashed upon his altar.

Men had forgotten, as men were wont to do. But he had not forgotten. The taste. The smell. The delicious power that flowed into his veins as he feasted. His chest swelled, contorting his misshapen form. Muttering words of power that had not been heard in centuries, Crom Cruach reclaimed a piece of who he was, who he had been, in the days when mankind had crawled weakly on their knees, cowering at his idols. They would cower again.

They would remember their proper place.

He would be the elf king's captive no more. The iron prison to which he had been bound would never again find him within its powerful walls. Weakened though he may be, when his strength fully returned, no sigil or spell would be strong enough to keep him under Rygeil's thrall. With the blood he'd spilled, he felt those bonds eroding. There would come a time when Rygeil and his descendants would kneel at his feet, as would the entire world.

He moved toward the small village, listening to the ring of a bell and watching men swarm from houses with makeshift weapons while the four soldiers spilled from the tavern, swords drawn. They never had a chance. They were cut down, all of them. Ribbons of blood streamed from their bodies, soaking the hard ground while women and children ran in terror, their voices silenced mid-scream. It was not war. It was murder. Brutal. Horrific. Crom Cruach danced through the melee, cackling as he swept his arms in huge arcs, knocking full-grown men to the ground in tangled heaps.

Aos Sí warriors, who had honed their skills for battle, raced into the village, their faces devoid of feeling as blades severed lives with a neat slice. But every death took its toll. These were not soldiers they killed. They were farmers and wives. Children and the elderly. This was not the way of elves. Calum raced toward the demon, rage thundering through his veins. Crom Cruach saw him coming and bolted, speeding past the warrior who took after him.

"Cease!" Calum yelled.

The demon stopped and dug his foot into the chest of a corpse, causing the ribcage to crack under the pressure. "Eh?" he asked slyly.

"You heard me, abomination." Calum stepped forward, careful of the bodies that lay at awkward angles on the soiled ground. "Remove yourself."

He smirked, the expression ghastly in his deformed face. "You would deny me my playthings?"

Elven faces reflected a myriad of emotions, from indifference to disgust, as they ceased fighting and held the villagers at bay. Some started to shuffle uncomfortably under the demon's brooding stare, their lean bodies shifting in a breeze that carried the scent of death—distaste for him, the only common emotion flashing across their features.

The elves will learn to kneel alongside the children of men, Crom Cruach mused. *Their offspring will find their way to my altar.*

Calum clutched the medallion, commanding him to stop as the demon darted forward and snatched an infant from its mother's arms. "Mankind will once again worship me in fear!" Crom Cruach shouted, swinging his arm.

Riani gasped in horror at the evil act. Of late, her hatred for mankind had waned. She could trace the feelings to the massacre in the unarmed village of Belfirth. Her king had commanded his army to kill every man, woman, and child. Everyone. She'd felt a severing in her connection with Danu with each slash of her blade, each loosed arrow. Every slaughter that followed had taken a toll. Now she looked at Crom Cruach and saw herself. This was not the way of her people. This was not the path she wished to walk.

Calum stood a few paces from her, sword hanging limply, eyes fixed on the tiny bundle that lay still on the ground. He looked up at her, haunted. Gripping his blade, he wrestled his emotions, his weakness in the face of his enemy, and cut his eyes to the villagers. "Stand down before we slay every one of you."

A woman sobbed uncontrollably, the sound cutting through the angry mutters of the remaining men.

Motioning to a couple of his soldiers, Calum snarled, "Fetch that beast and let us leave this place."

Crom Cruach let himself be taken, his deviant appetites slaked with savagery, while Calum and Riani forced the survivors back at the points of their swords. They left the killing grounds at a run and did not stop until they found a large copse of woods not far from their destination. There was no talk as they took their rest, each of them lost in thoughts none cared to share. Riani set a guard to watch Crom Cruach, marking his movements and wondering if her king had overestimated his ability to control such a being. He had settled apart from the others, wedging himself into a dark crevice of rock, much like the prison he had lived in for hundreds of years. Perhaps he found comfort in that. She studied him, her violet eyes catching his, feeling a subtle thrum of power as their gazes locked. He was dangerous. Infinitely more dangerous than any of them had imagined. If he unleashed his power on her people, the Great Mother help them, because she feared even the strongest would fall.

She turned away and walked off, looking for solace among the trees.

Faraen joined her, slumping against a giant oak a few paces from where she sat. "I grow weary of what I am," he mumbled.

"Aye."

He leaned his head against the trunk and closed his eyes, reaching for the life within the tree. It was a faint connection when it came, an echo of what it could have been. "We've become monsters."

Riani closed her eyes and hung her head. "I know."

"The Great Mother will punish us, Riani. Her power will leave us, and what then? Are we to roam the world absent of her light?"

"I have no answers, Faraen." She sighed and looked

around. "Already, I feel a separation, as though she looks on me with sadness while letting me go."

"Perhaps it is not Rygeil, but Fiadh of Dorcha Wood who we should follow," he offered.

"That's treason," Riani whispered. "I fear it's too late for half measures now. The die is cast. A war of annihilation is upon us, and elves will either win or go down in flames."

"We—"

Calum's brisk stride cut him off, and they both sat up straight as he came among them. "Put what happened today behind you. It changes nothing."

Riani's eyes hardened, but she kept quiet.

"We leave in an hour."

He stalked away, and she looked at Faraen. He stared back, pained.

"Aye, my friend. I feel the shackles too," she said quietly, rubbing her wrists.

"Rygeil will stop at nothing." Faraen looked through the trees at the dark spot where the demon hid himself. "By unleashing that creature, we have seen it. Even in victory, we risk defeat. Do you honestly feel it will be any better when we return to Oadsera?"

"I must have hope that it will be."

He made a face. "I wish I had your optimism." Faraen settled his weary body against the oak, taking solace in the feel of the bark pressing against his back and the hum of life running through the trunk. But time marched on, and soon their rest was over.

Riani took on the task of guarding Crom Cruach when they left, ignoring him as he baited her. The last stretch was long, so much longer than any before it, as though the ancient one had become a cancerous rot among their group, eating away at each of them the longer they remained in his company.

A tangible weight lifted as the party finally came to the edge of Dorcha Wood in the late hours of the afternoon. They had bypassed the scorched section of the forest and stood at the northern border, far from the village of Felmore. The woods pulsed with knowledge and anger. Calum cocked his head and closed his eyes, feeling it. Part of him, a remnant of who he had been, connected with the trees, causing his body to rock abruptly as power surged in his veins.

Dorcha Wood welcomed him home.

CHAPTER EIGHTEEN

*V*eren came running as Krulan broke through the trees, yanking Fiadh from the Cù-Sìth's back and into a fierce hug. "I thought I'd lost you," he whispered.

She let out a small whimper as he crushed her in his grip, and Krulan growled.

He loosened his arms but kept her pressed to his body. His warmth felt good. "I'm alright. Eradar took me when I went for a swim."

Arms tightening, Veren snarled, "He will pay for that."

Fiadh arched her body away from his. "Nay, Veren. They have their reasons, and I will not retaliate." He argued, but she shushed him and pulled out of his embrace. Her legs were wobbly, but she could feel their strength returning.

Kaelari charged into the clearing on Meara's back, four other Aos Sí warriors not far behind. She swung off the unicorn in a graceful bound and came to Fiadh, pressing a kiss on both of her cheeks. "I will hear the tale when you are ready." Cupping Fiadh's face, she looked into her. "Come, you are weak, and I would see you restored."

Veren hauled her up against his chest despite her protests. She made a face and reluctantly looped her arm around his neck. Despite feeling like a child as he effortlessly carried her into the keep, it felt good to be home, to be in his arms among people she had grown to love.

Not to be left out, Meara whinnied and snuffled her neck and hair, earning a chuckle that turned into a coughing fit as Fiadh struggled to expel remnants of water from her lungs. The unicorn followed the party up to the courtyard, her soulful eyes watching as Fiadh was carried inside.

A short time later, Kaelari and Arel held their hands in a healing posture over her freshly clad form, spells filling the air and weaving themselves into her prone body. As they worked, Veren told her of what had happened over the last few days. She was shocked to learn that time had passed differently while she was captive in Abadon. What had been two days in that kingdom had been four in Erabel. It had been Dasha who alerted everyone to Fiadh's disappearance, having found Kaelari and coaxed her with alarm cries to follow him to the pool of still waters where they had found footprints leading out of the water and deep into the forest. Kaelari had followed the tracks until they vanished among craggy rocks to the north.

Seeing no clothing, many had assumed she had fled, which filled Fiadh with frustration and sadness. "How could you think I would leave?"

Letting her healing words drift to silence, Kaelari said,

"Because part of you is not of this world, and that piece calls you to another place, another people."

Fiadh tried not to be offended, but couldn't keep the hurt from her voice. "I would never abandon you! That you think I could…" she huffed, rolling into a sitting position. "I wouldn't do that. You're my family."

Veren smiled softly, the expression casting a radiant glow across his face. Fiadh felt flustered and ducked her head, switching the subject. "Krulan tells me that Rivya is missing."

She looked at the Cù-Sìth, who stood a few paces away, lashing his tail.

"Aye, we assumed she had gone with you," Veren told her. "She was lost to us, just as you were. Vanished. Even Krulan can't sense her."

"It's my fault." Her eyes grew moist as they fixed on Krulan.

"What is this?" Kaelari asked, looking between Fiadh and the Cù-Sìth.

Swallowing hard, Fiadh faced the elf. "I told her to leave me alone while I bathed."

"Why would you do that?" she asked, brow furrowing. "The Cù-Sìth are your protectors."

"I know." Her voice caught, and she balled her hands in her lap. "I was frustrated, feeling like you all think I need a nursemaid." Fiadh hung her head. "I wish I could take it back."

Veren and Kaelari gave each other a long look.

"Are you certain the Merrow did not trick her into entering their waters after you had been taken?" Veren asked. "We found her tracks, but they were scattered and directionless. Some were found at the pool."

"I… I never saw her, and they didn't speak of it. I don't think they took her, but—" She paused and looked through the open doorway to the forest beyond. "I suppose they could have."

Mayhap, they took her to keep her from alerting us of their foul deed, Krulan said with a menacing growl.

Her heart wrenched at the hope Krulan was hanging onto. "I don't believe they did, my friend."

Kaelari huffed and folded her arms across her chest. "Would you tell us if they had?"

"Kaelari," Veren said with a warning. "Do not cross that line."

The elf threw up her hands. "She's said she won't retaliate! If she knew Rivya had been taken, would she tell us now when we know she'll refuse to attack the Merrow?"

Fiadh's eyes grew hard. "Because you're worried and hurting. I'll let that go. But please don't question my loyalty to you and my people again. I won't attack and kill those who've wronged me out of some need for gross revenge. They have their reasons for what they did and what they want. But I would sacrifice none of you in the name of peace."

"I've let my anger speak when I should have listened," Kaelari said. "Forgive me."

Lifting her arm, Fiadh opened her hand and held it out, squeezing gently when the elf took it. "Forgiven. I have made my share of mistakes and will no doubt make many more." Letting go, she sat back, her body slumping.

"You are weary," Veren said. "Perhaps you should sleep."

She shook her head. "Not yet."

Arel drew her attention when he asked, "How did you escape?"

She looked at him. He had always been quiet, keeping his distance as she trained with others. But she had felt him watching her on many occasions. "I took something from Eradar and used it to gain my freedom." Fiadh looked away, not wishing to explain further, though she could feel questions bubbling in every mind. "They meant to keep me, to use me to bring forth something called an Oilliphéist."

"A what?" Veren asked.

"An Oilliphéist. Ithraen called it the true ruler of the world." She shrugged at their looks of confusion, unable to tell them much more. "It's some form of dragon-like creature."

More Aos Sí had gathered and muttered to each other, words like fanatics and fairy tales peppering their conversation.

Kaelari cut her hand through the air. "It matters not what stories the Merrow believe. Fiadh is safely returned, but Rivya is missing and the threat beyond our borders remains."

Fiadh stretched and sat up straighter. "Tell me of Darragh's men. Have they continued their assault while I was gone?"

"There have been lulls between each attack, the most recent being the longest. I fear they are planning a larger strike," Veren told her. "We could surprise them if we attacked."

She made a face and shook her head. "I have not changed my mind, Veren." Fiadh rose, holding up her hand and shaking her head when Krulan walked toward her, offering his strong back. "Kaelari?"

"Aye?"

"I need to speak to the Great Mother."

Stepping to her side to lend support, she walked with Fiadh as they made their way to the ancient oak. Veren watched them go for a few moments, then looked at Krulan. "I fear for her."

The Cù-Sìth gave a distracted growl, his face strained as he looked toward the forest before he left the hall and followed Fiadh. He caught up with them moments later, noting how Dasha flew low around his mistress' head before landing on her shoulder as though he could no longer bear to be apart from her. It filled him with envy to see it.

With Kaelari's aid, Fiadh knelt at the base of the oak and pressed her hands to the surface, opening her entire being to Danu. The Great Mother greeted her as a daughter, but her voice was more distant than it had been in the past. She asked Danu about Rivya. The goddess could offer nothing, having lost a connection with the Cù-Sìth shortly after Fiadh was captured. Anxiety filled her at the news, and no amount of warmth and love from Danu could rid her of it.

What if the Merrow *had* taken Rivya? How many cells were in the bowels of their watery keep? They could've locked the Cù-Sìth far from where Fiadh had been held and she'd never have known her friend was there. Guilt and anxiety washed over her. What if they punished Rivya for her theft of Eradar's magic and escape from their kingdom?

With a shaky breath, she whispered her appreciation to Danu, pouring feeling into each word, then released their bond, coming back to herself and the prickly texture of the grass beneath her legs.

She could feel Krulan watching her and turned to him, slumping against the oak. "I can't find her." He came to her side and laid his massive head on her lap. She ran her hand between his ears, to the base of his skull. "Krulan, I won't stop until she's found."

A rumble vibrated through his chest. She felt it travel through her legs and leaned down to press her lips to his brow. He closed his eyes, and she pressed her cheek to his head, inhaling his musky scent—so like Rivya's. Tears pooled, slipping between her lashes and into his fur. Dasha hopped to the ground and haltingly came toward her. He croaked softly, cocking his head. Fiadh sighed and reached for the raven, running a finger through the feathers below his ear canal when he nudged her with his beak. In moments, her hand fell to the ground, face drooping. Krulan's warmth and the steady beating of his heart lulled her, and she let her heavy lids slide shut.

That's when he found her, tapped into her mind with a mental dart that jarred her to awareness. Calum.

ister, Calum called, the word tugging at Fiadh's mind.

She jerked upright and craned her neck, looking north. Krulan rose and followed her gaze. He barked, and she turned to him, mouth parted.

Kaelari, having been watching, ran to Fiadh, sliding to her knees. "What is it?"

Looking through the trees again, Fiadh said, "I hear my brother. I hear Calum."

Snarling, Kaelari rose and let loose a war cry. Aos Sí came running, Veren leading them.

"What is it?" he shouted, looking around for a threat.

"Calum has come," Kaelari said.

Veren looked at Fiadh. "Where?"

She ran her fingers along Dasha's back. "I need your wings, my friend."

He croaked at her and launched into the air, a black form against the pale sky. She closed her eyes and merged with him, unaware of the new ease with which she did so. Her body titled as she rode the wind with Dasha, seeing the whole of Dorcha Wood spreading out before her in a carpet of green and brown. He banked east and searched the burned remains of Darragh's assault, then headed north. They hid among the trees, but the raven's sharp eyes caught their movement. From his vantage, he couldn't make out their number. The trees were too thick, and they blended into the foliage like ghosts.

Sister.

Fiadh cocked her head and listened to Calum's voice, commanding Dasha to fly low, wanting—needing—to glimpse her twin. The raven swooped toward the tree line, sharp eyes piercing the shadows, but seeing nothing.

I see your pet, sister. How sweet. Would you like to see mine?

A murder of crows burst from the trees, aiming at Dasha.

How powerful are you, Fiadh? Powerful enough to protect your spy?

Calum, no!

The crows surrounded Dasha, forming a cloud of black feathers and shrill caws. Fiadh gritted her teeth and poured her energy into the raven. Dark magic, stolen from Eradar and unnatural for her kind, traveled through their connection and sank into Dasha. His eyes grew wide, their purple hue ringed with red. But it was too much, too strange, and their connection wavered. In that moment, a crow slammed its body into Dasha, sending him reeling to the ground.

Mind severed from her raven, Fiadh screamed, throwing off Veren's arms as he grabbed her. Hunching, she snarled and ripped her mind through air, finding Dasha as he plummeted to the ground and flooding his body with power. Mouth turned down, she relaxed her shoulders as the raven caught the wind, wings flapping as he retreated to Erabel.

Not bad, sister. But why leave so soon? The fun has only started.

Birds of every type flew into the sky, all aimed at Dasha as he struggled to out-fly them. Like a living thing, Calum's connection to Dorcha Wood crawled across the forest, and everything from songbirds to hawks rose from trees at his command. Cries from hundreds of flapping bodies filled the air. They came from all sides, surrounding the raven.

Do you have the power to stop me from loosing them on your pet?

Please, Calum, she begged, desperately holding onto her connection with Dasha. *Don't!*

Stop me, sister. Take their minds from my control.

Fiadh whimpered, wanting to rip the birds away from her twin to save her raven. But her connection with Danu felt strange, dull. She feared if she lent her will to the birds threatening Dasha, she'd lose him.

Can you not? Calum asked.

She tried to block her brother from her mind and focused on Dasha. His heart beat wildly as she poured magic into him. Fiadh drew the raven to her like a fish on a line, mumbling words of power to give him faster flight.

Ah, sister, you disappoint me. I thought you had more power than that. I expected more. It seems Rygeil overestimated your power. You're not so strong after all.

Dasha breached the barrier and entered the protection of Erabel. The birds at Calum's command followed, scattering when his magic lost its hold as they passed over her kingdom. Fiadh sagged to the ground, keeping her mind on Dasha as he came to her, landing in an exhausted heap a few paces away. She crawled to him and cradled his weary body against her chest, crooning as her hands raced over his form, checking for injuries. He gave a tired croak and went limp.

Calum tapped at her mind, and she brushed him away, but not before she heard the whisper of his thoughts.

You can't keep me out, sister. We share the same blood. Danu lives in me, just as she does in you.

Fiadh closed her eyes at the truth of his words, finally looking up to find Kaelari and Veren hovering by her side. "They are coming from the north."

"Fight him!" Kaelari yelled. "Dorcha Wood is yours to control. Beat him back!"

Her mouth turned down. "I can't. He's too strong."

"He is not stronger than you. Dorcha Wood is *your* domain. Not his. Why are you letting the beasts answer to him?"

She looked at Kaelari. "My connection with Danu…" She shook her head. "Something's not right. I can't stop him."

"To arms!" Veren yelled, casting a worried glance at Fiadh before turning his attention to his fighters. "I want archers in the trees along the northern border and fighters on the ground. No one is to cross the barrier." He said the last with a hard look at each face and waited for curt nods. "Go and send a warning should Rygeil's warriors come within sight of Erabel."

They fled on swift feet.

Fiadh hugged Dasha to her chest and got to her feet. "I want to help."

Veren shook his head. "Your body is weak, but your mind cannot be." His eyes darted to the sleeping raven. "I have no doubt he will pit his will against yours, and you must be strong enough to fight him."

She frowned, feeling Calum prodding at her mind. "You'll stay within our borders?"

"Aye. We will keep watch and wait for his next move." Veren cupped her cheek. "I will return with word."

"I want to be with you," Fiadh whispered.

"I know, but you're needed here." He laid a hand on Dasha. "Tend to him and leave this work to your warriors."

She swallowed hard and nodded. "Will the barrier keep him out?"

Kaelari gave Veren a look.

"Tell me."

"We don't know," Kaelari said. "In ordinary times, any of our people could travel in and out of Erabel. Since we arrived in Erabel, Veren and I have done what we could to instill protections that repel anyone who's heart and will are not aligned with yours."

"I don't understand. Are you saying the barrier has a… a mind of its own?"

"In a way, yes."

"How?"

Kaelari pursed her lips. "It is born of Danu. Its power, our power, comes from the Great Mother. When Veren, I, and others reinforce it, we also imbue it with the knowledge to discern an ally from an enemy."

"So, it has a will?"

"To some extent. But it is not a free will. It can't decide on its own to let in or keep out those who seek to cross over." At Fiadh's look of confusion, Kaelari continued. "You understand the barrier works by sensing those who try to cross it, right?"

Fiadh nodded.

"That discernment comes from the magic we use to build and strengthen it. This is another layer that—we hope—enables it to determine those who wish harm from those who are our allies."

It was a lot to take in. If passage into Erabel depended on whether the barrier could see into those who tried to enter, it could be fooled. "Does Calum know how it works?"

"We must assume that he does," Veren said.

She made a strangled sound.

"That doesn't mean it won't work against him," he assured her. "Kaelari and I have spent many hours adding layers of protection. I believe they will hold."

"If I were Calum," Kaelari said, looking between them both, "I would send one of my fighters to test it."

Veren frowned. "I will warn the others."

He left, followed by Kaelari. Krulan rose as she watched them go, planting himself in front of her—a menacing guardian. Growls rumbled through his chest, and she put her hand on his shoulder.

Could you drive him out, Krulan?

Calum is too powerful.

Fiadh eyed the Cù-Sìth. *Are you saying you can't fight him or won't?*

He shares your blood. The blood of Erabel. If my fighters and I attack him, he could overpower us. I will not risk leaving you unprotected.

I thought he was weak. That Rygeil had taken much of his power.

The Cù-Sìth grumbled. *Even if he had, Dorcha Wood has powers of its own that Calum can tap into. He, too, is a child of Danu.* He paused and Fiadh nudged him.

What aren't you telling me?

I do not know if we can fight him. Krulan ducked his head and looked away. *It is like asking us to harm you, even if doing so means saving you. I do not know if we can bring our teeth, our claws, our powers down on him, or if when we charge him, we would simply halt and bow our heads, unable to draw his blood. It is too great of a risk to send us against him. Understand, we would want to obey you. Our loyalty is for you. I would charge him at your command, but when it comes to it... I do not know. It is like asking me to harm you, Fiadh, to draw your blood. No matter what the cause, I cannot do it, and I do not know if that extends to Calum. I fear it may and that this is why Rygeil has sent him. It is too great of a risk to send us against your brother.*

She stroked his back. *I understand, my friend.*

Fiadh found a soft patch of moss and laid the raven down to rest and recover. Too wired to sit and wait, she paced while Krulan watched her. Eventually, her constant motion irritated the Cù-Sìth, and he snapped at her. She made a face and found a bench while she awaited word from Veren. He returned as one hour became two, striding toward her with a black look.

"He waits beyond the border of Erabel. I don't think he'll attempt breaching our protections yet." He sat next to her and took her hand in his. "You must be vigilant, Fiadh. Do not allow him into your mind."

How am I supposed to keep him out? she wondered. *He's too strong.* But she said nothing, only nodded her head. "I won't."

The mood was quiet as they settled in to wait for Calum's next move. Kaelari and a few others returned, and food was brought. Though appetites were sparse, everyone was too edgy to feel the pangs of hunger.

The day wore on, interspersed with warriors arriving and departing as they took shifts along the border. Dasha woke and flew onto the low branch of a tree, tucking his head between his wings while keeping one eye on his mistress. To keep her mind occupied, Fiadh begged to train with Veren or Kaelari, each protesting that she needed to save her strength. "Does a soldier take his ease when preparing for battle?" she snapped. "No! He trains, and that is what I must do."

They gave in, though she couldn't help note the look that passed between them. "Stop coddling me!" Fiadh threw her arms out and called to the wind. It stirred, but there was a new quality to her connection. It was stronger, but also more separate, as though it came from a place that was detached from the Great Mother. She tested it, a smile curving her lips as she shaped it into a tight funnel that reached beyond the trees and toward the low-hanging clouds. "I won't stand aside as if I'm not part of this world. I can protect my home as well as you can," she grumbled.

Veren sighed and joined her. "I can see that." When he

joined his magic with hers, his brow wrinkled in confusion, and he glanced at Kaelari.

She went to his side and lifted her arms, merging her own power with theirs, feeling the difference in Fiadh's magic. "What is it?" she whispered to Veren.

"I don't know."

Ignorant of their worry, Fiadh poured herself into her magical training, relishing the feeling of magic singing in her blood. *I can protect us,* she thought as she brought a thin bolt of reddish lightning into the vortex. *I can protect all of us.*

Kaelari stepped away to mull over what she felt while Veren continued to practice with Fiadh. It bothered her not to understand this new well of magic. But she couldn't deny its power. And where there was power, there was an advantage.

Eventually, Fiadh dropped her arms and staggered to a bench, where she collapsed onto her back. "I feel stronger."

Veren snorted and pushed her legs aside to sit next to her. "Aye, you look it."

She kicked his thigh. "Not now, you dolt! Then," she flung her arm toward the field, "when we were training. I felt...different. It felt good, like I could protect our home and our people."

"I felt it too," he said quietly.

She sat up. "What's wrong?"

He shrugged. "You seemed different just now, when we were training. I wondered about it."

Fiadh looked away, mashing her lips. "You've just forgotten how it felt to train with me."

His eyes narrowed, but he didn't push her further.

A few minutes later, Fiadh huffed. "This cannot be the best course, Veren. This waiting."

He chuckled. "Be grateful for the lull, Fiadh. You will look back on it and realize what a gift it was."

She rested her arms on her knees, hands dangling to the ground. "Do you think he'll attack?"

Veren's mouth turned down. "I would imagine he'll take advantage of an opportunity should one present itself."

"What do you mean?"

"There are many eyes fixed on Erabel. If Darragh were to unleash an army, we would be forced to fight." He held up a hand when she tried to argue. "We would have to fight, Fiadh, and in the heat of battle, things could happen." He looked away for a moment, then snagged her in his gaze. "You must stay here if Darragh attacks."

"What? No! I can help!"

He sighed. "Fiadh, if Calum captures you, then all of this, everything you're fighting for, ends."

She looked around, agony marring her face. He was right, of course. In fact, she had already come to that conclusion but had said nothing, her pride and desire to feel like she was doing her part overriding reason. But hearing it made it more final. "I don't want to hide behind barriers while you and others fight to protect our home."

Veren took her hand, stroking each finger, then turning it over to trace the callouses on her palm. Tingles of aware-ness traveled up her arm and into the pit of her stomach. "You have to live, Fiadh. Without you, all is lost."

A lone tear slid down her cheek. Resignation was a bitter taste on her tongue. "Let's hope it doesn't come to that."

He nodded and tucked the messy tangles of her hair behind her ear, tracing its mangled remains. She forced her body not to pull away from him in shame at the deformity. He felt it and leaned forward to kiss the ruined tip. The action touched her core, and a sob broke from her chest. Wrapping his arms around her, he mumbled words of comfort, passing a look to Kaelari, who heard the crying and came to see what was wrong.

Fiadh gave into his coaxing words, releasing pent-up fear and grief. When she finally spent herself, she rested her head fully into his chest and simply lived in the moment—feeling his heart beat against her cheek. The sensations as his fingers trailed down her back.

When she was ready, she pulled away, and he let her go. "It feels as though the world is closing in on me and I'm powerless to stop it."

"Aye."

Wiping her nose on the sleeve of her tunic, she took a shaky breath and said the thing she had been wondering since all of this started. "What if we can't protect Erabel?"

"There has always been that probability. We are outnumbered on every front."

Fiadh looked to the north, where she knew Calum waited. "You can't let him take me, Veren."

"He won't," he said, playing with her fingers.

She pulled her hand from his and turned to face him fully. "You don't understand what I'm saying. You can't let him take me. You know what will happen if he does."

Veren's forehead creased. "You won't be captured, Fiadh. Krulan and I won't let that happen."

"I know you believe that, but if he does or if Darragh's army somehow manages to breach our protections, you can't let them take me."

"What are you saying?"

"I think you know," she said softly.

He jumped to his feet. "I will not kill you, Fiadh! That's obscene!"

Krulan snarled and shot to his feet. *You will not speak such evil!*

She stared at him. *You must understand, Krulan. If I were taken, he could… he could use me against you. I've already lost Rivya. I can't lose you.*

You have not lost her, he snapped. *She will be found, and we will deal with those who took her in time. But I will not hear of you sacrificing yourself out of some misplaced sense of honor.*

"Veren——" She paused and hung her head. "You and Krulan must accept that you may have no choice."

Cursing, Veren strode away, back and shoulders rigid, only to spin around, pinning her to the bench with a hard look. "That is a vile wish, and I will not do it! If you are captured, I will find you and set you free!"

Knowing it would hurt, she said, "Like you did when Eradar took me."

Her words hit their mark and brought him to his knees. He hit the ground hard, as though she had knocked the breath from him. She rose and came to him, placing her hand on his bent head. "I know you would protect me with your life."

"I would," he said harshly.

"I need you to protect the future of this world too, and that won't happen if I'm taken."

She knew she had won at that moment and walked away, collecting Dasha from his roosting spot. Krulan watched with guarded eyes as she slipped into the shadows of the hall.

CHAPTER TWENTY

iadh writhed beneath the coarse fabric of her blanket. Covered in a fine sheen of sweat, her hands twisted under the covers, fisting the wool as they grasped for the owner of the voice that called to her. Her body arched off the bed, neck bending as she dug the back of her head into the cushion of her raised pallet, trying to escape it, longing to go to it. War raged in her mind, finally wrenching her awake with a muffled scream.

Sister.

Clamping her hands to her ears, she squeezed her eyes closed, shushing Dasha when he squawked from his roost in the corner.

Come to me, Fiadh.

Soothing the raven with honeyed words, so he didn't rouse anyone, Fiadh threw off the blanket and swung her legs to the floor. The room was cast in shadows that moved erratically as leaves tossed in the breeze outside her window.

Calum's voice was an echo in her head, bouncing off her skull.

You think I am your enemy? That I wish for you to be a slave to Rygeil? You are wrong. Come with me, Fiadh. I will train you, and we will be more powerful than Rygeil. Together, we can take the throne and rule as brother and sister.

Clutching her chest, she sobbed, her heart longing for her twin while her mind screamed at her to be wary.

Fiadh. I know you hear me. I can sense you in my mind. We are family. We belong together, you and I. I am bound to Rygeil only because alone I am not strong enough to challenge him. He thinks me his pawn—broken and subservient, but I remember. I remember what he did to me, what he stole, and all these long years I have waited. Waited for you, my love. Join me. Free me from him. And together, we will unleash your true power—the children of Threa united.

Each word cut deeper than the last, and she felt her will falter. Fiadh held onto the threads of it, but they were wasted tendrils against the constant barrage of his appeals.

I want to know you again, sister. You were lost to me. You and Mother were taken. Come to me. Tell me of our mother.

She clamped a hand over her mouth and sobbed, shoulders shaking as she struggled to contain the sound. Her memories of Calum were borrowed from Riona. Mother had told her stories to keep him alive, even as she believed her son to be dead. That was what Fiadh knew of Calum, snippets of the boy he'd been as they'd played together in her youth. Of the man, she knew nothing more than what she had been told, and those tellings had not been kind.

Fiadh, please. I've missed you all these years. I need you, sister.

Her knees popped in the quiet as she rose. Unable to

stop herself, Fiadh left her room and made her way through the maze of hallways into the courtyard. Creatures who used the cloaking darkness of the night watched her pass, their eyes glowing in the pale light of the moon. She spoke to them in her own way, touching their minds and feeling their response. There was no desired destination, only a fierce need pulling her away from the keep.

Calum's voice grew quiet, and she sighed with relief. Erabel looked different at night, secretive, alluring. She smiled as she took a path through the forest, trailing her fingers through the leaves and flowers that grew along the edges. With a start, she saw Meara materialize from the darkness, her black coat blending so completely she had been invisible until she stepped from the shadows. With a low nicker, the unicorn came to her and snuffled her hand. Fiadh stroked her face, then looked north, her mind, once again ensnared by the sound of her brother's voice.

I feel you, sister. Your power is so like my own, but you are untrained, and it makes you weak. I can make you strong.

It was a powerful lure.

Warriors are watching the northern border, she sent to him.

Ah, my sweet sister. You are looking out for me as I will look out for you. There are troops with me who are loyal to Rygeil. For them, I make a show. Pretend I am loyal to the king. Pretend I too wish to see you on your knees. Follow the tenor of my thoughts, and you will avoid them.

She tilted her head and looked west. There, along the border, she felt him. Meara fell into step behind her, becoming one with the night, her hooves muffled by layers of leaves as she followed Fiadh. Lifting her hand, she commanded her to halt and came to the edge of the western border of Erabel. Her feet planted themselves on the ground just beyond the barrier, as though rooted. Fiadh looked at them, perplexed, then lifted her gaze and came face-to-face with someone she would know anywhere.

He stood among the trees of Dorcha Wood, just beyond the barrier that pulsed with powerful energy, facing her. His was a beautiful face, pale with piercing green eyes that matched her own, and long black hair that hung in fine strands past his shoulders. Calum lifted his hand and smiled, making her breath catch in her chest as though he had reached across the expanse and into her.

"Fiadh," he said, his voice resonating with power and feeling. "Sister, I have missed you so much."

Her eyes went wide, then pooled with tears. "Calum? Is it really you?"

He nodded, lips curling to show his perfect teeth flashing in the darkness. "I thought you were lost to me."

Fiadh gulped. "Mother thought you died. If she had known…" She lifted her hand and dropped it. "She would've given anything to see us reunited."

"Aye, I imagine she would have. She was a good woman, though I remember little more than the sound of her voice and feel of her arms as she held us close and sang us to sleep with lullabies."

The memories he conjured sent a pang of loss through her body.

"Perhaps, you can tell me more of her."

She nodded. "I would like that."

Calum's mouth curved in a small smile, though his eyes

remained distant. "Will you come with me? We can leave this place, all of it, and know each other again."

He reached for her, fingers passing into the barrier. With a hiss, he jerked them back. "What is this? You've used magic to keep me out of my home?"

She shook her head. "I didn't!"

An ugly look passed over his face. "Your precious Veren must have."

"Calum, please, don't do that."

"I? I've done nothing but come for my sister, my blood. And you hide behind this barrier!" He whipped a hand through the air and flung a bolt of electricity at it, glowering when it bounced off the protective layer with little more than a sizzle. "Why do you hurt me like this? I've done nothing to you!"

"I'm not hurting you! Please don't be angry."

"Then, come to me. Cross over and join me. Let us be a family again." He held out his hand, his long fingers unfurled and inviting.

Fiadh looked at it, felt the pull to reach out and take it. Her arm lifted, and she flicked her eyes to his, seeing a cold look of triumph. She balled her hand into a fist and forced her arm to fall to her side. "You've changed."

His jaw ticked as he tracked her movements. "Have I? I cannot say the same for you. I… there is much I don't remember." He looked abashed and shrugged. "I didn't have a mother who kept your memories alive."

"Nay, you did not, and I wish you had."

His eyes narrowed slightly. "Will you join me? I want nothing more than to know my sister again."

Within his words, she felt his power, it slipped into her mind through their twin-bond, flooding her limbs with the urge to cross the threshold that kept her safe and take his outstretched hand. How would it be to know her twin? To have a family again. Her legs trembled, and she felt her body begin to rock forward, drawn to him. He grinned and opened his arms, ready to embrace her.

She pressed her hand to her lips as tears made tracks down her cheeks. Nodding, she said, "I would go anywhere with you."

Joy, and something darker, flashed across his face. "Come, sister. Let us be away from this place and start anew."

"Aye, that is the dream." Fiadh looked wistful. "If only I could embrace it."

His smile faltered. "What?"

She gazed at him sadly. "I can't leave them."

"Who? The traitors who hide with you?"

"Don't call them that!"

"Why? It's what they are." He lowered his arms and schooled his face. "Fiadh, they turned their backs on us. Even now, we fight the humans, and let me be clear, our cause is desperate. We're winning many battles, aye, but for every one of them slain, ten more take his place. Each day there are more, and unlike them, we cannot afford a defeat. We do not have the numbers." He paused and looked beyond her toward the seat of Erabel. "And all the time, warriors refuse to help us. Tomorrow we could lose, or the day after, when these soldiers of yours could make all the difference. And what then? The humans will come for you here to finish the job at their leisure." He leveled a hard look at her. "They are traitors to our people. How can you trust them?"

She turned her head as though she could see the keep through the trees. "They're not traitors. They're my friends. My family."

"*I'm* your family! They're just using you. Can't you see that?"

Fiadh could feel his anger. "They're not using me, Calum. Rygeil is using *you*. You said so yourself."

"Rygeil may not be the leader we want, but he is the leader we have. The humans are the true enemy, sister. They must be exterminated. But our people need all three of us combined as one force to defeat them. And then, once they are defeated, we can deal with Rygeil. So let us play as the king's pawns for now, and then once the war against man is won, our knives will find Rygeil's back. He shall fall to our combined powers, and it will be us to sit upon the throne. Together."

"Oh, Calum, how did you become so filled with hate and anger? I... I've heard what he's done to you over the years."

Resentment and pain flooded his face. "You know nothing of my life."

"You're right. I don't. But I want to know."

"Then, come with me, sister! Let us be away from all of this!"

"I can't do that." Fiadh started to back away.

Meara stepped from the shadows, a dark presence at

Fiadh's side. Calum glanced at her, eyes traveling to the deadly tip of her horn.

His face crumpled. "You would turn your back on me? Your only family?"

"Goodbye, brother," Fiadh said, voice catching in her throat.

Turning from him, she swung onto Meara's back. Just then, Krulan materialized, his yellow eyes finding Calum in the darkness. They stared at each other.

Krulan, don't hurt him, she pleaded.

He ignored her and stared at Calum.

Her brother studied the Cù-Sìth. She watched in confusion as Calum's face went blank, and his hand drifted to the dagger in his belt.

"Calum? What are you doing?"

He didn't answer. With wide eyes fixed on Krulan, he pulled up the sleeve of his tunic and ran the blade along his arm.

"Calum! Stop!" Fiadh screamed, clutching Meara's mane.

"Help me, Krulan," Calum whimpered.

The Cù-Sìth's body trembled as blood dripped down her brother's arm.

"It's Rygeil… he's making me!" The blade cut another furrow into his skin. "Please, help me, Krulan." Calum's face contorted, and the dagger shook as he lifted it for a third time.

Krulan, what's happening? Help him! Fiadh pleaded.

His massive body twitched as though at war with itself. She saw the sharp tip of a fang flash in his muzzle, but he said nothing.

The dagger hovered above Calum's arm, blood dripping onto the dirt. Fiadh was about the leap off the unicorn when her brother's hand fell to the side. Scowling, he said, "I see she has you firmly in her grip."

Fiadh gasped, and Krulan's body unlocked. Snarling at Calum, he spun around and nudged Meara, forcing her to turn. *Go!* Krulan commanded.

Pressing herself to Meara's back, Fiadh whispered and hung on tightly as the unicorn lunged into a full run, Krulan beside her. Three more Cù-Sìth burst through the trees, two at her back and one at her side. Fiadh craned her neck just before they tore through the trees and saw Calum watching her, his face a mask of anger and grief.

He was toying with you, Krulan snarled. *With me as well.*

I don't understand.

Calum was testing me, seeing if I would breach the barrier and save him from himself.

Fiadh's heart ached at her brother's deception. Was he truly lost to Rygeil's madness?

When they returned to the keep, Veren intercepted them. "Fiadh! Where did you go?"

She looked down at him, grief pulling at her mouth. "I saw my brother."

He scowled and reached for her. "That was reckless."

"I know, but I had to see him."

"You could've been captured!"

"But I wasn't," she said, brushing his hands away. "I'm tired. I'm going to bed."

Veren stepped aside to let them pass and watched as

Krulan kept pace with her. In moments, they were swallowed by the shadows of the keep. Looking west, he closed his eyes and reached out his senses, calling on an owl to scan the western border. He saw only Calum's retreating form in the bird's eyes. Releasing a frustrated breath, he strode inside.

Her door was open when he made his way to her room. Krulan lay on the floor, her stalwart guardian. Veren glanced at the Cù-Sìth, then at her small form as she curled onto her side.

"I don't want to talk about it, Veren," she said to the darkness.

"Sleep well, Fiadh."

He left, pulling the door closed behind him.

CHAPTER TWENTY-ONE

*D*arragh stalked into the hall, bellowing for Donal. Under his breath, he cursed Haegna, damning her for her refusal to give him counsel. She was punishing him for some imagined offense, turning her back and refusing to speak like a spoiled child. It had taken all his will to keep from wringing her neck.

Growling to a servant for a cup of ale, he threw himself into his chair and glowered. A young maidservant held out a tray with his drink, keeping her eyes cast down as her arm shook under his glare. He grabbed the ale and took a deep swallow, releasing a loud belch as she backed away.

"What is your name?" he barked.

"M—Mabel, milord."

Eyeing her youthful curves, his loins began to stir. "Come to my chambers after the evening meal."

She darted a fearful glance at him, face paling. Giving a short nod, she scampered away.

Darragh settled back and scratched his groin, imaging the evening to come. After a few moments, Donal came through the door and strode to him, bowing when he came to the edge of the dais. "My lord."

"The young lord of Belfirth continues to badger me to press our advantage with a large force now that the witch's beast has been slain," he said. "And while I'd rather see his back flayed beneath the lash for his impudence, I acknowledge that he may have a point."

Donal cleared his throat. "It is true that the men have grown restless since they slaughtered the creature. The small bands you've sent to menace her people have proved fruitless. Another hunt may slake their boredom and draw her out."

"Aye." Darragh drummed his fingers. "Though I admit I had thought killing her beastly protector would've been enough. Perhaps, she is a callous bitch who cares nothing for those who guard her. Either that or she is weak and lacks the stomach for a fight."

"There is only one way to find out."

Darragh grinned cruelly. "True enough. Let Gideon lead a contingent into Dorcha Wood. Have him slay every creature they see. By the day's end, I want the forest to flow in rivers of blood. We shall see if that sways her inhuman heart."

His commander nodded. "A sound plan."

"You know, she would be quite a prize to present to the king's men when they return with reinforcements," Darragh said, running his finger along the rim of his mug. "Mayhap, he'd offer a kingly reward upon hearing of it."

"Aye, it would be a show of strength King Stephen would be unwise to ignore."

Downing the rest of his ale, Darragh said, "See it done. I want that witch brought to me by day's end."

"Very good, my lord." Donal bowed and left the hall, striding to the training field where Gideon practiced his swordplay.

"Gideon!" Donal shouted above the grunts and raucous laughter of soldiers.

Backing away from Quinn and sparing a few words to compliment the young man's skills, Gideon strode to Donal, letting his blade swing toward the earth, its point digging into the soil. "Aye?"

"Lord Darragh commands you return to Dorcha Wood and draw the Aos Sí witch out. You mentioned she has an affinity for the wild things that live there. It is time to test that bond."

Gideon studied him for a moment, thinking of the many animals that had come to Fiadh's hand. Some had come to his as well. "You wish me to slaughter them to force her out?"

"Aye, a hunt like we haven't seen in many a year! Dig them out, hunt them down, shoot them from their trees. Ah! What fun! Mayhap that will draw the bitch out from behind her cursed fortress and dark magic barriers!"

Shifting his weight, Gideon cast a glance at the forest. "I will need men."

"You have them," he said, nodding to Gideon's soldiers.

He shook his head. "They're not ready for this. Most of them had barely held a sword before coming here."

"Choose five from my ranks but take yours with you as well. It is past time they learn the ways of war."

This isn't war, Gideon thought. "Tell your men I will let them know who will join me by nightfall. We will leave at dawn."

Donal nodded. "Choose wisely, little lord. Darragh expects you to draw the witch out."

Gideon stalked away, having a brief word with his men before leaving the field. Splashing water on his face from a trough, he leaned on the edge and looked at his reflection. His face was covered in a week's worth of growth. It had been too long since he'd had a bath. Too long since his last sound sleep. The image that stared back at him looked haggard and haunted.

Gideon hung his head. "I want to avenge you, father, but I've lost my way. I don't know if I'm fighting for our people or just to slake my rage," he whispered.

Aishling's face filled his mind as it often did. Has she received my last letter? he wondered. The runner he'd sent had yet to return, but he could be on his way back with a reply from his foundling. When all of this was over, would he take her into the Scarlet Mountains or to Belfirth? He wondered if his home was overrun with elves. Mayhap, Quinn and the others would join him, if there was anything left. He sighed. If not elves, it was filled with ghostly memories.

Wiping his hand over his face, he took himself to the kitchen for bread and cheese. He would eat alone, as he often did, taking his meal to a fallow field just outside the forest. Why he had chosen that place, he couldn't say, but there was a comfortable boulder to perch on, and it was quiet, away from the misery of Darragh's people.

Tearing off a hunk of bread with his teeth, Gideon chewed and looked sullenly at Dorcha Wood, dredging up his hatred, detesting the fact that it had grown weaker since he had helped catch and kill the Cù-Sìth. In truth, it had begun to waver long before that awful event. What kind of man felt pity for a beast such as that?

Losing his appetite, he threw the heel of bread into the trees and stalked to the pasture where Aridius grazed with the other mounts. Whistling, he watched as the gelding whinnied and trotted toward him, a gray mare at his side. Gideon chuckled and said, "Who's your friend?"

The horse tossed his head and nickered, snuffling Gideon's hand, where he'd tucked the apple he'd snatched from the larder. Breaking it in half, he held the pieces out and smiled as two sets of horsey lips clamped onto the fruit. Aridius finished his treat and stepped forward, bumping his head against Gideon's chest. He reached up and scratched between the horse's ears and along his jaw, digging his fingers into all the itchy spots that couldn't be reached. Giving a throaty moan, Aridius leaned into him. The mare, not to be left out, nudged Gideon's other hand, and he soon found himself rubbing down both animals as they closed their eyes in bliss.

"That's enough, you greedy beast," Gideon said when Aridius demanded more.

The sky was darkening. Soon it would be night, and

come the dawn, he would enter Dorcha Wood and begin the slaughter. Part of him hoped Fiadh would stay away. Another part hoped she wouldn't.

CHAPTER TWENTY-TWO

"I am told Calum remains just inside the northern border of Dorcha Wood," Veren said to Fiadh when he joined her at the table to break his fast.

"You're certain?" she asked.

He nodded. "Kaelari sent for a púca who will keep watch and report any movement."

"That could be risky," she said, frowning.

"How so?"

"What if Calum's connection to Dorcha Wood is like mine, and he senses the púca? He might retaliate. I don't want anyone killed for my sake."

He made a frustrated noise. "You can't control that, Fiadh. This is a dangerous time, and we've all accepted the risks in coming here. So should you."

"I understand the risks, but that doesn't mean I'll deliberately put someone in harm's way. Perhaps, you should call the púca back."

"She volunteered for this role. It would be an insult to force her return."

Her mouth turned down. "I won't force her to do anything, but I hope she isn't being reckless for my sake."

"Calum will never know she's there."

They ate the remainder of their meal in silence. As Fiadh scraped the last of her porridge onto her spoon, Krulan came into the hall, tail drooping. Her face looked pained as she watched him find a quiet corner and curl into a ball. Tucking his head along his side, he watched her with yellow eyes.

"We should take advantage of this lull and find Rivya," she whispered to Veren.

Krulan's ears perked at the sound of his mate's name.

"I will not allow you to enter Merrow waters in search of her. It's too dangerous."

"Not that I need your permission, but I wasn't talking about looking there," she said caustically. "I want to search Dorcha Wood. Maybe she went there to hunt and got injured. We could find her tracks and bring her home."

He frowned. "Calum is still a threat, as is Darragh. It's not wise to leave the safety of Erabel. Besides, Krulan searched Dorcha Wood and found nothing."

Fiadh turned to the Cù-Sìth. *You found nothing?*

Only old tracks.

Where did you look?

I searched our hunting grounds.

What if she didn't go to your hunting grounds? Fiadh asked.

She would not stray from those, he told her, rising to his feet. *At least, I had thought she wouldn't.*

We'll find her, Krulan.

Fiadh got up, stopping when Veren grasped her arm. "It's not safe to leave."

"You can stay here or come with me," she told him, easing her arm away, "but I'm going to search for Rivya."

"Has anyone ever told you that you're reckless?"

"Frequently." Fiadh strode to the door, Krulan at her side. Turning around, she said, "I will stay well away from the northern part of Dorcha Wood. That should ease your mind."

He sighed and held out his hands, palms up. "May the Great Mother give me patience."

Muttering, Fiadh left the hall.

Veren shook his head and jogged after them. "Fiadh, you do realize that if she is not within the boundaries of Dorcha Wood, you and Krulan cannot search for her."

Krulan growled. *I know my duty and need no reminders.*

Fiadh clutched Veren's hand and squeezed. "He understands."

They went to the southern border of Erabel, well away from Calum's encampment and far from Krulan's hunting grounds in the west. Dasha flew low through the trees, dipping in and out of her vision until she commanded him to return to the keep and wait for her. He went with a collection of throaty complaints, and she watched his departure until his dark form disappeared among the trees. Meara stepped from the shadows of an oak then, the blackness of her coat hiding her until she stood in the light.

Smiling, Fiadh went to her and ran a hand down her soft neck, fingers sifting through her thick mane. While she could cover more ground on Meara's back, it would be more difficult to see any tracks from that height. "You will remain here too, my friend."

The unicorn nickered, nudging her in the chest and looking toward Dorcha Wood.

"I know you would, but I need you here."

Meara gave a horsey snort and ambled away.

Fiadh could see and feel the barrier, just as she had the night before. It was like a living thing, pulsing with power, reminding her of a beating heart. In the light filtering from the trees, she could make out the tiny rainbows of its shimmery form when she titled her head. Reaching out a hand, she touched it, feeling an overwhelming surge of power.

It unlocked something within her, and she grew rigid, teeth clenching, nostrils flaring. Her muscles burned as magic shot through her body. Power born of Danu waned just as the stolen power of the Merrow exploded, coming to vibrant life. Her eyes grew round, pupils dilating as stars danced within their center, galaxies circling slowly in a cosmic rhythm. Fiadh looked at the landscape in front of her and saw every creature as a pinpoint of light. Even the trees, their roots buried underground in a complex network of communication and life, throbbed with awareness and power. And beneath the forest, she sensed a river—ancient and dark—its waters flowing as they had since the dawn of time. *The Merrow swam those waters as they traveled between their realms,* she thought. Giving the river a gentle tap with her mind, she felt it respond, heard it welcome her as though she were part of it. Smiling broadly, she turned to Veren and Kaelari and saw them take a step away from her.

All is well, she said, her words never leaving her lips, inserting themselves into their minds with a subtle command. It was so easy. Why hadn't she done it before?

Veren was the first to register her thought and nodded warily, gripping his bow so tightly his knuckles turned white. Kaelari shot him a look and pulled herself into a fighting stance.

Krulan let out a low growl and pawed the ground.

Aye. I am ready, she told him.

Fiadh's eyes cleared, returning to their normal, brilliant green, though swirls of shadows lingered in each iris. She put her hand on Krulan's back and passed through the barrier into Dorcha Wood. The forest welcomed her in its embrace, trees bending to stroke their leaves or branches through her hair and along her limbs. She reached out to the them, greeting each one as an old friend as animals appeared from every direction, falling into step or flight as she moved through the woods.

They had gone only a few paces when Fiadh stopped and tilted her head, spinning slowly to look toward the north. Her brow creased. There was something there, with Calum. Something old and cruel. Powerful and dark. Part of her wanted to go to it, was drawn in an indefinable way, but the larger part of her was repelled by its nature.

"Something travels with Calum," she said.

Whatever was traveling with her brother sensed her awareness and reached for her mind, its will testing the mental shields she threw up. A sly laugh echoed in her brain when it prodded at them, and she flinched.

I feel it, Krulan said, hair on his back bristling.

Do you know what it is? she asked, focusing her power to keep it from entering her thoughts.

Teeth flashed in his muzzle. *I have never sensed it before. Evil surrounds it. That much I can feel.*

Kaelari strode to them. "What is it?"

"We don't know, but it's powerful and… ancient."

Veren and Kaelari looked at each other.

From Erabel came two members of Krulan's pack, having been summoned by their leader. With Krulan at the center, they formed a wall of bodies behind Fiadh.

They will search with us, he said.

She looked at each of them. *Perhaps, we should separate. We could cover more ground that way.*

We search together.

Fiadh's mouth made a thin line, but she didn't argue.

"Fiadh," Veren said. "You should return to the safety of Erabel."

She shook her head. "Whatever is with Calum, it watches. Nothing more." Glancing at Krulan, she added, "He will keep me safe."

"I don't like this," Veren said, notching an arrow and scanning the forest.

"Nevertheless, we will go on."

Kaelari chuckled. "She has truly come into her own."

"Don't encourage her," Veren groused, following as Fiadh began to search the woods for signs of Rivya.

Tracks were found, dug into the soil, and a few days old. Krulan and Vaymir, his second, sniffed the ground and looked toward the south.

Why would she come to this part of the forest alone? Fiadh asked.

She wouldn't. Not of her own free will. Krulan eyed the signs of Rivya's passing, tail lashing.

They followed the tracks, noting the broken stalks of plants, signs of a quick passage. Krulan's anxiety was palpable, and Fiadh kept her hand on his shoulder as they walked deeper into Dorcha Wood.

"Stop," Fiadh said, mouth parting as her eyes grew wild. "They're killing them!" She took off running, screams filling her mind, making her stumble.

Veren picked her up. "What is it?"

She sobbed and clenched the fabric of her tunic. "Soldiers. They're here." Fiadh spun around wildly and clapped her hands on her ears. "They're killing them! Don't you hear it?"

Alarm spread across the group with swords slipping from sheaths and bows gripped in skilled hands, postures of readiness marking every form.

Krulan snarled, flecks of saliva dripping from his muzzle. *Where are they?*

Everywhere! It's too many… I can't… they're screaming!

She turned to him and their eyes locked. In a moment of connection, they both heard it. The sounds of slaughter coming from the direction of her childhood home—the hut tucked safely in the depths of Dorcha Wood. Fiadh climbed onto Krulan's back, and they raced through the trees, Veren and Kaelari quickly falling behind.

Stay with the elves, Krulan commanded, and the two Cù-Sìth skidded to a stop and spun around.

Wind whipped through her hair as Fiadh clung to his back. Her mind was chaos, drowning in the fear and pain of so many creatures. With a whimper, she pressed her head between his shoulder blades, grounding herself in the jarring motion of his body and the rapid beating of his heart. By the time they reached the small clearing outside her former home, Fiadh had regained control. She swung to the ground as Krulan charged for one of two soldiers who had a large wild cat pinned against the wooden wall. They didn't see him coming. Krulan's presence made itself known as a spray of blood hit the soldier's face. There was no time for the man to scream before the Cù-Sìth brought him down next to his dead comrade.

The cat bolted to Fiadh, practically climbing up her body, its powerful frame shuddering. She dropped to her knees and held him, slipping into his mind where she saw what he had seen. The men. The killing. The image of one who had betrayed her. Him… again.

A cold look fell across her face like a shadow while in her mind she felt a dark power slither, awakening, warping her to its will. Fiadh rose and jerked her head to Krulan. Wiping his face in the dirt to rid himself of the blood, he came toward her, kneeling as she climbed onto his back.

Sister, Calum's voice called, slipping past her defenses. *I feel them. I feel the soldiers in the woods. They are violating our home, killing everything we hold dear. You can stop them.*

Fiadh shook her head, at war with herself as dark magic bloomed in her chest.

Can't you hear the screams of the dying? They're calling to you. Begging you to save them. Are you going to let them die?

I won't become a monster, she said, gritting her teeth.

Krulan's body trembled with pent-up rage. She felt it beneath her skin where she clutched his thick fur. *There are more men in the forest,* the Cù-Sìth said, his mind red with anger.

Find them, sister. Show them they are not welcome in our home.

Her mind broke, fed by the darkness that flowed in her veins and the barrage of anger from Krulan and Calum. "To Felmore," she ground out, and Krulan launched into a run.

Go, sister. Go and find them. Kill them all.

She gripped Krulan's scruff. *I do not go to kill.*

But you will when you see what they have done, Calum warned before his thoughts drifted to silence as Krulan raced through the trees.

At the edge of the forest, on the border between the Dorcha Wood and Felmore land, they stopped. Fiadh slid from Krulan's back. She stalked along the edge, toward the outer walls of the castle. The forest had grown quiet, animals hiding or fleeing. She could sense the presence of men nearby.

Are the Cù-Sìth still with Veren and Kaelari? she asked.

Aye. They will not leave them unprotected.

Fiadh turned her attention to Felmore Castle, and her mouth dropped open in dawning horror. There, just above the outer wall, were three huge pikes. On the center pike, tilted at a grotesque angle, was Rivya's head. A yelp of shock ripped from her chest as she noted the spikes on either side held the remains of two pups. Rivya hadn't told her she was pregnant. *My fault,* Fiadh thought. *If I hadn't sent her away she and her babies would be alive.*

Fiadh collapsed with a cry of rage and grief and looked at Krulan who stood shaking at her side, his eyes fixed on the corpses of his unborn children and mate.

He threw back his head and loosed an ear-splitting howl. From the depths of the forest came responses from the rest of his pack. Fiadh tapped at his mind but it had become nothing but blind rage. Krulan lunged toward Felmore.

"Stop!" Fiadh shouted, imbuing the word with a command.

Let me go, Fiadh. His body grew rigid.

Krulan no! They'll kill you!

Let him go, sister, Calum said. *He has the right to seek vengeance. Look at what they did to his mate. They murdered his children.*

"I won't lose him too!" she cried.

They are a plague, her brother told her. *You need to stop them before they kill the rest of his pack.*

Fiadh's eyes grew round, and she looked behind her, scanning the forest, though she could see nothing but trees and bracken. Would Darragh's soldiers try to take down another of Krulan's pack?

Killing is not the will of the Great Mother, Fiadh argued.

Danu has no will, Calum said. *She is energy, power. The Great Mother is not some human playing plots and strategies. She is raw. She is pure. If she gives you the power, then you owe it to her to use it to save her children.*

You're wrong.

You don't believe that, sister.

This is not the way! If it were, why aren't you doing it?

The Great Mother has given me many gifts, but I am not the chosen one. You are. Her true power runs in your veins, not mine. Danu has blessed you, sister. All you have to do is reach out and take it.

It's not right, she pleaded.

Look at what they did! Calum demanded in a voice that shook her body.

Her gaze swung to the gruesome remains. One of Rivya's eyes was missing, and her mouth hung open, blackened tongue lolling from her muzzle. Shifting her eyes, she looked at the babies, really looked. They were so small. Twins. Digging her hands into the dirt, Fiadh sobbed so forcefully she retched, crawling away from the mess as her body heaved. A chasm of sorrow opened within her, like the gaping maw of a horrifying creature. It threatened to swallow her in its misery, but she fought it and forced her body to stand. Clumps of dirt and leaves fell from her hands as she spread her fingers and anchored her feet into the earth.

That's it, Calum coaxed. *Feel her power. You know what to do.*

Magic spread through her veins, twisted and amplified a hundredfold by that of the Merrow. Danu's connection dimmed, taken over by a darker force. Air churned all around her, picking up debris from the forest while clouds coalesced across the sky, darkening until day became night.

Become vengeance, sister!

Fiadh's eyes began to glow, an inner light spilling from them as she glared at Lord Darragh's stronghold. Lightning flashed, followed by cracks of thunder so loud the ground shuddered. The storm grew, expanding to fill the horizon in ominous spirals of black and gray. People shouted, but their voices were nothing more than the drone of insects as Fiadh lifted her arms, calling on the particles of water in the air itself. They came to her, drawing together and hardening into chips of ice, a massive cloud of crystals that bobbed and spun until she threw her arms forward.

Hail, sharp as daggers, rained down on Felmore, cutting through thatched roofs, gouging wattle and dub walls, knocking down those who did not seek shelter. The entire village erupted into chaos. Soldiers manning the wall walks fled inside the keep while people who'd been milling about scurried into doorways, some dragging those who had fallen behind them.

Ah, I can feel your power! You are a goddess, my love!

Fiadh curled her hands in circular motions bringing a funneling cloud from the sky, watching with grim pleasure as it touched the ground just beyond the outer bailey of the keep. It rolled across the ground in a deafening whir, coming to a stop at the portcullis. She held it there, showing the lord who cowered inside the power she could wield, daring him to come out and face her. With a sweep of her arms, it dissipated.

Turning away with one last, long look at what was left of Rivya and her pups, she walked into the forest and stood among the trees, Krulan, a sinister shadow, at her side. The soldiers were still within Dorcha Wood's borders, creeping through the trees in search of safety from the storm that still churned slowly above them. Closing her eyes, Fiadh took hold of her fury and poured currents of energy into it, felt it bloom, becoming a tangled thing within her mind. She used it to reach into the soil. Like the roots of trees, it snaked through the ground, touching everything, imbuing it all with dark purpose. The forest groaned, took on new awareness. Branches bent and bark thickened, turning black as the leaves, leached of fall hues, flushed to a bruising purple.

Her power crept through the woods, reaching into every living thing, and finding the men who hid there.

Reach beyond Dorcha Wood, sister. Feel the wraiths of old. They await your command. Find them. Call to the Hunt.

Fiadh opened her arms and reached for the dark creatures—luring them with the promises of violence.

CHAPTER TWENTY-THREE

*M*ist, so thick it hid the trees, crawled across the forest floor. Gideon halted his soldiers and tried to get his bearings, spinning in a slow circle while looking up to search the sky for a sun that hid behind dark masses of clouds. A startled shout had him swinging his head, but all he could make out were the shadowy forms of his men, and they appeared to be drifting away from him.

"Stay with me!" he shouted, but his voice was caught in the fog and swallowed. Another yell had him jumping to his left, where he thought he saw a man go down, but when he ran toward the blurry form, all he found was a sword. "Quinn! Where are you? Quinn? Brody? Shout out so I can find you!"

He held his breath and listened, turning his head this way and that as voices called back, sounding farther away each time. A flash of movement made him spin, sword in his hand, but the only thing he saw was the branch of a tree swaying. As he watched, he realized it did not sway in a breeze, it was bending, reaching for him, its twigs curling into claws. He yelped and ran, fear clouding reason. Gideon leaped and stumbled over rocks, his feet catching on roots that rose from the earth.

And then a noise split the sky, loud like thunder, but sharp and high-pitched. It grew in intensity, becoming an inhuman shrieking. Gideon fell to his knees and clutched his head, a hoarse roar erupting from his lips as the sound became a nauseating din. Through slitted eyes, he saw a shadow whizz by, its ghostly form followed by more horrible wailing. Not a moment later, he heard another scream that turned into a squeal of pain before it was silenced.

Heart thundering, he staggered to his feet, blindly running, looking over his shoulder as shadowy creatures gave chase. Fear gave him strength. He slashed wildly as branches clawed at him, trying to drag him to the ground as he careened through Dorcha Wood.

His legs almost gave out when he finally saw a break in the trees. Gasping, he pushed himself to the limits, suddenly finding his body in the air and flung to the ground. Stars exploded behind his eyes, and his lungs seized. Gideon's mouth opened and closed like a fish, arms numb at his sides where his sword lay useless. The rustle of leaves sent him into a panic, and he blinked rapidly, forcing his chest to expand and retract until breath finally rattled out of him. Craning his neck to the sound, he saw the spindly legs of a creature stalking toward him.

Gideon's body screamed as adrenaline fled from his

muscles, leaving him weak and vulnerable. A loud panting filled his ears, his own, as he watched a nightmarish thing emerge from the mist. Its legs were black like tar, leading to a torso of sickly gray with leathery wings fanning out behind it. He tracked the body to its skull-like head and froze, caught in twin orbs, so black they were nothing more than dead pools that sucked him in, pulling his mind into a ghastly haze of misery.

It was a Sluagh. A creature from childhood stories, tales that had left him clinging to a candle in the night, wishing the flame would never go out.

The Sluagh came for him, slowly, chittering its teeth with a beetlish sound that sent shivers up his spine. It opened the slash of its mouth, white fangs dripping black drops of saliva, and hovered above his face, so close he could feel the coldness of its breath, smell the rankness of death each exhalation wafted into his nostrils.

"Leave Dorcha Wood," it hissed. "If I see you again, I'll kill you."

Gideon's eyes widened hearing the words he'd yelled at Fiadh on the crest overlooking Belfirth thrown back at him. "F—Fiadh?"

"Get out." The Sluagh canted its head at an unnatural angle, dead eyes boring into him. "Leave!"

Its roar echoed through the forest, the force of it propelling him to his feet. Gideon lurched to safety, turning back just once to see the Sluagh watching him before its head shifted, and it fixed its stare on a point behind him. He turned and saw the remains of the Cù-Sìth and her pups staked upon the pikes. Darragh had done such a craven thing to draw her out. Now, something unrecognizable had been unleashed. The girl he had known was gone, and he feared what she had become.

CHAPTER TWENTY-FOUR

iani screamed at Calum above the roars of thunder and dreadful wailing that ripped through the sky. "We must go!"

He looked at her, mouth splitting into a triumphant smile as trees contorted and blackened, becoming something with a monstrous will. The elf grabbed his arm and tried to drag him away, but he shoved her aside. A few paces away, Crom Cruach held out his arms, laughing and dancing in circles.

Calum clutched the medallion around his neck and whispered, "Go and find Darragh's men. Kill them. Kill them all."

Cackling, Crom Cruach bolted into the forest, bloodlust lending him speed as he searched for the soldiers. They had scattered, hunted by elves and Cù-Sìth. He threw the hood of his ragged cloak over his head, obscuring his face to appear as an old man, and stalked toward three young soldiers who hid among rocks and shrubs. They spotted him and shrank away.

"Come, come, I will take you to safety," he said, motioning for them to rise.

Shrieking from Sluagh ripped through the sky, and the men jumped to their feet, running toward the demon. At the last moment, he whipped the hood from his head, relishing the flash of fear on every face before he cut them down with spells that tore through flesh and bone. Flitting from one body to the other, he consumed their blood, feeling his power growing with each sip. Once finished, he danced through the forest, searching out others who'd escaped the elves and Sluagh.

The demon chased them down, shrieking laughter, picking them off one by one. Sated, he stood over the corpse of one of Donal's soldiers and reached for Fiadh, sensing her power and the strange darkness that ran through it.

That is not Danu's magic, he mused, closing his eyes to touch her mind. She recoiled from him, her thoughts black with fury. *Interesting. I would not have thought the chosen one would turn her back on the Great Mother.*

Though his hunger was appeased, Fiadh's strange power was an enticing lure. He followed the tenor of her mind, stopping with a curse when a command burned through his skull.

Return to me! Calum demanded, channeling his power into the medallion.

Crom Cruach gnashed his teeth, body trembling under the weight of the magic that compelled him to give up his pursuit of Fiadh.

Come to me! Calum's voice screamed into his mind.

From the corner of his eye, a dark shadow broke from the trees. Covered head-to-toe in a cloak, the figure came toward him as he stood immobile.

Crom Cruach, you will obey my command! Return to me. Now!

The force of Calum's will when channeled through the medallion, shook the demon. Biting his tongue so hard he drew blood, he stood his ground and waited for the cloaked figure to come within a few paces. Peeling back the cowl, the mage, Xander, revealed himself. The demon's face lit in a maniacal smile.

"My master wishes to set you free," Xander said.

Still frozen under Calum's spell, Crom Cruach could do little more than nod. The mage muttered, hands moving in broad sweeps as magic leaped from his fingers and fused with the old god's. Xander's magic was not as powerful as his master, Dothur's, but it was enough to release the bond that held the demon captive.

To the north, Calum gripped the medallion. The disc throbbed with power as he worked the spells Rygeil had taught him. It grew hot, scalding his palm but he clenched his jaw and held tight. Suddenly, a flare of power seared through it, cutting through his hand. He cried out and dropped the medallion, watching the grass beneath blacken. Crouching, he reached a finger out and touched the sigil.

I am free, my prince, Crom Cruach said, splitting the disc and severing its power over him. *Run back to Rygeil, now. Warn him not to seek me out again.*

With a bellow of rage, Calum jumped up and stalked into the woods, refusing to let his grandfather's prize escape so easily. Hearing his yell, Riani, Faraen, and the others scrambled after him, falling often in the thick mist that covered the ground like a blanket. Above, they saw streaks of gray shooting through the thunder clouds, ghostly screams in their wake.

"What are they?" Faraen shouted to Riani.

The elf ran at his side, shaking her head before falling hard on the nub of root that shot from the ground. "What's happening to the wood?"

"I don't know!" Faraen yelled above the din. "It is as if something has taken hold of it. Do you think… do you think it's Fiadh?"

The idea startled her, and she cringed. Whatever was happening to the forest was dark and unnatural. It was not the Aos Sí way. Nothing of Danu lived in the wrath she felt emanating from Dorcha Wood. Just then, something slithered past, cold and fast. Faraen yelped and shot to his feet, grabbing Riani and hauling her toward Calum. Behind them, they heard shouting as others struggled to break free from a forest that had grown dark and angry.

Fear flooded their muscles, lending them strength as they ran, not stopping until they found their prince standing in a ring of oaks. He turned at their approach, and they paled at his expression.

"Crom Cruach has escaped," Calum ground out.

Riani gasped. "Escaped? How?"

He tossed the two halves of the medallion at her feet.

She bent to pick it up. "The Great Mother help us," she whispered, dropping the shards as if they were tainted with the demon's evil. "That cannot be."

"It is done," Calum said.

The remainder of Calum's fighters joined them. They stood and listened to the hell that had been unleashed in Dorcha Wood. Their faces were masks of horror at what Danu's landscape had become.

"Is this the demon's doing?" one asked.

Calum shook his head. "Nay. What you are seeing is the power of my sister."

Shocked mutters circled the gathering.

"Aye, believe it." He eyed each of them. "We must capture her before she grows too strong."

"How can we do that without the demon's power?" Riani asked.

Calum felt for his sister's mind, tentatively piercing her consciousness. She brushed him aside, but not before he saw the darkness swirling through her like a living thing. *She is ripe for the taking,* he thought. *Together, Rygeil doesn't stand a chance.*

"The demon isn't going anywhere. We will lure him to us when we have Fiadh."

Riani shifted her body, uneasy with Calum's decision. "Are you sure he'll fall for that?"

He shrugged. "If he eludes us, so be it. Once we have her, it matters little."

Calum turned away from the sounds of the dying and headed to their encampment on the edge of the woods. The elves followed, watchful of the trees and wild things that had become sinister. When they arrived, Calum separated himself and reached out to Fiadh. If he could bend her will, feed whatever dark power she had harnessed, their combined strength could be greater than Crom's. They could rule and shape the world as they saw fit. The kings of men would kneel, as would all Aos Sí.

Closing his eyes, he concentrated on Fiadh. *You've done so well, sister. Find them all. Make them pay.*

CHAPTER TWENTY-FIVE

Fiadh came for them, tracking Darragh's men as they ran from the shadows lurking in the mist, the Sluagh screaming overhead. Heart beating so fiercely it felt like a hot coal in her chest, she walked through the forest, Krulan at her side, leaping at and tearing apart interlopers who crossed her path. Her magic sang through Dorcha Wood—a sinister song that called to terrible anger buried under layers of living.

Body thrumming with dark power, Fiadh reached for every creature within the forest, commanding them to come from their hiding places and fight. Bodies contorted as her power flowed through them, turning eyes blood-red, suffusing every mind with ravenous violence.

Good, sister. I feel your power. Unleash Dorcha Wood on our enemies!

Birds of every type swarmed through the trees, their cries mixing with the Sluagh in a cacophony of shrieks and caws. While those on legs became packs of every variety tearing through the underbrush with thunderous beats of their passage.

The trees groaned and turned black, twisting their branches into deadly spears as panicked men fled the forest. In the thickening mist, the hunters became the hunted.

She and Krulan followed the sounds of a skirmish. Cocking her head, she watched a soldier spy her and charge, his accomplice already engaged with Krulan in a match that was decided the moment the man faced the wrath of the Cù-Sìth.

Kill him! Calum shouted in her mind.

As if he moved in slow-motion, Fiadh saw the soldier raise his sword with a battle cry and hurtle toward her. She lifted her arm, and a root shot from the ground, wrapping itself around his left leg and breaking it with a loud snap. He shrieked and fell as more fibers erupted from the soil and twined around his body. Growing frantic, he waved his sword and began to scream, his voice devolving into desperate cries as one of the blackened roots snaked around his neck. His eyes bugged as he stared up at her, growing frantic when Krulan stepped to her side, his muzzle covered in blood.

"You should not have entered Dorcha Wood," she said, turning away as his face purpled under the pressure around his neck, mouth going slack with a final gurgle.

Good, sister. It's so easy, is it not?

Fiadh rubbed her stomach, queasiness making it clench. When it passed, she listened for more yelps or signs of passing from the remainder of Darragh's men.

They're hiding from you, sister. Seek them out.

Frustrated by the limitations of her hearing, she tapped into more power. She found the mind of a badger, its lithe body slinking through the debris on the forest floor. Fiadh reached out to it, but it shrank from her. Gritting her teeth, she tapped into her stolen power and ruthlessly took over its mind, smothering its will completely. She forced its body to run along the needle-littered ground. Scenting the sweat and fear of men, the badger turned east, stopping when the smell grew strong. From the shelter of a holly bush, she spotted a young soldier through its eyes, back pressed against the face of a boulder, sword clenched in hands that shook. She roughly let the animal go. *There must only be a few left*, she thought.

Her gut churned, and she grimaced, but, even with growing nausea, magic dripped from her body and poured into Dorcha Wood.

Search out the others, she told Krulan.

I will not leave you.

You need not worry for my safety, Krulan. Go.

He looked uncertain, but heeded her command, unable to refuse the power behind it.

As soon as he left, she found a quiet spot away from the bloodied grounds of combat. The oily feel of the Sluagh's mind still lingered. She paced, shaking her head, trying to rid herself of it, and the image of Gideon's terrified face when he'd realized it was her voice coming from the creature. She couldn't kill him. Not even now.

You show weakness by sparing him, Calum said.

I won't kill him.

Are you so sure he deserves to live? his voice whispered.

Get out of my mind! She clutched her head and sent a dagger of power at Calum, feeling him flinch.

Breathing deeply, she closed her eyes and let her shoulders drop. Her stomach roiled. Fighting queasiness that bubbled inside, she gulped hard to keep bile from crawling up her throat. Beneath her hand, her gut clenched, spasming so violently it felt as though something writhed inside of her. Doubling over, Fiadh retched, throat distending painfully as tears leaked from her eyes. With a violent lurch, her stomach twisted and disgorged a slick, black mass. It landed on the ground with a soft thump. Panting, Fiadh stared at it, watching with dawning horror as it twitched and flopped, elongating into a wormlike creature.

Her mind went white and she heard the voice of Aelrah speaking of Caoránach, the Oilliphéist. With horrible clarity, Fiadh relived the invasion she had experienced in the oracle's chamber—the tendril of something reaching into her through her nostril, traveling down her throat and into her body. Her head swam with the memory of it, going blank as she had done in that moment when it dove into her so deeply she felt it in every part of her.

Something had been left behind.

Fiadh trembled, her power leaching into the soil where she crouched, as though pulled by the creature that turned its sprouting head toward her before diving into the ground like a snake, sealing the earth behind it as though it had never been. She sat on her heels, sweat running down her face in the chill air. Had that really happened? Had that *thing* been growing inside her? Her mind recoiled. With shaking hands, she touched the ground where it had disappeared, but all she felt was packed dirt, not even an indentation to indicate its passing.

Words swam in her head. Worm. Dragon. Ruler.

Aelrah had said both she and Ithraen were needed to perform the magic that would unleash Caoránach—the power of Danu and that of the Merrow as one. With sick realization, Fiadh acknowledged that the power she had stolen from Eradar had made her a perfect vessel to birth the creature all on her own. Thoughts raced through her mind as she was filled with indecision. Glancing back at the ground, she knew there was nothing to be done. It was loose now.

Staggering to her feet, Fiadh got her bearings and reached out to Krulan. With a last look at the deceptively undisturbed earth, she made her way back to where he had left her to await his return. By the time Krulan broke through the trees, Fiadh had collected herself and reignited the power running through her body.

We must find Veren and Kaelari.

They are with my pack. The others returned to Erabel.

If you lead, I will follow, Fiadh told him as she took one last look toward the section of forest where the creature she'd spat out had vanished before shutting the experience from her mind.

CHAPTER TWENTY-SIX

Her heart ached with sadness and burned with anger as Fiadh walked through Dorcha Wood, pulling the bodies of slain animals into the earth where they would become a deeper part of the forest. Kaelari and Veren followed at a distance, wary of the power she wielded while also eager to use it to their advantage. They needed the edge against Darragh's army. Krulan, on the other hand, did not shy away from her. His rage matched her own, and he clung to her side. She kept a hand on his shoulder, feeling his strength while soothing the pain that gripped him.

She stopped when she came to the body of the young soldier she'd killed when she'd pulled roots from the ground and strangled him. His vacant stare held her where she stood and, like a mirror, showed her what she had become. Her mouth twisted. *Blood on my hands,* she thought, turning her palms up. They were pink beneath the grime. Fiadh curled them into fists and looked at the fallen man. With whispered words, she called on the earth and gently pulled his body into its womb.

Turning to Kaelari and Veren, she said, "This is not the way. I've become a monster."

Veren wrapped her in his arms, stroking her shoulders as her body shook. "Shh. This is war, Fiadh. All of us feel the stain of it. But it is a necessary evil."

She shook her head. "What I did was not necessary."

"It was not your hand that ended this one's life," Veren said, looking at the wounds. "It was a Sluagh."

"That doesn't matter. If not for me, they wouldn't have come." *If not for Calum, I'd never have reached out to them,* her mind shouted.

"Come away. Let us return to Erabel."

"Not yet. I started this path, and I must end it before it's too late."

Do not take away our advantage, Krulan said. *You need to bury your tender heart and do what you must to secure your future.*

Not like this, Krulan. There are other ways.

If you go the path of the weak, this world will consume you! he raged.

She sighed and took his massive head in her hands, tugging at him until his eyes were level with hers. *You are my good friend. My protector. My Champion. But I need you to listen to me. I will not become this thing that I let loose today. I can't. If I let it take over again, I fear I'll lose myself forever.*

He growled but didn't argue.

Dropping her arms, she looked to Kaelari and Veren. "Darragh's men will return."

They nodded.

"I can't undo what I've done. I can only fight for what's left of me." Brows furrowing, they looked at each other, then back at Fiadh. "There will be no more killing."

Closing her eyes, Fiadh lifted her face to the sky and called to the Sluagh. A small group of the creatures whipped through the air, inhuman wailing following their flight as they streaked past. The elves watched warily, edgy as the dark forms of the Sluagh sailed over the trees. Kaelari blanched when one landed in a flurry of leathery wings and scuttled toward Fiadh. Krulan snarled softly, hushed by the press of Fiadh's hand.

Its head bobbed from side to side as it marked each of them before fixing its gaze on Fiadh. Eyes—endless pools of black—studied her. When it spoke, its voice sent tremors down the elves' spines, and they gripped the hafts of their blades tighter.

"You are either brave or a fool to call upon us," it rasped.

Fiadh tilted her chin in acknowledgment. "You are part of this world, and it has many enemies. Your people are not among them."

A white film flashed over its eyes as the Sluagh blinked, mouth curling in a smile that revealed needle-like teeth. "We had not expected one such as you to call us from our slumber. Long have we hidden in the dark, forgetting who we were. Riding the skies in righteous fury brings back memories of better days. We are the Hunt," it said, and one black leg dug a small furrow into the soil, "What is your will?"

"I seek allies, but not executioners."

An eerie sound, like a hundred beetles scurrying across

the ground, filled the quiet as the Sluagh considered the offer. "You cannot change who we are, young one. The Hunt are the harbingers of death. You should have known this when you sent for us."

She wanted to blame Calum for the presence of the Sluagh. How had he even known of such beings? She longed to rage that it hadn't been her plan to bring forth such a ravenous band of creatures. That she hadn't wanted to kill Darragh's men. But those arguments were lies that tasted of ash in her mouth.

Frowning, Fiadh said, "I've seen the cost of killing, and I refuse to be a part of it again."

Don't push them too far, Krulan warned. *They are dark creatures.*

"I seek an alliance."

"An alliance without death?" the Sluagh asked. "Tell me, how would that work?"

"The people of Felmore fear you."

Sharp teeth flashed in the slash of its mouth. "As do yours."

"That is true. If you wish to fight alongside us, I ask that you leave the soldiers unharmed. Only frighten them."

"Hm. We could do that without your alliance."

"Then why didn't you?" Fiadh challenged.

Be careful, Krulan said, back bristling.

The Sluagh stared at her, mouth clicking. "It has been centuries since we rode the skies. We had forgotten."

Fiadh sensed there was more unsaid. Tapping at the Sluagh's mind, she found a dark chasm of thought, and, within it, longing for the one who had led the Hunt long ago. They were like a rudderless vessel now. Lost in a world that had forgotten them just as they had forgotten who they were. Not wanting to become lost in the creature's head, she pulled back.

"I will lead you." The Sluagh's eyes widened. "I only ask that you abide my wishes. When I call on you, remind them why they fear the Hunt. Keep them from our borders, but don't kill."

The Sluagh considered her offer. "I accept. For now."

Fiadh nodded.

"I am Troya, speaker for my people." Behind her, others of her kind shifted in a tight group, their wings scraping against each other with a whispery sound. "My sisters and I will reclaim the skies when you call."

"Thank you, Troya." Fiadh leaned around, making eye contact with each Sluagh, many of whom stood fidgeting. "You are welcome to remain in Dorcha Wood." Kaelari gasped, earning a glare, before she continued, "I only ask that you do not hunt within the forest."

"We hunt what we have always hunted, and they do not live within these woods."

Fiadh clasped her hands loosely and looked to the south, where Felmore sat like a boil on the landscape. "Lord Darragh has many soldiers at his command. This attack was a small taste of what I know will come."

Troya cocked her head. "What would you have us do?"

"Keep watch. Should more soldiers enter the forest, drive them out."

"Until then?" Troya asked.

"There is something else in the forest. Something old and cruel."

"Aye, we have felt it." The Sluagh looked to the north. "Some were slain by its hands."

"Could you find it?"

"We will try." With that, she turned and spoke to her sisters, and they launched into the sky in a mass of pale wings and unearthly wails.

Kaelari hissed and clamped her hands over her ears while Krulan's went flat against his head.

Veren flinched but stood stoically, eyes fixed on Fiadh. "What have you done? Those are evil beings from ancient legends!"

"They're lost. Whoever once led them is dead, and they've been in hiding ever since."

"And you think it's safe to set them free?"

Fiadh looked away. "I can't take back what I've done, Veren! I called them. I brought them here, and they slaughtered people! Young men just following orders! People my age. What do you think that makes me?" She sobbed. "Don't ask me how I did it or why, just accept that I did this. I'm trying to make it right now."

Walking away from the look in Veren's eyes, she headed toward Erabel, Krulan at her side. The moment they crossed the border, Dasha bounded toward her, dancing at her feet. Smiling, she leaned down and rubbed his head. "I missed you too."

Flying to her shoulder, he preened her hair as they made their way to the keep. Fiadh felt charged. Awakened. But she knew that given a moment of privacy grief and fatigue would consume her and she had no desire to fall apart in front of an audience. So, she focused on Dasha, listening to his thoughts as he told her about his day. Wishing she had stayed with him.

Somewhere, in the back of her mind, Calum prodded at her, his voice distant but there. Cutting herself off from him, she walked into the great hall where a group of warriors waited. They looked worn, but well, with only a few superficial wounds here and there. It was a relief to see them whole.

Begging exhaustion, Fiadh patted Krulan, sending him away, and headed for her chamber. Moments later, Veren knocked on her door. She opened it and went to her pallet, perching on the edge. Dasha croaked at him from his spot in the corner. He nodded to the raven, then folded his legs and sat on the floor facing her.

"Want to talk about it?" he asked.

She shook her head, but a ragged sob betrayed her. It came spilling out like a river. She told him about Rivya, swallowing hard when an image of the Cù-Sìth's remains flashed in her mind. He kept silent as she glossed over the skirmishes she and Krulan had taken part in, shame clouding her mind at the knowledge of the lives she'd taken. She left out Gideon, never mentioning how she'd somehow taken control of the Sluagh at the height of her rage and come for him. It was too awful to share. Veren listened, then spoke briefly of the soldiers he and the others had taken down and the surety that this was another test for a greater attack to come.

"Lord Darragh may very well be trying to draw you out, Fiadh."

"I know."

"We were lucky that it was another small band of men." Veren scooted back to rest against the wall, shoulders sagging. "Next time, he may send the whole of his army."

Fiadh sighed. "I don't think his soldiers will be too keen on entering Dorcha Wood after today."

"That may be true, but they'll come when he commands it. I know how you feel about killing, but you may need to face that inevitability again."

She looked away. "I won't be a part of that again."

Resting his leg on his upraised knee, Veren said, "I understand. It changes you."

Fiadh gulped, face crumpling. "I've got blood on my hands, and it'll never come off."

"I'm sorry, Fiadh. I wish the world was different. But we have to fight for what we want."

She took a deep, shuddering breath.

Veren eyed her as she fought for control, marking the power that throbbed in her veins, so strong he could feel the gentle vibration of its existence. "I've never seen power like what you showed today."

She made a non-committal sound.

"How did you do it?" he asked.

"Do you remember when I said I took something from Eradar to escape the Merrow?"

He nodded.

"I stole his magic." She paused, gauging his reaction. "It… did something to me. I feel different. Detached in some ways, connected in others. It's hard to explain." Fiadh looked at her lap, twisting her hands in the hem of her tunic. "When I saw what they had done to Rivya, something... broke free inside of me," she lifted haunted eyes to his, "and I welcomed it."

CHAPTER TWENTY-SEVEN

*C*rom Cruach holed up in the massive trunk of a dead tree, wedging his body so deeply the mage could see nothing but light reflecting off his eyes. Its confines, so like the cell he'd lived in for hundreds of years, hugged his form. Drawing on Xander's magic and the dark power that flowed from Fiadh into Dorcha Wood, the demon set his will to the only thing that could hold him and spat a Word into the wind. It was carried across leagues and into Oadsera, where it found the idol hanging from Rygeil's neck and sundered the bond that held him. The moment the sigil's power was rendered impotent, Crom Cruach crowed in triumph.

Smiling cruelly, he pressed a finger into the decaying wood of the oak, channeling his power and hurling it like a spear into the earth where he felt it hit its mark. Danu flinched, and the forest shuddered. Crom Cruach sniggered. The Great Mother was weak, and it was not from him.

Rygeil's lust for power and Fiadh's unnatural magic had taken a toll. *How wonderful,* he thought.

"Rygeil's spawn wields power not her own," he said to the mage. "An interesting turn of events."

"She is of no concern to us," Xander said.

Crom Cruach frowned. Fiadh would make a delightful plaything, while she lasted. And her blood. Her blood would be exquisite. The demon flicked through memories of the events of the day, relishing bits and pieces. It had been entertaining, made more so by the naked terror of Darragh's men upon seeing the Sluagh. He pursed his lips. That had been a handy trick on Fiadh's part, and it gave him pause, as they were creatures with a dark history, not the type elves aligned with. And they were formidable.

He eyed the mage. "Was it you who called upon the Sluagh?"

Xander shook his head. "I come on behalf of my master. I have no interest in skirmishes between men and elves."

"But there is such fun meddling in their lives!" He dug his fingers into the dirt, stabbing at Danu. "If you haven't come to join me, why are you here?"

"My master requests your presence."

The old god cocked a brow. "Oh, does he? And who is this exalted master of yours that I should heed his invitation?"

"Dothur, son of Carmun."

"Carmun and her offspring are dead," he sneered. "You have been fooled."

Xander rose, his body unfurling beneath the lengths of

his black cloak, and looked to the south. "Go to the witch of Felmore, and you will see I speak the truth."

He considered the mage, tapping his fingers on the rotted sides of the fallen tree. Xander's magic was weak compared to his own, but it had been enough to aid in destroying the power of Calum's medallion, and for that he was grateful. But he had no wish to enter a new prison with a new master. Freedom was still fresh on his tongue. He had yet to plumb its depths and reclaim his place among the realms of men. And yet, if the mage spoke truth, aligning with the spawn of Carmun was a tantalizing lure.

"Leave me, and I will consider your words."

Bowing, Xander left in a swirl of fabric and spells. Crom Cruach waited until the mage was gone, knowing he would likely remain nearby at his master's bidding. Dothur. The idea of his existence had a strong appeal. If true, he would be a powerful ally. But he could be an equally powerful enemy.

Curious about the witch Xander spoke of, he closed his lids, sent out a thrum of power like a beacon, and waited, batting aside Sluagh who sensed it and sought to find its source. It took half of the night, but eventually, Haegna felt him and responded. He hooked her mind and, like a fisherman, reeled her in with promises of blood and magic.

In the hours before dawn, he left his hiding place. Using spells of concealment, he passed by guards on the outskirts of the castle. Leaving them shuddering and looking over their shoulders as they felt his presence but saw nothing. Whispering a word, he opened the outer door to the dungeon and stole into Felmore Castle, unerringly finding his way to Haegna's door. Using magic to unlock it, he entered and found her sitting above the dark pool of her scrying bowl.

She stiffened, sensing him, and he cast a spell, holding her rigid upon her stool as he imprisoned her mind. Looking about the small cell, he noted the sleeping form of her servant on a pallet in the corner. She would not trouble him.

Shuffling to Haegna's bent form, he looked over her shoulder, smiling grotesquely at his reflection next to hers. Her eyes were round and clouded by age, staring fixedly at what he conjured in the black liquid. It was too easy to hold her, spinning fantasies of blood and power, and he enjoyed the moments, seeing what she saw. As his eyes drifted along the surface, he caught a glimpse of something else in the pool, something that stared back at him sardonically. His eyes narrowed, and for a moment, it revealed itself, pale and wretched. Then it was gone.

Crom Cruach hissed and ruthlessly wrenched Haegna out of her stupor. "You seek those you should not toy with, my dear."

Haegna looked at his image upon the surface of her scrying bowl and slowly turned to face him. "I didn't. He sought me."

"Oh? More dangerous are those you do not seek." He dragged her rocking chair from its spot by the fire and settled himself. "Do you know who I am?"

She looked at him warily and shook her head.

He laughed, the sound bouncing off the stone walls. "The children of men have short memories. I have a mind to remind them why they should not have forgotten. But that is for another time."

"Why have you come?" Haegna asked, adding slyly, "Are you here to curry favor with the future king of the western reaches?"

"A future king, you say?" He leaned forward, glowering at her from beneath his deformed brow. "What use is your spawn to me?"

"His army is great and more men flock to him each day. Even King Stephen is sending men. Soon, he will unleash them on Dorcha Wood and take Erabel's heir. With her, he will wield even greater power."

"You think she is so easy to catch?" He tsked. "Hers is a power far greater than yours, old woman. But the idea of an army of men has its appeal, though not for the capture of the Aos Sí witch."

Haegna's lip curled. "I will have her, and none shall stop me!"

Crom Cruach muttered a string of words and watched with glee as Haegna's face grew still, her mouth pulled in a grimace of pain. Body locked, her only indication of awareness came in the slight ticking of her eye. Whispered words curled around her still form, and her mind flinched, too weak to keep him out as he brutally carved his way into it, callously boring through her memories. When he'd finished, a trickle of blood slid from her nostril and over her clenched mouth, trailing around the curve of her chin and down her neck. She gasped, her body sagging as she fell to the floor.

"You seek the elven witch? I could bring her to you, should you prove worthy."

She lay on her side, heaving.

Hauling himself to his feet, he stood over her, back hunched and protruding beneath his tunic. "Defy me, and I will kill you."

Turning her head, she eyed him. "What would you have me do?"

"Tell your son to alert his armies and ready themselves to set a trap."

CHAPTER TWENTY-EIGHT

*C*alum reached for Fiadh as she writhed in the throes of a nightmare. She whimpered, body soaked with sweat, mind conjuring the face of the young soldier whose dead eyes had stared into hers. He tasted her grief in the tenor of her thoughts.

Sister, I feel your struggle. It will get easier. I promise. You have done a great thing. Humans are a curse. You should feel no remorse, only joy for cleaning the world of more of their kind.

She curled onto her side with a hoarse sob.

Come to me. I can heal your pain, ease your worry. Together we can leave this place behind and start again.

"Calum," she whispered in her sleep.

Fiadh. I hear you. Come to me.

Jerking awake, Calum's voice lingered in her mind like an echo. She looked around, shushing Dasha when he stirred. Bending her knees and hugging them to her chest, she clenched her eyes and tapped into her twin bond.

Brother, I need you.

I am here, sister. I am with you.

Tears spilled down her cheeks. *I feel so alone.*

You are not alone, Fiadh. You need never feel alone again. I want to take you away to someplace we can know each other again and be a family.

She nodded, longing to get up and go to him, knowing she couldn't. *Leave Rygeil, Calum. Be with me, here in Erabel. Your true home.*

His mind went blank.

Calum? Did you listen to my words? Abandon Rygeil. Stand with me.

I… I cannot. We need him … for now. His power is great. Only with him, with all our bloodline's powers combined, can we be sure of victory over the humans. Otherwise, the best we may achieve is to hold out a few more years in the far wildernesses of the world, the deepest forests and wild lands.

She felt his uncertainty. Rolling onto her knees, she looked out the window, seeing the pale face of the moon. *Please, Calum. He's manipulating you. We need peace with the humans not war. Don't you see that?*

Silence.

Calum?

What game are you playing at, sister? There can be no peace with humans. Why can't you see that? How many do they have to kill? How much must they burn? Our people, our animals, our birds, our trees? How many? They will keep coming again and again. They will wear you down, and each of us will fall to their armies one by one—you, me, Rygeil. Save your desires to move against Rygeil for another day.

For now, we must unite with him against mankind. If we fight amongst ourselves, all is lost.

You claim you're not a pawn, but those are Rygeil's wishes I hear.

You think so? Or has someone else been whispering in your ear? Has that traitor, Veren, told you I'm nothing more than a puppet? He knows me not.

What? No! It's not like that!

He laughed, forcing the sound and cold feel of it into her head. *You're so pliable, sister. So easily led. Why would I abandon the greatest army in the world to stand with you and lose everything? I'm offering you more power than you could imagine! Once we have exterminated the children of men, we can take the throne!*

I won't walk that path, Calum.

You disappoint me, sister.

Fiadh felt the moment he severed their connection. She reached for it again, but it was as though she hit a wall. Dropping her chin, she cried quietly until her body felt wrung out. Exhausted, she curled to her side, pulling the blanket over her head. The feel of a hand on her shoulder made her yelp, and she threw a pulse of energy in all directions, knocking Veren onto his back.

"Fiadh, it's me," he whispered harshly. "I heard you crying."

She sat up and rubbed her eyes, a sob catching in her throat when she found him in the shadows, sprawled on the floor. He sprang to his feet and gathered her in his arms, words of comfort filling the quiet.

Fiadh clung to him. "I keep hearing Calum's voice."

"You have to block him out."

"It's not just him. I... I keep seeing the face of the

soldier I killed. His eyes. I still feel them on me. I'm so ashamed of what I've done," she said wetly. "I never wanted to hurt anyone… I didn't…" She shook her head, wishing the motion could cleanse her mind of the awfulness.

Veren ran his hands along her spine, the tips of his fingers sending tiny tremors through her body. She burrowed into him, feeling the solid pounding of his heart against her cheek. They spent many minutes in each other's arms, but eventually Fiadh got a crick in her neck and pulled away. When she looked at him, he couldn't hide what shone in his eyes.

Fiadh stared, seeing his raw emotions, the turmoil of trying to mask them and failing. It was a look she had seen before. Only, then, it had been from one who knew only part of who she was, having shunned the rest of her as though she were a leper. Gideon had awakened her, pulled at her heart until she thought she loved him with the whole of it. But she hadn't seen all he was either. She had been too young and too blinded by infatuation. It was a cruel lesson.

"Fiadh," Veren said, licking his lips nervously, "when we met, I told myself that I would stand at your side in the dark days to come, never wishing for more than to be the hand that shields you. But, I cannot deny—" He made a frustrated sound. "I think you know how I feel. I think you know that I've fallen in love with you."

Her eyes grew soft. "Aye. I've seen it." She put her hand on his chest. "And I care for you too, Veren. I care very much."

"But you don't love me." He smiled crookedly.

"I can't… I want… I—"

"Shh," he said, pressing his finger to her lips. "He hurt you."

She gulped and looked away.

Cupping her chin, he turned her head. "It's alright to be hurt. It's made you strong, and I love the strength I see in you."

Fiadh sobbed and threw herself in his arms. "Make me forget him," she begged. "Make me forget."

Veren pressed his lips to her head, kissing the skin along her hairline and trailing his mouth down her face, around her chin to her neck. She tilted her head back as he flicked his tongue on the lobe of her ear, then snagged her mouth, nipping at her lower lip.

"Are you sure?" he whispered, nibbling and kissing her jaw.

Fiadh nodded, surrendering herself to the moment, forcing her mind to let go of the hurt, at least for one night, and open her heart again.

Lowering her to the bed, Veren tugged gently at the lacings of her chemise, slipping it over her shoulders and halfway down her arms so the tops of her rounded breasts swelled above the fabric. His lips followed his eyes, raining kisses on every inch of exposed flesh, lingering on the skin above her heart as it stuttered in her chest. She moaned as his hand cupped her, needing her flesh, until her nipples throbbed, and then went lower, sliding his fingers along the apex of her thighs. She parted them at his questing, giving as much of herself as she could.

Crouching at the foot of her pallet, he tugged her

chemise off and looked down at her pale form with hungry eyes. "You're so beautiful."

She sat up and pulled at his tunic with shaking hands. He closed his fingers around them and took over, gauging her reaction as he removed each piece of clothing, noting her eyes go round with a flash of fear when she cast a glance below his waist. He made her forget that fear as he plied her with touches that made her stomach flutter and her skin burn. When he finally rose over her, she held him in a limpid gaze, knowing it would change everything and nothing. Veren ground out her name between clenched teeth and claimed her in a way no man had. In the glow of their union, her heart felt whole.

They held each other after, reality slowing creeping into the residual warmth of their joining. Outside her window, the first blush of a red dawn stained the sky, bringing with it a new day and the cold truth that the longest of those days was yet to come.

"There's something I've wanted to ask you," she said against his chest, where her head rested.

He trailed his fingers along her shoulder and back. "Oh? And what is that?"

"Do you think I'm wrong, not wishing to fight like Kaelari wants me to?"

Moments passed as he stroked her skin, considering. "I would say that you must follow your heart. Yours is the purest I have ever known. You know the path you must take. You'll lead, and I will follow."

"Thank you," she whispered.

"It is I who should be thankful. You've brought such

hope, to all of us." He kissed the top of her head, and they watched dawn spread across the horizon. The colors reminded her of the Ruby Cay in Abadon.

Leaning up, she rested her arm on his chest and looked at him. "Do you remember me telling you about my time with the Merrow? About Aelrah and the Oilliphéist?"

"Aye."

"Do you think they're real?"

His hand stilled as he considered. "My first reaction would be to say it is just a story, but I have come to understand that some stories have kernels of truth. Why?"

She shrugged, remembering the feel of vomiting up a wormy mass and watching it disappear into the ground without a trace. For whatever reason, she was reluctant to tell him about it, part of her thinking that maybe she had imagined it. The other part knowing she had not.

Locking away the bizarre memory, she said, "I've been thinking about it, wondering what kind of creature it would be if it were real."

"The Merrow likely have many stories of creatures that roamed the earth when they were a more powerful people. Perhaps, this Oilliphéist is a reflection of who they once were, and bringing it back is a desire to reclaim what they lost."

She hummed and turned her head into his chest. "I think we're all trying to take back something we lost."

Veren nodded. "Aye, I suppose we are." He gave her a squeeze as he looked at the lightening sky and rose from the bed.

Her stomach chose that moment to loudly protest its emptiness. She slapped her hand on it and giggled.

He arched a brow. "I believe I have discovered what you seek."

Fiadh threw her pillow at him, laughing as he caught it and tossed it back. She got up and grabbed her clothing, darting glances at him as he slipped his tunic over his head. Heat filled her cheeks as she remembered the feel of his chest pressing against hers and the slow grind of his hips.

"I feel you looking at me," he said.

"It's your own fault I'm looking."

He chuckled and pressed a kiss to her lips before striding to the door and opening it. "I will meet you in the great hall to break our fast." He winked and shut the door.

With its closing, the last of the soft glow of their night together left, leaving traces in the air itself, intangible things Fiadh wanted to grab and hold on to even as they drifted away. Sighing, she finished dressing and plaited her hair, blushing when she saw the knowing look Dasha gave he when eyed the rumpled bedding.

"What?"

He swooped down to her pallet and croaked at her, clacking his beak.

"That's none of your business." She huffed and tugged the neck of her tunic.

Dasha flapped his wings and danced in a circle, eliciting a small smile that turned into a laugh when he wasn't looking where he was going, and tumbled onto the floor. If ravens could scowl, he did as he glared up at her and pigeon-walked to the door, pecking on it twice.

"I'm coming. I'm coming." She opened the door, and he flew on ahead, cawing about his superior ability to navigate the halls. She shook her head and followed, but with each step, it felt as though the outside world also took one step closer, pressing down on her like a storm cloud. Looking out the archways lining the hall, she scanned the sky, a sense of doom washing over her mind.

Something was coming. It was almost here.

CHAPTER TWENTY-NINE

Stalking from his tent, Calum looked around at his warriors breaking their fast and announced their immediate departure. They would return to Oadsera and inform Rygeil of Crom Cruach's disappearance. His grandfather would be angry, but he would tell the king Fiadh was close to breaking. He needed more time.

Breaking camp, Calum glared in the direction of Erabel. His sister hid behind those barriers, tempting him to join her, and he would be a liar to say he wasn't tempted. But it was too late for that. It was too late for him. Rygeil had spent years shaping him into the formidable fighter he was, had trained in him ways others of his kind deemed wicked. He knew the path he wanted to walk, and it wasn't with a pious group of elves. Mankind had to be defeated, everything else was second to that. When he returned to Dorcha Wood, he'd lay siege to Fiadh's mind, making what he'd done so far seem trifling.

She would turn, or she would die.

They kept to the trees when they could, camping in secluded copses at night, and taking too many risks in the open in their haste to return home. Once within the protection of Oadsera, Calum found Rygeil sitting in the solar with a missive open on his lap. He flicked his eyes to it, then focused on his grandfather.

"By your sister's absence, I see that you failed."

"She has a strong will and remains within the boundaries of Erabel."

"And these are barriers you cannot cross? Come now, Calum. You are of the same blood. Did you even try to breach them?"

Calum clenched his jaw. "They have been imbued with a spell to keep me out."

The king shook his head. "That is what the demon was for."

"He escaped, as I'm sure you know."

Rygeil reached for a blackened lump that sat on a small table. The idol was unrecognizable. Not even the sigil carved into its surface was visible. "Aye, when this happened, I knew you'd let him slip through your fingers. It seems I was wrong to trust you with such power."

"That thing should never have been released from its prison. It was only a matter of time before he escaped."

Leaning forward, Rygeil studied him, slipping into his mind like a needle. "You made a connection with her."

"I did."

"And, what did you tell her? I wonder. You keep those thoughts suspiciously hidden."

Calum lifted his chin. "If not for me, she wouldn't have

come so close to joining me and waging war on Darragh's men. She is wielding a dark power, one I haven't felt before."

"Oh?" Rygeil set the parchment aside and rose. "Tell me of this dark power."

Calum described what he'd seen and felt, the way the forest had grown dark as the creatures within it fought back against the invaders, commanded by Fiadh. "And she called upon the Sluagh."

The king's eyes widened, then wrinkled as he chuckled. "Was it you or Crom who put that idea into her innocent mind?"

"It was I. Though, I wonder if the demon fed on the magic she used. It was… unnatural. I felt nothing of the Great Mother in her mind as she attacked the soldiers."

Rygeil flapped his hand. "Danu doesn't understand the ways of war. She would have us live side-by-side with the children of men. Mate with them."

Disgust filled Calum's face.

"I see the thought repels you, as it should." He wandered to a window. "The loss of Crom Cruach is great. Without his power, we lose our greatest advantage. Their numbers have grown. Already, our army was defeated outside Kelholde. But," he said, turning around to face his grandson, "if what you say is true. If your sister has somehow harnessed dark magic, she is even more valuable to us. I must have her."

"And you will, my king."

Picking up the missive he'd set down, he looked at Calum. "Do you know what this is?"

He shook his head.

"It is a letter from Lord Darragh to King Stephen, intercepted by our warriors. In it, he congratulates the king on his victory in the borderlands outside Taigon and requests reinforcements to root out the last of the elves in Dorcha Wood. They think us beaten." Walking to the fire in the hearth, Rygeil tossed the paper into it, watching the parchment fold in on itself and blacken along the edges before catching fire. "There will be no more communications between the lord of the western reaches and Taigon. I will recall what is left of my army. Let King Stephan think we have been cowed and retreated." He lifted a jewel-encrusted goblet and took a long pull of wine, gently wiping the corner of his mouth when he finished. "We will march on Erabel—our entire force—and this time I will lead it. I wish to see this new power of hers."

Calum's face twisted in an ugly smile.

Rygeil grabbed a quill and parchment, scratching out a message before rolling it and sealing the paper with a daub of wax. Glancing at Calum, Rygeil walked toward the door and paused as he opened it. "You will turn your sister or I will kill her. Either way, her power will be mine."

Shutting the door, the king strode to the parapets and called to his owl. The bird shrieked and came on silent wings. He stroked its feathers, eliciting a happy clack. "Take this to Khaeris." Snatching the parchment, the bird spread its wings and took to the skies, banking south toward Rygeil's army. It would take a few days for them to return, longer if they came upon men who would likely have scouts posted along every route to the Felraine Vale. He took a deep breath, filling his lungs and letting it out slowly, feeling magic race through his body. Patience was a learned skill, one he had been forced to hone over many years. Fiadh's time would come. She would surrender to him, and he would consume her power, carving a path through the realms of men so deep they would be cowed for all time.

CHAPTER THIRTY

In the western reaches, Gideon strode through the inner bailey of Felmore Castle. Shoving open the doors to the great hall, he searched for Darragh, finding only Donal, who was deep in conversation with three men.

"Where is your lord?" Gideon asked.

Donal glared at him, then turned his back to finish his conversation.

"I said, where is your lord?"

Turning slowly on his heel, Donal faced him. "He is occupied. And may I remind you that you are here at his whim? An invitation that can be rescinded."

"I care nothing of his whims," he said caustically.

Donal sneered. "Have a care for your neck then, young lord, lest you find it wearing a necklace of rope."

Gideon's teeth flashed between the thin slash of his smile. "I have greater things to worry about than a noose. You would do well to think on that."

Arching a brow, Donal batted his hand at Gideon as

though he were a pesky fly and fetched his lord. Gideon paced, too wound up to sit, and waited for what felt too long for Darragh to make his entrance. It surprised him to see the lord come from the dungeons, and he wondered absently if he had captured the mage once again.

Gideon strode to him and gave a curt bow. "My lord, I lost many men. All but six of those under my command." He clenched his hands, thinking of the young soldiers who never made it out of Dorcha Wood. Too young. They should never have been there.

Adjusting his tunic, Darragh looked bored and sat back in his chair, gesturing for him to continue.

"We both know the storm that rolled through Felmore was no natural event." Gideon shifted his weight and darted a glance at the stained-glass window that bore a new hole where a shard of ice had pierced it. "She has grown stronger and used that strength to bring about the wind and rain and… other things."

"Other things?" Darragh smirked. "Is that why you failed me? You had one task, young lord. Draw her out and, yet, where is she?"

Gideon stiffened.

"I had not thought she'd pose such a problem." He scowled and drummed his fingers.

"Perhaps, attacking Dorcha Wood is not the best course of action."

"You think not?"

"She only fights back when we enter the forest. We cannot afford to lose more of our men. They will abandon you if they see these attacks as losing battles. Already, there is talk of returning to their homes."

"Who threatens to leave?" Darragh's eyes narrowed.

"It matters little who said it. The fact that it's been said is enough."

"I ask for men, and these country lords send me boys."

Gideon's face hardened. "Those *boys* bled and died for you."

"I meant no offense, young Lord of Belfirth. I weep for those men, but this is war. And soldiers die in war." He picked up a mug of ale and drank it down, eyes never leaving Gideon as his throat worked. Resting it on the arms of the chair, he said, "Our soldiers will not be the ones dying in the battle to come."

"My lord?"

"King Stephen has sent a legion of his army to aid us." Darragh watched Gideon's face as the news sank in. He'd sent three runners to request the king's aid after the envoys had departed. Two had returned with word from Taigon. When they arrived, he'd do as Haegna had instructed and command King Stephen's legion to hide beyond the hills outside of that accursed forest until the time was ripe to attack. And as the king's army overran the elves, he'd watch safely from beyond the forest—his troops hidden from sight by Haegna's spells—and claim victory when they'd done their work. Aye, let the king's men bleed and die in Dorcha Wood. And if the elves slaughtered them? At least his men would be spared while King Stephen's bled. "They will arrive within a fortnight, and when they do, we'll see how strong that elven witch really is."

Gideon left the hall in search of Quinn. He found the young soldier with Brody in a healer's tent. His face was pale and haunted as he looked up at Gideon.

Waving his hand when Quinn began to rise, Gideon said, "Sit down. I came to see how Brody is faring."

Quinn looked at his friend. "He hasn't opened his eyes."

There was a thick bandage around the soldier's head, but it was the one covering the wound in his gut that drew Gideon's attention. He could smell the rot. It wouldn't be long before Brody succumbed. He only hoped his soldier never wakened to feel the pain of dying.

He rested a hand on Quinn's shoulder. "Have the healers seen him?"

"Aye. They've done what they could." Pain flashed across his face. "He's going to die, isn't he?"

"He is. I'm sorry, Quinn." Dropping his hand, he recalled his first battle—the screams of the wounded and dying. They were things he'd never be free of. The lucky ones were those who lost their lives before they knew what felled them. Looking down at Brody, he knew naught could be done.

It's my fault, Gideon thought. *I should have refused to let them enter the woods.*

The opening to the tent flapped in the breeze, drawing his eye to the shrouded bodies outside of it. More of his young soldiers lay there, cold and still on the dirt. Why was he doing this? What was he fighting for? Did he even know anymore?

If what Darragh said was true, King Stephen's army would arrive and attack Fiadh and her people. She would fight back, as she already had. And when she did, how many men would she and the elves kill? Hundreds? Thousands? For what? Who would win? Darragh? He'd be named ruler of the western reaches, perhaps. And King Stephen would be able to claim a victory against a race his ancestors had all but wiped out. *But, what of me?* Gideon asked himself. *What do I get out of waging war on the Aos Sí? Revenge? Revenge won't bring them back.*

Quinn's quiet gasp had him turning back and kneeling at Brody's bedside. The young soldier's face was yellow as he labored for breath. Gideon heard the death rattle and put his hand on Quinn's shoulder, feeling the shudder of his body as he tried not to sob. In moments, it was over.

"I didn't think it would be like this," Quinn whispered.

Gideon rose and looked into his face, seeing shattered innocence. "None of us did."

CHAPTER THIRTY-ONE

A púca, in the form of a deer, burst into the hall just after dawn eleven days later. "Rygeil is at the border of Dorcha Wood!"

Veren glanced at Fiadh, his hand griping the spoonful of porridge halfway to his mouth. Jaw clenching, he dropped the spoon and rose. "Send out a warning."

With a jerk of its head, the púca left, bounding through the courtyard in huge leaps. Fiadh watched him go, then looked up at Veren, who stood bellowing orders to those who were now entering the hall.

Sister, Calum's voice called to her. *We have come. Join us or be annihilated.*

Don't do this, Calum.

You force my hand.

Leave him! She screamed at him. *He's using you. It's not too late.*

But it is for you if you continue to hide behind your barriers.

She wanted to weep for her brother, but clenched her

fists, blocking him out, and looked at Veren. "Do you remember what I asked you?" she said quietly.

His eyes swung to hers, going wide. "I remember, but do not ask that of me."

"You're the only one I trust to see it done."

"Even if I agreed, which I do not, Krulan would not allow it."

"Then you must keep it secret from him."

Veren's face crumpled for a moment. "I will not let it come to that." Striding to Kaelari, who had just entered, he gave Fiadh a look and began barking orders, putting Fiadh's morbid request far from his mind.

Krulan eyed her. *What did you say to Veren?*

Only that we must defend Erabel to the last.

He looked at her suspiciously, but let it go. Moving to her side, they left the hall amidst the chaos of readying for attack and went to the barrier that protected Erabel. Dasha swooped between the trees overhead while Meara trotted to her, bumping her shoulder with her muzzle.

Fiadh stroked her velvety nose. "We ride into the storm today."

The unicorn bobbed her head.

Tugging at her ears to pull her down, Fiadh pressed her forehead to Meara's, just below her massive horn. Giving her sips of power, she readied Meara the best she could, knowing it may not be enough in the face of battle. With a pat on the neck, Fiadh looked around and found Dasha.

Show me Rygeil's army but be wary. Calum may sense you, she told him, and he took off, wings beating against the lightening sky.

Closing her eyes, she reached for the raven, becoming one with him as he flew above the tops of the trees. She could feel the lift of the wind beneath his wings as he banked right, eyes scanning the forest's edge, finding thousands of Aos Sí amassed to the north in the same area Calum had set up his encampment. He flew low, trees a blur beneath his body. She looked through his eyes at the sea of warriors preparing for an invasion, feeling his body shift on the wind as he looped around to fly past the gathering again.

Suddenly, Fiadh let out a gasp as Dasha's head turned sharply, his eyes tracking an arrow that came hurtling toward him. He tilted his wings and flapped harder, aiming for the clouds overhead, and shifted his eye to watch the arrow pass by harmlessly, never seeing the other that pierced his body and sent him plummeting from the sky.

Fiadh screamed, the sound ripping through Erabel like a shockwave. Every Aos Sí froze, then Veren ran, Kaelari at his heels, passing him as she leaped over obstacles.

"Fiadh!" Veren yelled, feet pounding on the earth. "Fiadh!"

"She's here!" Kaelari shouted, and Veren followed her voice, finding the two kneeling on the ground, Fiadh keening.

"Dasha! Dasha!" she screamed.

Kaelari looked at Veren, and he paled.

"Fiadh, I'm so sorry." He reached for her, and she shook him off, curling into herself. Veren stood helplessly as grief tore from her chest.

Fiadh threw her head back and roared in anguish. The

sky turned into a black roiling mass, lightning shot through the clouds in jagged bolts as deafening cracks of thunder shook the forest. Arching her back, Fiadh stretched her neck and turned her face to the storm. Anger burned, erupted, morphing into rage. And her rage *sang*. The stolen power of the Merrow flowed through her in a violent river, smothering the gifts of Danu completely. It blossomed—a molten flower—within her core, dark and distorted.

I feel your rage, sister, Calum crooned. *You have so much power. Just think what you and I could do with it.*

Fiadh's body twitched, violence simmering under her skin. *You mistake me. I will never join you, brother.*

"Ready our people," she said coldly, getting to her feet. "Drive Rygeil's forces away from Erabel and out of Dorcha Wood." Her eyes glowed as she looked at every face. "But you will not kill."

Raising her arms, she called to Troya, watching with grim pleasure as the Sluagh streaked across the sky before circling like a funnel cloud and landing a few paces away.

Kaelari and Veren took a step back, their distrust of the monstrous creatures so ingrained they could do nothing else.

"Rygeil and his army are just within Dorcha Wood," Fiadh said.

Flashes of light from the storm lit Troya's skull-like face as she stared at her. "What will you have us do? Spill their blood?"

"You and your sisters aren't here to slaughter elves."

"Pity."

Fiadh pinned her with a hard stare. "Let them see your

power. They are afraid of you. Use their fear to drive them out."

"Do naught but menace your people?" Troya asked.

Fiadh jerked a nod.

Troya grinned, flashing the sharp points of her teeth. "Very well." With that, she loosed a horrendous wailing, echoed by her sisters who joined her as they beat their leathery wings, bending the branches of trees with their passing.

Turning to Kaelari and Veren, Fiadh said, "Reinforce the barriers. They must hold should his army come through Dorcha Wood."

"Where are you going?" Veren asked.

"To stop him from reaching our border."

Kaelari stepped forward and grasped her wrist. "Fiadh, you cannot stop him."

"You have no idea what I can do."

She shook her head. "He is too powerful."

Fiadh looked down at her arm, then into Kaelari's face. "Let me go."

Whatever she saw and felt snaking through her mind, made her release her hold and back away.

"Fiadh," Veren pleaded, his heart in his eyes. "Don't do this!"

"I am the only one who can." She strode forward and hooked her arms around him, pulling him down to her mouth. Their tongues twined, his desperate, as he tasted goodbye on her lips. "Keep the barriers strong," she said. "I'll come back."

His hands balled into fists, but he let her go, his will

bending and breaking beneath the awesome power she wielded. He knew at that moment that if he fought her, tried to prevent her from leaving, she'd lash out at him. Darkness dimmed the vibrant green of her eyes, turning them a dull red. He sent a look to Krulan, who flashed the wicked point of a fang.

Fiadh leaped onto Meara's back, and they sailed through Erabel, bursting through the barrier and into Dorcha Wood, coming to a halt in the disturbingly quiet forest. Above her, banks of turbulent clouds blocked the light, turning day to night, blanketing the wood in gloom. Krulan circled, low growls rumbling in his chest. She hopped off Meara and walked a few paces through the forest, opening herself fully to the power flowing through her veins, feeling it throb in her fingertips. In the distance, she heard the ghostly wails of the Sluagh and followed the sound, cocking her head and closing her eyes to sense it better.

Rygeil's army spread out, remaining at the edge of the woods, not having breached its border. She felt their fear as they caught distant glimpses of the Sluagh. Fiadh bent and pressed her hands to the ground, sending currents of energy through the mantle, reaching for Danu. The Great Mother felt her and responded weakly. Brows creasing, Fiadh delved deeper, confused at the pale tap of awareness from the goddess.

Great Mother, she called out, *we are under attack. Your people need you. Our barriers must hold.*

Daughter, Danu sent back, though it was very faint, *darkness surrounds you. I cannot…* The voice faded to nothing.

Fiadh reached for her again and was met with silence.

Clutching her chest, she looked at the ground, imagining she could see Danu's pale face. The sorrow she was certain would be there. Shouts and the sounds of the Sluagh wreaking havoc brought her head up. She focused on the power that radiated through her body and threw out her hands, channeling it into the trees. Oak and ash groaned and swayed, their branches twining together to form walls as roots contorted beneath the forest floor in freakish undulations. Sensing Rygeil's army readying themselves, Fiadh shifted her body and sent a wave of energy through the earth. It rolled along the ground, thick mist following behind it. Every animal it touched linked with Fiadh's mind until her head swam with hundreds of voices. She took control of them, bending them to her will. No longer was it a shared bond between animal and elf. Fiadh became the master. She commanded the forest to rise up, to become her soldiers, and unleashed Dorcha Wood onto Rygeil's army.

CHAPTER THIRTY-TWO

Fiadh bent low on Meara's back, knees hugging her sides, as they raced through the trees, Krulan and a host of predators—from wolves to wild cats—at their sides. Heavy mist hid their forms as they traveled north, turning just before the edge of Dorcha Wood to hurtle through the trees parallel to Rygeil's army. Shifting to sit upright, Fiadh pumped a fist into the air and let out a battle cry. Birds of every kind burst through the trees, coming at Rygeil's army like rain, dive-bombing, shrieking, talons and beaks finding soft flesh, before sailing into the air.

Shouts cut through the chaos as Aos Sí warriors called on the wind, throwing huge gusts at the birds who kept coming, many falling to the ground, necks and wings broken. And then the Sluagh arrived in force, adding ghastly wails to the melee. Rygeil watched them come. *Not bad, granddaughter, not bad,* he thought. *Your powers will be even more beneficial than I had hoped.* Raising his arms, he hurled balls of hail at the creatures, knocking a few to the ground, where they hissed and spat before taking to the air again. His own pack of Cù-Sìth stood among the Aos Sí army, waiting for their king's command.

Meara wheeled around, bounding over logs and between trees, while Fiadh scanned the pandemonium just beyond the forest, looking for Rygeil. Lightning arced across the sky, bright as the sun, and it was in that moment she saw him, helmet glinting under the bolt of electricity. His face was a cool mask of indifference. Fiadh frowned, eyes narrowing, and reached out to Troya. The Sluagh tapped her mind in response, but refused to go after the king, fearing for the safety of her sisters should he target them. Fiadh muttered and gripped Meara's mane. The unicorn came to a stop, chest heaving, not with fatigue, but with energy. She was ready to charge the field.

Where are you hiding, sister? Calum called to her. *Are you too afraid to leave your woods and face me?*

I wait for you here, Calum. Come and get me.

He snarled. *You'll regret not joining me by the time this is over.*

We shall see. It's not too late, you know. You can still redeem what's left of yourself.

And join the losing side? I think not.

So be it, brother.

She cut off their connection and ran a hand down Meara's neck, soothing the animal as she pranced. "Let them come to us."

Meara snorted and shook her head, tufts of her mane flapping.

Krulan stood, glaring at the Cù-Sìth in Rygeil's army. The massive beasts stood together, their leader a female with a darker pelt than Krulan's. He reached out to her, but she refused to respond, only stared at the trees as though she could see him.

I will not fight my own kind, he told Fiadh.

I would never ask you to. You are not here to kill. We must keep them away from Erabel.

Fiadh looked out at the field and saw Rygeil's soldiers gaining the upper hand, beating back the birds and Sluagh with powerful spells. Fiadh called to the flocks, commanding them to fall back to the forest. Hundreds of predators awaited Rygeil's troops as he shouted for them to advance. Fiadh watched them come, felt the trees bend and twist with awareness, forming barriers to block any who tried to pass. Those who slashed through the tree line were met with claws and fangs. Unprepared, the first to enter the forest were knocked to the ground and dragged away, injured but not killed. The surety of an easy win faltered among the soldiers, but they kept coming.

Suddenly, a voice like thunder filled Fiadh's mind, echoed a hundredfold when it filled the minds of every creature she was connected to.

I do not wish for you to die, all my wild things, my foxes, my robins and ravens and wolves and wildcats, my children of the forest, Rygeil said. Do *not give up your lives for my wayward granddaughter —my misguided heir who would shed your blood for her ambitions. Go back to your burrows and trees and live in peace. This is not your fight but ours, mine and hers. I wish you no harm, only love. Please go now and live in peace.*

Every animal stopped. She reached out to them, but her

link to their minds was lost, broken. Reaching for Danu, she felt nothing.

Did you think you had the power to stop me, young Fiadh? Rygeil asked. *You belong to me. We are blood. Enough of this paltry show of strength. You are nothing compared to me.*

If you are so powerful, why do you hide behind your army? Fiadh challenged, keeping her growing panic from her thoughts as she tried again to reach for the creatures of the wood. *Come and get me yourself.*

Rygeil's warriors advanced. Fiadh sent bolts of lightning at the king to force him to call them back, but he raised his hands, turning them back on her with flicks of his wrists. Electricity crashed and banged, striking all around her as Meara pranced in nervous circles.

Whispering to the unicorn, they spun around, and she hugged her knees to Meara's sides. Bent low, they tore through the forest when alarm washed red across her mind.

Pulling up on Meara's mane, she whispered, "No."

A legion of King Stephan's army spilled over the grassy hills that had concealed them, swarming in numbers far beyond her imagination. They had lain in wait as Rygeil amassed his people and entered the wood. Now, men, drunk on victory over the elves in Kelholde, fanned out in the thousands, engulfing the northern stretch of Dorcha Wood. Fiadh gave Krulan a frightened glance and kicked Meara's sides, hugging her neck as they raced for Erabel. They tore through the trees, twigs snapping loudly under Meara's hooves as they veered away from Rygeil's forces. Fiadh clutched Meara's mane, glancing back often.

Aos Sí war cries rent the air. In their haste to capture

her, they were blind to the armies of men that had begun to press forward into the forest. The mist lifted and the storm ebbed as Fiadh's mind was consumed with urgency and fear. Meara leaped over a fallen log just as Rygeil sent a blast of power through the forest, sending her crashing to the dirt in a cloud of thrashing legs. Fiadh flew through the air, smacking into a jut of rock. Krulan grabbed her tunic, yanking her off the ground, and ran, her body dangling from his mouth.

Behind them, Meara screamed in frustration, finally finding her footing and breaking into a gallop. The world swam before Fiadh's eyes, blood dripping onto her face from a gash on her head. Rygeil felt her weakness and pursued her, searing her mind so that it became a miasma of pain and confusion. She slapped at him weakly, her body coming to painful life as Krulan growled and pushed himself the remainder of the distance.

Her mind went blank the moment they crossed into Erabel, the barriers shielding her from the king's mental assault. Shouts and hands rained down on her as she was hauled into Veren's arms. Meara roared a warning with a strident whinny as she passed into Erabel. Kaelari, with the other elves making a loose circle around her, looked to Veren.

He clutched Fiadh tighter and focused on the unicorn, moments passing as they communicated. "Rygeil's forces have entered Dorcha Wood," he told the group surrounding them.

"I couldn't stop them." Fiadh's voice broke.

Veren's mouth turned down as he glanced at her before

cocking his head as he listened to the thoughts Meara passed to him. "The king has sent an army, and they have flanked Rygeil's fighters."

Krulan growled, back bristling, and whipped his head toward the southern border of Erabel. *Do you feel that?*

Fiadh followed his gaze and took a deep breath, focusing her sight to blend with Krulan's. She gasped when she felt a dark spell waver at the border of Dorcha Wood, giving her glimpse of what it hid. "Darragh's men wait in the south." She paled. "We're trapped."

Kaelari clenched her jaw. "We were never going to stop them army from entering Dorcha Wood, but we can keep them out of Erabel. Mayhap they will destroy each other."

"Whoever wins," Veren said, "they will come for us next."

"We will remain with Fiadh," Kaelari announced. "The rest of you, spread out along our borders. Our barriers must hold!"

They left in pairs, less than thirty against thousands of men and elves. The odds were too great, and they all knew it.

Kaelari watched them go. "We cannot hold them off forever," she said.

"I know," Veren said, easing Fiadh onto the ground.

She looked up at Kaelari as she began to chant, hands sweeping over her body in healing waves. The wound was minor, and her skin sewed itself together under Kaelari's ministrations. Head clearing from the jolt of the fall and Rygeil's mental attack, Fiadh sat up, taking Veren's hand when he offered.

"Rygeil doesn't of Darragh's armies," Fiadh told them.

Veren's brow shot up. "Oh? We could use that to our advantage. Are you strong enough to keep fighting?"

Fiadh gave him a look and jerked her head to Meara. Hopping onto her back, she said, "To the end."

Meara took her along the border of Erabel. As they went, she reached into her core, tapping into Danu's power. It was all but gone. Frowning, Fiadh felt for her darker magic, knowing it would continue to weaken her link with the Great Mother, but desperate to use anything to protect her home and people.

Troya swooped past, and Fiadh reached for her, begging the Sluagh and her sisters to make themselves little more than ghosts in the eyes of the armies of men until the time was right. The Sluagh reluctantly agreed. She then reached for the animals of Dorcha Wood, but felt only a lingering awareness. Rygeil had damaged that connection, and she had no idea how to repair it.

The storm, which had dissipated to banks of gray clouds when Fiadh had fallen from Meara's back, regained its strength. She channeled it at the king's army, pelting them with rain and shards of hail, prodding them away from the forest but they continued to advance.

Her face crumpled when Calum reached out to her again.

Sister! There are too many!

She sobbed, feeling his fear and rage as hordes of men broke through the trees.

Run, Calum!

He heeded her words, leaping into the trees.

She felt Rygeil lash out, roaring in a voice that boomed through the forest, resonating with power. His warriors renewed their battle cries and charged the men. Desperate, Fiadh reached out again to the wild things that cowered in the woods, sagging with relief when she felt the pale response of a weasel. The sounds of steel meeting steel rang out amid a whoosh of arrows. She gasped as one of Rygeil's elves fell to the ground just beyond the weasel's hiding place. Not wanting to watch as one of the king's men advanced with sword raised, she cast a mental net, searching for another open mind until her thoughts snagged, coming to a stuttering halt.

"Dasha," she whispered and leaped onto Meara's back, kicking her into a full gallop.

Veren yelled, his voice mixing with Krulan's angry howl. Fiadh ignored them and placed her hand on Meara, muttering a spell to give her speed, losing them in their pursuit. The forest blurred as they barreled through it. Heedless of the men and elves that blended into the trees, Fiadh pushed Meara, her mind fixed on the fragile link with Dasha.

Madness filled the forest as men and Aos Sí attacked each other. Shouting to the sky, Fiadh called on the Sluagh, listening as they filled the air with their awful song. Men screamed in terror as the wraiths dove at them, trying to drive them away. Within the chaos, she heard laughter as something sinister danced among the fighting, its foul will so thick it hung over the forest like a fog. She blocked it out, all of it, and leaped from Meara's back, running to a cluster of rocks and thorny bushes. Sweeping leaves aside, she dove her hands into the greenery and pulled Dasha out. He croaked weakly as she stared at the arrow embedded in his shoulder. She whispered words of comfort and cradled him to her chest.

Fiadh turned, and Meara let out a scream, thrusting her horn into the heart of a soldier who'd snuck up on them. He fell, mouth working for a few moments, then going slack. The unicorn pranced nervously, the whites of her eyes showing as five more men circled them. One charged Meara, slashing at her leg, aiming to sever a tendon and bring her down. She swung her massive body, slamming into him so hard he flew through the air, striking a tree with a sickening crunch.

The remaining four descended, swords swinging wildly. Fiadh, hampered by Dasha's limp form, lashed out, sending two sprawling into unconscious heaps while Meara slashed her hooves and swung her head. She never felt Calum creep up behind her. Using the hilt of his sword, he cleaved downward onto the back of her head, and all went dark.

CHAPTER THIRTY-THREE

Gideon watched from the cover of a fallen tree as Fiadh was flung across the back of an Aos Sí warrior. He had abandoned Darragh when he saw the lord had no plans to advance his army to aid the king's men, sneaking into the woods where the fighting was thick. He followed the pair from a distance, fending off an attack when he broke through a cluster of bushes. For a few moments, he thought he'd lost them, but racing through the trees, he caught sight of Fiadh's slack form as they headed away from the tree line and deeper into the forest. Shouts and screams grew fainter as he tracked them.

Stopping behind the massive trunk of an oak, Gideon peered around the tree, watching the pair leave the forest and head into a meadow where a dozen elves milled around, conferring. He glanced from face to face, eyes finally resting on one he knew. Gideon glared at Rygeil, mouth pulling down as he saw the elven king's delight when his gaze fell on Fiadh.

She was dropped roughly on the ground and engulfed, arms and legs pinned. Her head flopped to the side, face caked with blood. He watched the shallow rise and fall of her chest as rope was brought, and she was bound and staked. The one who had captured her spoke briefly to Rygeil, swinging around toward the forest with rapid gesticulations. Gideon ducked around the tree, hand gripping his sword, ears trained for the sound of approaching feet. When none came, he crouched low and resumed his watch.

Rygeil stood over her prone form, a grim smile on his face. He barked an order to those around him, sending three off on some errand. In the distance, the fighting continued, but it was impossible to say which side was winning. Though the elven army was outnumbered, they had abilities that gave them an edge, and the forest itself was fighting, wild things of every type attacking both sides. Add the Sluagh and Darragh's self-serving inaction to the mix, and the battle could go either way, as impossible as that seemed.

Gideon's jaw clenched as Rygeil bent over Fiadh and slapped her so hard her face was flung to the side. She coughed, body jerking, and the elven king straddled her, grabbing her face, and digging his thumbs into her cheekbones. He could hear nothing of what was said but saw Fiadh blink and flinch as Rygeil leaned in close, his nose almost touching hers. He must have done something because she bucked and screamed, the sound traveling across the distance with awful clarity.

Something in him snapped. His body shuddered with the force of it, anger swamped his mind, leaving as quickly as it came, and replaced with anguish. She continued to scream, under some mental assault she could not escape, and with each cry, Gideon's resolve fractured until there was nothing left but desperation.

Heaving himself from the tree, he grabbed his sword, ready to fight his way to her, but knowing he'd be struck down before he even got close. He turned his back on the tortured sounds coming from the meadow and ran. It was a death sentence, his mind hammered into him over and over as he careened through the forest. How he found the border of Erabel, he couldn't say. It was as if he was guided by an unseen hand. He slammed into the barrier, body flung backward as its power repelled him. Reaching out a hand, he felt blindly, hissing when a painful current burned his palm.

Realizing he'd reached Fiadh's stronghold, he closed his eyes and prayed. *Great Mother… I… I know that I am far from your sight. But your daughter needs you. Fiadh needs you. Please help me find her people.*

A gentle breeze, at odds with the chaos enveloping the forest, passed over his face, and he could've sworn he heard a woman's voice. *My son.*

His fingers curled as he reached toward what he couldn't see. He flexed them and pressed his hand forward, feeling the moment the barrier gave way. Stumbling forward, he fell to his knees in Erabel.

It didn't take long for the Cù-Sìth to find him.

It came through the trees. A monster. Hate spilled from his yellow eyes, and foam dripped from his snarling mouth. Gideon fell to his knees before it and hung his head, dropping his sword to the ground. He could feel the beast's hot breath on the back of his neck and knew it would be over quickly. A quick jerk. A tear. And it would be finished. Vicious snarling radiated down his spine as he fought against his body's drive to run or fight.

"Fiadh," he said, voice shaking.

The snap of teeth next to his ear had him falling to the side. He rolled onto his back and yelped in pain as the massive creature slammed a paw onto his chest. Its muzzle, hovering above his face, curled, revealing fangs that dripped saliva onto his cheeks. The Cù-Sìth increased his weight, pressing down until Gideon felt as though his ribs would break.

With a wheeze, he said, "Fiadh… they took her."

Teeth gnashed, their whiteness stark against the dark fur of its muzzle.

"Fiadh… he's killing her."

The weight of the Cù-Sìth suddenly lifted. He tilted his head back and howled, the sound returned by others of his kind. Gideon remained on the ground, gasping, as the sound of many feet grew louder. In moments, he was surrounded.

A striking male elf strode toward him, the deadly tip of an arrow aimed at Gideon's head. "Speak now or take your words to your grave."

Gideon eyed him coldly, the spirits of his family telling him to fight, to kill this enemy. He shut them away and focused. "Fiadh was captured. Rygeil has her now and he's… doing something to her. She was screaming!"

Another Aos Sí stepped into view, pinning him with piercing blue eyes as the tip of her sword pressed against his throat. "Where?"

"In the meadow, just beyond the edge of the wood." He

jerked his head, feeling the prick of the blade and the warmth of blood drip down his neck.

"Veren," she said, sheathing her sword. "Lower your bow."

Veren took a step back but kept Gideon in his steely gaze. "Lead us."

The Cù-Sìth growled threateningly, the sound echoed by the others who stood in a loose circle. Gideon stopped moving and held up his hands in surrender.

"Krulan," Veren said. "We need him."

Krulan's lip curled, but he backed off.

"Fiadh charged into the wood, and we lost her," Veren said.

Gideon looked at him. "She's a fool."

"Aye."

"And the world cares for fools." Gideon began walking, at war with himself, as he felt the eyes of Aos Sí on his back. He should be fighting them to his last breath, seeking vengeance. But they were fighting Rygeil, which made this a confusing mess. In the end, Gideon had to let go of his hate and embrace what he knew was right. Fiadh was innocent. He had wronged her, and if he meant to have the chance to beg forgiveness, he had to save her first.

CHAPTER THIRTY-FOUR

Rygeil tore into Fiadh's mind as she lay helpless beneath him. His eyes, cold and hard, bore into her, flaying her open with terrible power. She fought, throwing up mental barriers, but they were feeble, her mind having been drained, her connection with Danu weakened. He pressed his fingers into her skull, driving his will like daggers. She screamed through clenched teeth, trying to reach out to Krulan, but unable to find him.

There was nothing but pain.

Rygeil let go and straddled her chest, panting. She turned her head and found Calum. "Calum," she whispered, "please don't let him do this. Help me."

He stared at her, torn. "You should have listened to me!" Then he turned his back on her.

She sobbed, her body spasming as Rygeil held his hands above her face and began chanting. The spell wove through the air like a web, falling lightly over her and then tightening. Fiadh struggled, eyes going wide as it began to smother her. She could feel her power—her life-force—slipping away, caught in the net Rygeil was spinning.

Dorcha Wood grew quiet, and the wind died down, the storm dissipating to little more than weak gusts and misty rain.

"Calum," she screamed, wrenching herself from the weight of Rygeil's magic. "Help me!"

"I can't, sister," he whispered.

Tears spilled from Fiadh's eyes. Somewhere out there, her people were fighting and dying. She tried to reach out to them but there was almost nothing left, only a shadow of what she'd wielded. The ghostly shape of a Sluagh flew across the sky, and she called to it, but her words drifted uselessly in the air. The light was fading, the world going dark. She let go then, unable to hold on.

"You're killing her," Calum told Rygeil.

"Her death will not be in vain. With her power, the armies of men will crumble once and for all."

Calum looked down at her in agony. "But, she's my sister. Your blood. Take her power, but let her live."

"She had her chance!" He glared at Calum, knocking him to the ground with a spell, before turning back to Fiadh, who lay helpless and unresponsive. "I will have every ounce of her lifeblood, every bit of her power."

Her brother lay on his side, looking from Rygeil to Fiadh, watching her grow pale. Flicking his eyes to the king, he slipped a magic-imbued blade from his boot and sprang, stabbing it into Rygeil's side. The king snarled and lashed out. Magic slashed through Calum's body followed by a sudden burst of shouts and snarls. Krulan roared as Calum fell, charging into the meadow with pack mates and elves at his sides.

From outside herself, Fiadh felt Rygeil's weight lifted abruptly, but she lay unmoving, unable to open her heavy lids. Yells and snapping teeth were all around her, but she couldn't rouse herself to escape them. The feel of coarse hands on her face broke through her listlessness, and she turned toward them.

"Fiadh, come back to me."

She felt tugging and heard the sawing of a blade on the rope that bound her. When it was cut, her arms twitched, but were too heavy to lift.

"Fiadh," the voice said.

Whose voice was that? It was so achingly familiar.

"Fiadh, you need to wake up." Hands gripped and shook her, causing her head to loll. "Fiadh!"

Her eyes fluttered, the world coming into focus by slow, painful degrees. The first things she heard were shouts, and she tried to turn toward them, but her face was caught and held. Fiadh looked into Gideon's eyes and flinched.

"It's alright," he said. "I'm not going to hurt you, but I need to get you out of here."

He tucked an arm beneath her back and lifted her. She whimpered, her body a mass of pain. Jostling her gently in his arms to get a better grip, he turned and took a step toward the forest.

A tearing sensation ripped through Fiadh's heart as she

saw her twin lying on the ground gasping for breath. "Stop," she begged, thrashing her way out of Gideon's arms.

He set her down, and she crawled to Calum.

"Sister," he whispered, chest rattling from the wound Rygeil had inflicted. His mouth gaped open. "Sister, I'm sorry. Forgive me."

She cupped his face. "There is nothing to forgive. Stay with me, Calum." Holding her hand over his wound, she spoke words of healing but they were weak, tied to a connection with Danu that she had turned her back on.

"Fiadh," he called out. "Fiadh, I'm sorry." His body went slack.

Krulan howled as a hoarse sob ripped from her chest. She grabbed at her tunic, trying to hold herself together. It felt like she was being rendered in two. One half of herself, stranger though he had become, splintered. Her body swung drunkenly to the side. She clutched Gideon as he kneeled next to her before looking up to find Rygeil staring down at her with murder in his face.

Run! Krulan commanded, fending off the advances of one of Rygeil's guards.

I can't.

Her grandfather barely glanced at Calum's fallen body before carving his way through two of Fiadh's warriors with a swipe of his blade and a muttered spell. His body wobbled, weakened, as they fell to the ground. Veren roared from nearby and charged. The king's eyes swung to him, and he lifted his left hand, red with blood from the gash in his side, sending a gale of wind at the elf. The force of the gust pushed Veren back but wasn't powerful enough to knock him down as the elf's feet dug into the soil.

Gideon rose and stood next to Veren. They glanced at each other, then drew swords and rent the air with battle cries. Rygeil fought them off, but they kept coming. The sound of metal rang through the meadow alongside yelps and grunts, as others engaged with the last of the king's guard, trying to drive them off while the Cù-Sìth pinned others to the ground, saliva spraying from snapping teeth.

Krulan faced off with a female of his kind, Rygeil's protector from Oadsera. Nearly as massive as him, she growled and paced, finally backing off at some communication from Krulan and disappearing into the woods. He ran to Fiadh then, lending his back as she struggled to get to her feet.

Are you hurt? he asked.

Only my heart, she told him, thinking of Calum.

Anchoring herself on the trampled ground, she reached again for Danu, but the Great Mother was little more than a vestige of what she had been. Rygeil caught her eye and sneered, whispering a Word that violently shook the earth beneath their feet, knocking both Veren and Gideon to the ground. They sprang up, but he stabbed his cruel will into their minds. Their eyes went wide, bodies rigid, hair whipping about their faces as a small maelstrom of wind wrenched their swords from their hands.

Rygeil held Fiadh's gaze, swinging his sword at Gideon as the man unlocked his muscles and bent to retrieve his weapon. She screamed a warning and watched in horror as Gideon spun around to see what was wrong. She saw him fall, body bouncing against the flattened grasses, pinned beneath Veren's, who'd crashed onto his a moment later.

Krulan's pack circled Rygeil.

"You can't kill me, Krulan. You know the law. I am of Erabel, just as Fiadh is."

He growled and snapped his teeth, every movement mirrored by the other Cù-Sìth. Lunging, Krulan tore a piece of Rygeil's tunic, revealing the seeping wound in his side.

The king's face contorted in an ugly grimace as he pressed his hand to the gash and spun on his heel, running into Dorcha Wood with spells to lend him speed and repel those who tried to follow. He slipped into the trees, calling on the healing magic of the forest to replenish what it could. But the wound was deep and rank with a deadly spell from Calum's blade.

Fiadh watched until Rygeil disappeared from sight, then staggered to Gideon and Veren. From his prone position, Gideon blinked at her, his chest compressed so he could do little more than wheeze.

"Veren!" she cried and tugged his shoulder, struggling to roll him off Gideon and onto his back. Kaelari was there, and the two peeled him away, gasping when their efforts revealed a deep slash across his chest. She looked at Kaelari, stricken.

"Veren," Fiadh said softly, smiling as his eyes fluttered open.

Drawing on the remains of her power, she began to chant, holding her hands above the wound. Kaelari joined her, their voices blending, becoming one. As the spell ended,

Fiadh looked down at him and found his eyes on her. He mouthed words he was too weak to utter.

"Shh. Save your strength," Fiadh whispered. He nodded slowly. She pressed a kiss to his forehead and laid her hand on his chest, feeling his heart beat slowly beneath her palm.

Until it didn't.

CHAPTER THIRTY-FIVE

Kaelari prowled the meadow while Fiadh sat on her heels, hand still pressed to Veren's cooling chest. She heard Gideon moving nearby but couldn't look away from the elf's fixed gaze. *He's still beautiful,* she thought, as memories of the sweetness of his embrace filled her mind. He had healed a piece of her wounded heart, and now he was gone.

How could he be gone?

Fiadh looked around, lost. Calum lay nearby, another casualty of the madness. His loss was a tangled web of emotions. How had the world come to this? Men and elves at war. For what? Power? Land? Blind hate? How many had to die before it ended?

Her eyes snagged on one of Rygeil's soldiers who kneeled at the feet of Vyami, Krulan's second. Fiadh stared at her, slowly rising. Krulan was at her side in a flash, a hulking beast filled with violence, as she walked toward the

Aos Sí fighter. He gave a short bark, sending his pack mate off, and slowly circled the female as she sat looking up at Fiadh. He growled and snapped.

Kaelari came to Fiadh's side. "She surrendered."

Fiadh raised a brow and crouched in front of the prisoner. "Why did you surrender?"

"Because I refuse to fight for a king who puts his lust for power above his people." It sounded rehearsed, but Fiadh said nothing as she continued, "Rygeil has wronged many in his quest to conquer, yourself included. I am done with him."

"What's your name?" Fiadh asked.

She lifted her chin. "Riani." Her eyes flicked to Veren's body, and Fiadh saw grief in their depths. "I loved him once. He… he was the best of us and refused to pay homage to a king who abused his throne. I… I should have gone with him but I lacked the strength."

A single tear slipped down Riani's cheek. Fiadh marked it, but hardened herself, fearing that if she let herself feel anything, she'd feel all of it and, like a giant boulder, it would crush her. "I give you leave to come to Erabel, but I don't trust you. That's something you will have to earn."

Riani nodded, eyeing Krulan as he growled at her. "Rygeil will not stop, even with his army dwindled, he'll command his warriors until there's no one left," she warned. "He broke the laws of Danu and sought an alliance with Crom Cruach."

Kaelari's face was a mask of horror. "Say it is not so."

"He freed the old god in the hope that he could wield

him like a weapon against the armies of men." Riani shot a glance at Fiadh. "And you. I have seen that creature's foul work and want no part of it."

"He escaped?" Kaelari asked.

"Aye, when Calum first came," Riani said. "He was released into Dorcha Wood and could not be called back. I have not seen him since."

Kaelari met Fiadh's worried stare. "Could this be the one you spoke of?"

She nodded. "I still feel him. He is darkness itself."

"He's evil," Riani told them. "And powerful, far stronger than any Aos Sí."

"Why would he wait to escape? Why did he not leave the moment he was freed?"

"Rygeil gave Calum something to control him, but, somehow, the demon severed that power," Riani explained. "If you sense that foul being, then he has not left those woods."

"Perhaps, he means to align himself with Lord Darragh," Gideon said, drawing everyone's eye. He jerked his head toward Dorcha Wood and added, "The soldiers you see swarming the forest are the king's men, sent to aid Darragh in his quest to crush your people. But he hasn't sent his troops. He waits and watches with his army."

Fiadh studied him and saw his eyes flash to hers before he met everyone's hard stare.

"Why would the demon want an alliance with mankind?" Kaelari asked.

Gideon looked down and dug his feet into the ground,

gouging a furrow in the grass. "There is evil in Felmore Castle. Some say it is a witch." He shrugged. "I saw… someone… not long ago," he said, remembering when Aishling was almost taken. "I cannot say what she is, but there is a fell presence in the keep."

Kaelari muttered and stalked away, coming back in a fury. "If Crom Cruach is truly free, the Great Mother help us all! That demon was consigned to an impenetrable iron prison. He was to be held there for all time lest his evil spread through the world again. If he is truly free, it will take power far greater than ours to capture or kill him."

A pall of silence followed her pronouncement. Fiadh felt Gideon glance at her, but refused to meet his eyes. Her emotions were too raw, her heart too broken. She couldn't face him. Not yet.

The rumble of battle drew closer as they stood in the clearing. Fiadh turned her head and studied the tree line, seeing wisps of smoke curling in the air. "They're burning the wood," she whispered. "Will this never end?" All eyes followed her line of vision.

"We must return to Erabel!" Kaelari shouted, motioning for elves to lift Veren's body onto Krulan's back while his pack mates took the bodies of the others who'd been slain. Gideon helped, feeling hostility in every look, but refusing to shrink from it.

Their pace was slow as they crossed into Dorcha Wood. Smoke hung in the air, growing thicker the deeper they traveled. Krulan growled a warning as the rustle of a body drew their attention. Gideon drew his sword as elves notched arrows and gripped blades. Vaymir lunged into a thicket and dragged a screaming soldier out, tossing him at Krulan's feet. Kaelari lunged.

"Stop!" Gideon and Fiadh yelled at the same time.

Tossing his sword, Gideon dropped to the ground shielding the young soldier. "He's one of mine."

"Kaelari, back away," Fiadh said, putting her hand on the elf's shoulder.

She gave Fiadh a look, then bowed her head and stepped back.

"Quinn, what are you doing here?" Gideon asked.

He looked from Gideon to the Cù-Sìth to the elves, eyes wild, chest heaving.

"Quinn, it's all right. They won't hurt you."

Fiadh crouched next to Gideon. "Be calm. You won't be harmed."

Quinn looked at her face and nodded, sitting up slowly, before turning to Gideon. "I saw you leave and went to find you."

"Foolish boy! You could've been killed." Gideon rose and held out a hand, hauling Quinn to his feet. "Are you hurt?"

He shook his head and licked his lips, eyes darting to the hostile stares surrounding them. "I wanted to fight with you. To have your back."

"You are a hindrance until you've mastered your skills. I left you to keep you safe."

We must go, Krulan told Fiadh.

She nodded. *In a moment.*

Krulan growled, drawing the soldier's attention. "Aren't they the enemy?" he whispered, edging closer to Gideon.

"Not anymore. I was wrong, Quinn. I was blinded by hate and… I was wrong." Picking up the sword Quinn had dropped, he handed it to him and said, "You must return to Felmore. This is no place for you."

"Darragh refuses to let our army march," Quinn said, voice wavering as elves crowded closer. "I overheard him tell Donal that we'll wait until the king's men are spent. I went to find you and let you know what I'd heard, but I saw you slip into the forest and tried to follow."

"He plays a dangerous game. But if he will not advance his army, then you are safer there."

"You're not coming back?" Quinn asked.

"Not yet," he grasped Quinn's shoulders. "I need you to return to Felmore. Be my eyes and ears. If you hear that Darragh searches for me, tell him you haven't seen me since the start of the battle. Perhaps, he'll think I joined the king's army and am dead."

"What should I tell the others? They'll wonder where you are."

Gideon frowned. "Feel them out. See if any would leave Darragh and join me."

Quinn's chest puffed. "They would all join you."

He gave the soldier a small smile. "Thank you, Quinn. But let's be sure of that."

"Vaymir," Fiadh said. "Will you escort Quinn back to Felmore to ensure his safety?"

The soldier's eyes went round, and he backed away from the Cù-Sìth as it approached with a menacing snarl. Krulan barked, and Vaymir's ears flattened.

He will do as you ask, Krulan told her.

Thank you. I know it's hard, but this is the path to peace.

"Go with him," Gideon said. "He won't hurt you, and he'll keep you safe."

Fiadh watched the Cù-Sìth escort Quinn from their group. The youth looked back often, fear evident in every pleading stare, but Gideon held his ground, folding his arms and refusing to call the soldier back. Soon, the pair disappeared among the trees.

"Thank you for keeping him safe," Gideon said quietly.

"It has to start somewhere."

They resumed their trek to Erabel, stopping again when Meara trotted toward them, nickering loudly while Fiadh frantically ran her hands over her body in search of wounds. Finding none, she hopped onto her back and led the party through the forest, skirting the heat of battle by traveling far to the south and curving back.

Gideon paused at the barrier then passed through. Gasps filled the air, and Fiadh's mouth parted in surprise. No human had ever set foot in Erabel. Fiadh scanned the faces of the elves, marking the shock, distrust, and anger she saw there.

He proved himself to the Great Mother, Krulan said as he took in Fiadh's expression. *He risked his life to find me when you were taken.*

She met his yellow stare.

There was begrudging respect when he added, *It was he who led us to you.*

What are you saying?

I don't know. Hate burns in my heart. Vengeance for the death of my mate, but if I slay him… it would be a murder.

Fiadh's eyes softened, knowing what it cost Krulan to say such things. She found Gideon watching her, drawn to her like a magnet. Breathing deeply, she accepted what her eyes told her. He had proved himself, and Erabel had opened to him. Gideon had passed into Fiadh's realm as though the Great Mother welcomed him as one of her own. Perhaps, she ought to see him as Danu did.

Aos Sí greeted the party as they traveled further into Erabel, panic on every face. Heiren, one of two Kaelari had chosen to organize their forces when they left to find Fiadh, met them a short distance from the keep.

He eyed Gideon with distaste, then shifted his attention to Kaelari. "Rygeil's forces began attacking the barrier along the north, more than a dozen broke through, before the king's men came upon them."

Fiadh blanched. "Did we lose any of our people when they came through?"

"Two."

She grimaced.

"Rygeil's forces have pulled back, but the king's soldiers brought their weapons of war through the forest and are heading this way."

Fiadh blanched, and she looked at Gideon.

His mouth turned down. "Can your barriers withstand a siege?"

"I don't know. Kaelari?"

"I fear even your power may not be enough to rebuild

what is already crumbling," Kaelari said. "It may be time to flee."

She shook her head and gritted her teeth. "I will not abandon Erabel."

"That is a fool's declaration," Kaelari snarled.

"Then I am a fool." Fiadh kicked Meara's flanks and made for the weakest sections of Erabel's defenses.

CHAPTER THIRTY-SIX

Fiadh stood at the nearly indistinguishable barrier that separated her from the madness consuming Dorcha Wood. Smoke permeated the air, passing through that thin protection, just as flames surely would if she failed to imbue it with the energy needed to sustain it. Meara wandered nearby, gorging on fruit and leaves, while Krulan sat at her side, staring into the woods beyond.

Someone comes, he warned, back bristling.

Fiadh's fingers curled and she followed his gaze, seeing nothing at first, then spying a shape bounding through the trees. At first sight, it was a fox, but as it came closer, she saw that was a mask. The púca darted through the trees, racing for Erabel, passing through the barrier and coming to a skidding stop.

In his mouth hung Dasha, one wing flapping weakly. Fiadh let out a cry and dove for him, gently pulling him from the púca's jaws. He croaked plaintively as a pain-filled eye fell on her. Torn between the need to replenish the barrier's strength and wanting to use that energy to heal him, she cast about frantically, surprise lighting her face when Gideon jogged into view. He slowed when he saw what she held.

"Is it dead?"

She shook her head.

Gideon came toward her cautiously, eyes flicking to Krulan, who stood at her side. "I can take it and find one of your people to tend its injury."

"Mistress," the púca said, pausing when Gideon gasped in shock at the sight of a talking fox. "Rygeil's army is being overrun, and the king's men will be here soon. They have weapons I've never seen with them."

Fiadh looked pained as she glanced at the barrier, then back at Dasha. "Take him." She carefully placed Dasha into Gideon's arms. "Find Kaelari. She'll know what to do."

He nodded, cradling the raven, and swiftly walked away.

"You put great trust in him to allow him here," the púca said as Gideon disappeared around a bend.

"I had no choice."

"There is always a choice. In this, I sense you have made the right one." With that, he sprang away, heading back into Dorcha Wood, where he would no doubt scour the forest for more wounded he could carry to safety.

Fiadh observed his passing until she could no longer see him, then raised her arms again—shutting away her worry for Dasha, grief over Veren and Calum, and mixed emotions for Gideon—and poured herself into fortifying the barrier. At the moment of contact, she felt how brittle it had become, leeched of Danu's power. It would not take much to bring it down. Focusing, she gave the last reserves of her strength, then sagged to the ground, head hanging in defeat.

Kaelari found her that way, saying nothing as she sat at her side and looked into Dorcha Wood.

"It's not enough."

She turned to Fiadh. "I know."

Distant screams and battle cries drifted on the wind, carried with ash and smoke. Above them, the Sluagh, having abandoned Fiadh's command to scare, not kill, dove into the trees, snatching soldiers before launching into the air and dropping them. Their bodies hit the ground in terrible, random thumps, each twisting her heart, eating away at her insides. Someone's son. Someone's brother. If any of them found her, they would kill her. She knew this, and yet, it still felt wrong.

"Your people look to you, Fiadh. You must be strong for them."

Fiadh stared at her with haunted eyes. "How do I do that?" She made a strangled sound. "Danu has left me. I can no longer hear her." Her face contorted. "I have something that was not mine to take, and I think… I think I must give it back."

"That power is the only thing that keeps us from what is coming. If you surrender it, you doom us all."

"If I keep it, we are doomed already."

Kaelari sighed. "You have no head for war. The enemy is out there!" She flung her arm to Dorcha Wood. "If Rygeil does not kill you, the king's men surely will. And with you, go us all. Every piece of this place, every living thing, will be at the mercy of those who seek to exploit or destroy it. You cannot let that happen!"

Fiadh got to her feet. "I won't. But I can no longer keep what was stolen. Send Heiren to the pool of still waters."

"Fiadh! Don't do this!" Kaelari yelled, balling her hands into fists.

She kept walking and grabbed Meara's mane to haul herself onto her back. Looking down into Kaelari's fuming face, she said, "This is the only way."

Meara lunged into the forest, Fiadh clinging low on her back. The water reflected the dark sky as she slid to the ground and came toward the pool. Shame mixed with anger made her muscles tremble as she lowered herself to the edge.

With a voice that shook, she said, "Eradar."

Many moments passed, the surface still and inviting. Behind her, Krulan stood, ready to grab her leg should she be pulled in. She leaned closer to the water, earning a low growl. Fiadh ignored him and whispered Eradar's name again, watching as the word traveled across the surface in tiny currents.

He rose slowly, head breaking the surface until she could see the coldness of his face. His eyes flashed, mouth turned down as he drifted closer, but not close enough to reach for her. "How dare you come here," Eradar hissed.

She took his ire as her due. "I'm sorry Eradar. I did what I felt I had to."

He frowned. "And now you'll die at the hands of men as Ithraen foresaw. I would say that I am sorry for it, but..." He shrugged.

"She cannot tell the future."

"You are a fool."

"So I've been told." She sighed and dipped her hand into the water.

Eradar tracked her movements, wary.

Fiadh closed her eyes and spoke softly under her breath, leaning back onto her heels when her voice faded. "I have given back what I stole."

He studied her, eyes going wide as his power was restored, though it was not as strong as it had been. "Why?"

"Because it was never mine to begin with." Rising, she looked down at Eradar. "I cannot promise that we will keep the armies beyond Erabel from breaching our borders, but I can promise to do what is within my power to shield your people."

At that moment, Heiren broke through the trees with a look of confusion when he saw Fiadh and Eradar. "My lady?"

She turned to him. "I wish for you to create a fortress of stone around this pool so that none can find it."

He nodded and raised his arms, pausing when Eradar spoke.

"You cannot win without my power," he said to Fiadh.

"I cannot win with it."

Eradar swam to the edge, grasping the rocky lip with his fingers. "Forgiveness does not come easy for my kind, but I give you mine. I was wrong to deceive you… to imprison you. My wife and son watch me still, and I would have them look on me with pride."

"Riona and Threa see me as well. I cannot keep what I wrongly took."

He nodded and drifted back to the center of the pool.

Fiadh motioned to Heiren to begin. The earth groaned as he pulled rock from the ground in jagged slabs that grew in height until they resembled an imposing mound among the trees. Surrounding the outside, were sharp points of granite and onyx, deterrents to any who might attempt to scale it and find what it hid at its heart. When the work was done, Fiadh thanked him and placed her palm on the rocky wall.

"You are safe now."

CHAPTER THIRTY-SEVEN

Gideon stood in the shadows and watched Fiadh return to the keep astride her unicorn. She looked so regal sitting atop a creature he'd long ago relegated to fairy tales. It suited her. She slid from her mount, stroking her hands across its head and neck, then sending it off to forage.

She didn't see him as she walked by, and he made no move to alert her of his presence. It was too strange to be here. He was at war with himself. One side shouting at him to avenge his family by slaying all who hid in this small kingdom. The other seeing them as a people struggling to survive, innocent of the atrocities in Belfirth. So, he kept himself apart. Watched. Waited. Relied on instincts that had kept him alive until now.

He looked up, seeing dark smudges of smoke creeping across the sky. It would not be long now. The king's men would finish off Rygeil's fighters and come for this place. At that point, Darragh may finally join the fight and come for

Erabel. For Fiadh. Gideon muttered and clenched his hands, finally stalking from the shelter of the tree he hid beneath and into the great hall.

Fiadh was there, speaking to a handful of her people. He came to an abrupt halt when he saw something move in the shadows beyond the group. They were creatures he'd only heard of in terrifying stories. And they stood just outside the ring of elves, watching him. They were man-wolves, the Faoladh. The reclusive people had arrived in Erabel only hours before when they caught the scent of war on the wind. He tried not to stare at them and failed, finally unlocking his body to move toward the gathering.

Talking ceased when Gideon came into view, faces growing cold and wary. He lifted his chin and said, "There is no time to waste. The king's forces will massacre the last of Rygeil's army, their numbers eclipse his, and when they are done, they will lay siege to this place from the north. If Darragh's army joins them from the south, you'll be trapped."

Separating herself from the others, Fiadh came to him, stopping when she had closed the distance and folding her hands. "Why are you here giving me counsel?"

Gideon wanted to look away. He yearned to scream at her that she didn't deserve his counsel, that she and every member of her race should die under his blade. That it would be a fair sacrifice for the death of his family and his people. But the moment the thought bloomed to vivid life, he felt ashamed. Aishling's face took its place. Her purity and innocence in the midst of so much savagery. What would she think of a man who slaughtered an entire people? Would she look on him with pride? Or with horror?

"I don't know why I feel compelled to help you, but I'm here, and it is within my power to aid you and your people."

"Tell me why I should trust you."

"You shouldn't." He looked away. "I have earned nothing but your scorn. And you have earned mine."

She lifted her chin, eyes growing cold.

"But, when I saw you taken, something… changed. I can't explain it. I know it had been there for a while, a growing resentment for what I allowed myself to be part of." Gideon stared at Krulan, who lay like a massive bear on the floor, watching him. "What Darragh's men did to your…" He lifted his hands, not knowing how to phrase it.

"His mate," Fiadh snapped.

Eyes going round, he glanced between her and Krulan. "I didn't know. I suspected, but I…" He shook his head and looked at Krulan. "I knew she was the mate of one of your kind. In the end, it mattered not which one."

A tooth flashed in Krulan's muzzle.

"He would like to rip out your throat, and he would not be unjustified in doing so."

Gideon scowled. "We each have people we would like to avenge. But, what then? When they are all *dead*, what does it solve?"

She pursed her lips. "It solves nothing."

He let out a gush of air and hung his head. "If I wanted to kill you, I would've done it."

"You would've tried, as you had threatened to do when you turned your back on me."

"I recall you telling me the same," he said, looking up from beneath his brow.

"So I did. And here we are."

"Fiadh." He swallowed hard. "You have no reason to trust me, nor I you. But it has to begin somewhere. Why not here?"

Moments passed with only the soft rustling of shifting bodies and the faint sounds of battle in the distance. "Go on."

"My people are superstitious." He flicked an eye to the Faoladh. "Many of the king's soldiers are likely young and fresh from training. They believe they will overwhelm the Aos Sí with sheer numbers alone, and they could if you let them."

"What are you saying? That we can win against so many?"

"You can… if they flee."

They sat down at a table, Gideon alone on one side with Aos Sí facing him. It was an awkward gathering, filled with the cautious glances of a tenuous alliance. His proposition was simple. Terrify the soldiers with shows of magic and the creatures of Erabel. Show them the power elves wield over the elements. With luck, the majority would retreat, leaving only the staunchest soldiers who could then be subdued.

It was a desperate plan.

Fiadh left the hall, cradling Dasha, and went to her room, gazing sadly at the rumpled bedding. She touched the pillow. Dasha croaked softly and pressed his head to her chest. She set the raven down and picked it up, pressing it to her face to inhale Veren's lingering scent, and let grief take her. Sobs shook her body, muffled by the pillow. When the worst of it was over, Fiadh wiped her eyes and gently set it on the bed, pressing her hand to its softness like a lover.

Turning, she left the room and went to the massive oak, the embodiment of Danu. There was an orange hue to the sky, the flames consuming Dorcha Wood having grown over the hours. She walked to the tree, kneeled, and laid her hands against the bark. Words spilled from her lips, nonsensical at first, just expressions of sadness, anger, and longing. They became something more as she kept talking, speaking to the Great Mother as if she spoke to Threa and Riona. They were one and the same.

A sound interrupted her, and she looked around to find Kaelari, Arel, Heiren, Riani, and the others entering the courtyard. They fanned out in a series of circles around the oak, the first wrapping themselves around the base with Fiadh. Linking hands and kneeling, they gave themselves over to Danu, greeting their mother and pouring their energy into her. Gideon watched it all, not understanding any of it, but somehow knowing what it meant.

The Great Mother writhed in the earth as their energy sank into the ground, spreading like the roots of a tree. She stilled, listening to her children, drawn by their voices and love. Wounds, brought on by the dark magic Rygeil and Fiadh had wielded, began to heal, leaving scars that would remain until the end of time. There were others there too, old scars from many peoples who had turned their back on the goddess. So it would always be.

Voices rose, blending together into a song that called to Danu, drawing her from her place of refuge. She reached for it, for all of them, absorbing their energy and giving it back tenfold.

As elven voices faded to silence, Fiadh opened her eyes and felt the gentle kiss of the Great Mother. *Daughter, you have come back to me.*

Mother, I never should have left. Forgive me.

All is forgiven. All.

Fiadh smiled, a lone tear slipping down her cheek. She bowed her head in thanks and stood, the power of Danu once again flowing through her.

Turning to Gideon, she said. "I am ready."

CHAPTER THIRTY-EIGHT

Night fell as Crom Cruach sat before the scrying bowl, watching the battle unfold, seeing Darragh's army held back and ready while the king's hunted down Rygeil's warriors amidst the flames of a burning wood. He cackled as Sluagh joined the fray, shrieking across the sky and diving into the melee, slicing through men like a scythe through wheat. And, when Rygeil and his paltry band of soldiers were dead or fleeing, both armies of men would join and march on Erabel, erasing that elven stronghold from the world.

Fiadh winked in and out of his sight, and he wondered at it, having felt her power, stronger and darker than any he had known in her kind. She felt different now, as though she had let go of the darkness she'd wielded. Foolish. If she had held onto it, she may have been able to save her people.

Soldiers, in numbers that dwarfed the Aos Sí, would break through the barriers protecting Erabel with their weapons of war. Danu was weak and would not be able to stop them. Perhaps, he brooded, he should stay and watch it all unfold, take the girl for his own. Muttering, he decided to let Darragh have Rygeil's spawn. She would bleed as well as any who fell under the blade. With her gone, none would remain whose power could rival his own.

A hand batted at his leg. He smacked it away distractedly and yanked on the other arm, holding Haegna's wrist to his mouth and sucking blood that had already begun to slow.

"Such sweet delights," he purred, feeling Carmun's power with every pull of his mouth.

Haegna whimpered and thrashed, calling weakly to Emer, who lay against the wall in a contorted heap.

He released his hold and licked his lips, smacking them loudly as he collected every drop. Gazing down at Haegna, he asked, "What promises did Dothur give you, old woman? What lies?"

She gurgled, rheumy eyes gone glassy.

"Did he promise youth? Power? Riches?" He tsked. "You were but a tool, sweetling. A lure."

He stood over her, stretching his humped back to his full height. Her eyes went wide as he flashed a grin and lifted his foot, slamming it down and cracking her skull upon the stone floor.

Crom Cruach left as Haegna's blood pooled, leaving her cell door open for any to find her. No doubt, Darragh would sense she was dead. Though Carmun's blood was thin in his veins, the connection was there. If he had been allowed to follow in his mother's footsteps, power would have been his to claim. As it was, she had hoarded her dark magic, dooming her son even as she sought to viciously carve out his place in the world. If he survived the battle, he may be of use and, if not, there were a thousand more who would vie to take his place.

He trailed his fingers along the damp wall, ragged nails scraping the stone. The chaos raging across Dorcha Wood was but a prelude of what would come. Carmun's son had great power, though he had not been strong enough to evade the Sight of the Aos Sí's most powerful seer. It was Zaeleria who had hunted Dothur down when he was weak, the foul witch. She had done it with old magic, forgotten magic, imprisoning Dothur in a ball of iron with spells born of Danu from the dawn of the Aos Sí.

But magic had rules—especially old magic. And Rygeil had broken those rules, his actions inadvertently weakening Dothur's cage as he turned his back on the Great Mother. Fiadh had unwittingly broken them too. He gave a sickening laugh that bounced off the dank walls of the dungeon. *To think, a pure one has fallen so far,* he mused.

Leaving the castle, he sniffed air heavy with smoke, and spun in a slow circle, eyes unerringly finding the one who awaited him. Xander came from the shadows and bowed low.

"Are you ready to join my master?"

He smirked. "And what does your master promise in return for my aid?"

"Whatever you wish, my lord."

"He may regret that offering." Falling into step beside Xander, the pair made their way to Malver Gorge, where Dothur waited, rattling the iron bars of his cage, tasting freedom and vengeance on the wind.

CHAPTER THIRTY-NINE

Creatures of every type poured out of Erabel in a flurry of feet, wings, hooves, and claws. They ran on two legs or four, rending the air with roars and shrieks—fairy tales and nightmares come to life. Both armies paused, ears trained to the sound of a thousand bodies crashing through the forest or screaming from the night sky.

Fiadh led them all astride Meara. She rode like the goddess of war, Morrígan. Arms raised and thighs hugging Meara's flanks, she called out to the wind and rain, which answered in huge gusts and torrents of water, dousing the flames that threatened to burn every living thing. Dorcha Wood stirred, wounded, struggling to release the darkness that had consumed it, but rallying to her.

Men shouted to each other through the pounding rain and roaring wind, gathering in clusters to regroup, uncertainty and exhaustion in every face. While the commander of the king's army rode just beyond the tree line, ordering those who began to flee to charge back into the woods and slay the enemy. Fear, palpable and infectious, strangled men's wills to fight as they saw what came for them.

Bands of Púca took the forms of wolves and wild cats, eyes glowing violet. While the gruagach, little people who lived throughout Erabel, left their groves and rode on the backs of hawks and owls, tiny spears in their fists. The Cù-Sìth ran among them, massive paws eating up the ground in thunderous strides as they tore through the underbrush, their greenish bodies nothing but hulking shadows in the dimness.

But it was the howls of man-wolves, the Faoladh, that provoked terror in the king's army. They slunk through the trees, running like men, though their faces and forms were that of wolves. Eyes glowing in the darkness, they broke off into pairs, claw-like hands and sharp fangs their only weapons.

Men saw monsters when they spied what came for them, and they ran, blindly charging through the trees, voices raised in fearful cries. They were easy pickings for what remained of Rygeil's army, leaping from the trees and spinning in the air with blades gleaming, cutting soldiers down before their feet touched the ground.

Gideon, riding on the back of Fionn—a huge white buck with antlers that spanned one and a half men—kept Fiadh in his sights. The animal displayed an intelligence that had startled Gideon when Fiadh had whistled shrilly, calling him to her hand. He had studied Gideon in his violet gaze, finally kneeling to allow him to mount his broad back. Clinging to the buck's neck, as the forest passed by in a chaotic blur, he kept his eyes on a woman who had been a shy girl when they had met.

Now, she was a warrior. Strong. Brave. Time and hardship made her a stranger, but within her hard eyes, he had seen glimpses of who she had been. Perhaps, she would let him know her again. If they survived this. If they could put the ghosts of their past behind them.

Looking up, he saw a dark shape circling. "Fiadh!"

She slowed Meara and craned her neck. Gideon pointed, and she tracked his hand, picking out what he had seen among the roiling clouds and rain.

The Sluagh hunted the king's soldiers, slaking their bloodlust in the lives they took as men tried to outrun them. Troya sailed past, her laughter sending chills down the spines of those who heard.

"Troya!" Fiadh screamed. "Stop!"

"You have no power over me, young one," the Sluagh shouted. "We are the Hunt, and now, we reclaim the skies!" With that, she banked to the right and plunged into the trees, where frantic screams followed.

Fiadh gripped Meara's mane to keep the animal calm, then turned to Gideon. "We have to stop them!"

"How?"

Her head swung to the sounds of slaughter. "I don't know, but I have to try!"

Fiadh whispered to Meara, who took off, veering to the left around the trunk of a tree whose limbs swayed as though it sought to caress her as she passed. Gone were their dagger-like limbs, replaced by the soft green of new leaves.

Gideon spoke to Fionn, feeling foolish in doing so, but unsurprised when the buck took off after Fiadh.

Kaelari and Riani bolted past as he rode, and he lost sight of Fiadh in the dense foliage. Coming to a stop, he followed the path the two elves had taken and gritted his teeth, seeing them engaged with a handful of the king's soldiers. Torn, he looked to where Fiadh had disappeared then back at her people. Growling in frustration, he leaped off Fionn's back and charged after them.

His battle cry had the soldiers grinning until they realized he had not come to aid them. He and the two Aos Sí worked together, disarming the men. They backed away as the three advanced.

"Kneel," Kaelari commanded.

One, a grizzled fighter with a thick beard and deep scar on his cheek, spat at the elf. "I do not kneel for Aos Sí scum."

Stepping forward, Gideon held his sword to the man's neck. "I suggest you do what she commands." The others sank to their knees. Pressing the tip of his blade to the man's throat where a drop of blood formed, Gideon said, "Kneel."

"You're a traitor to your race!"

Kaelari stalked to the man and swung her arm, knocking him out with the hilt of her sword. Catching the other soldiers in a hard stare, she said, "Leave these woods."

They grabbed the arms of their fallen comrade and left, dragging his unconscious form behind them.

Kaelari studied Gideon. "You have earned my trust. Now, you must keep it."

Nodding, he sheathed his blade, and the three set out in search of others.

Rygeil emerged from a copse of ancient oaks, having tried to use their sacred power to heal his wound. *Damn, Calum!* he thought, limping through the forest. The magic Fiadh's twin had permeated the blade with was powerful and taking its toll. But he was not beaten. Fiadh was close. He could feel it. If he could capture her, bind her, he could take what was hers and replenish his strength. Rygeil tapped at the minds of the remnants of his army, glowering at their dwindling numbers, and ordered them to rally to him. They raced through the trees, blending with the foliage as they dodged and slew men—the renewed strength of Danu fueling their powers—and found their king.

"The children of men believe they can best us with steel and numbers. Never have we cowered before the weapons of man!" he shouted, sweeping his gaze to catch every eye. "We will not begin today!" Rygeil paused and listened to the sudden barrage of shouts that filled the forest. "We fight two enemies and I will not accept defeat. Find Fiadh and bring her to me. Kill any who protect her."

Roars rolled across the wood. They bounded to their feet and raced into the forest, branching off in groups of three or four, two remaining at Rygeil's side to act as his guard.

The creatures of Erabel had taken their toll as the king's army fractured, losing their way amidst the smoke, wind, and rain while others fled the forest. The Sluagh, beaten back by Fiadh as she shielded a group of men from their fury with powerful blasts of magic, left with ghostly wails and promises that they would return, once again riding the skies as the Hunt.

Rygeil's fighters took advantage of those seeking to escape Dorcha Wood, springing from the forest like wraiths and cutting them down. Their haphazard path through the forest led them to Fiadh, who saw them coming and yanked Meara around, sending the unicorn straight for them. They jumped out of the way, too shocked to do more than watch her scream past.

Wheeling around, Meara pranced in a circle, then reared, hooves slashing the air. "Why do you fight?" Fiadh shouted. "You are my brothers and sisters!"

One stepped forward, yelling above the din. "We serve the king, not his usurper!"

Fiadh shook her head. "You serve an impostor who turned his back on our Great Mother."

Krulan prowled around the three, growling low in his chest and snapping his teeth.

They glared at her, eyes darting to her side, going wide when they saw Kaelari, Riani, and Gideon coming toward them.

"Faraen?" Riani asked.

His sword wobbled.

"Faraen, this is not the way."

Panic washed over his face as the two at his sides began to mutter.

Riani held up her hands, ignoring Kaelari's hiss as she stepped forward. "Please, we have a common enemy."

"*She* is the enemy," a dusky female spat.

"Nay. Fiadh is not your enemy, Nivaere."

"Riani," Faraen said, "What have you done?"

She lifted her chin. "What is right."

He shook his head in disbelief. "He'll kill you."

Riani's eyes pleaded with him.

"You tell us we have a common enemy, but I see the enemy standing with you." Nivaere leveled a finger at Gideon. "What are we to think but that you stand against us and are aligned with the children of men!"

"Our enemy is not the whole of mankind," Fiadh said, sliding off Meara. Without looking at Gideon, she walked toward Rygeil's soldiers. "We fight to protect our home, but that fight doesn't mean we have to spill blood. Look around you. They are fleeing in the face of our power. There is no need to chase them down and slaughter them."

Nivaere sneered and whipped her blade from its sheath, pausing with shock when she felt the tip of Gideon's sword at her throat. "Do it!" she yelled at him. "Your kind are no better than mindless beasts!"

Gideon said nothing, only glanced at Fiadh, who cocked her head. "If that were true, you'd be dead. This man fights at my side because—"

"I can no longer imagine a world without you," he whispered.

Pain flashed across Fiadh's face. There was so much darkness in their history. "There is another way, Nivaere," Fiadh pleaded.

"I would rather die than betray my king!" she yelled.

Riani sighed, gripping her blade tighter. Seeing this, Fiadh strode forward and took the elf's sword, walloping Nivaere in the head with the hilt and sending her crashing to the ground. Faraen looked at her, then back at Riani, taking a step away as she faced him.

"Will you follow in her path too?" she asked.

He glanced from one to the other, then at Fiadh and Gideon.

"Faraen, you saw what Rygeil has become, what he unleashed. Is that who you wish to fight for?" Riani asked.

There was a moment of indecision, then his shoulders sagged. "I don't know another life, but under his rule." He looked up and found Fiadh. "My arm is yours."

She watched him slowly go to his knees at her feet. "You will not kill men or elves," Fiadh commanded.

He nodded and looked at the quiet male standing next to him. "Iefyr?"

Iefyr glanced at Nivaere's unconscious form, then knelt next to Faraen and bowed his head.

Fiadh shifted uncomfortably as she looked at their kneeling forms.

They bow to their queen, Krulan told her.

She swallowed hard. *I don't know how to be that.*

You will learn.

"Rygeil is still a threat," Riani said, breaking the silence.

"I know."

The two elves before Fiadh got to their feet and stood next to Riani. They answered questions Kaelari posed about Rygeil's whereabouts, and it was decided to let him take the tatters of his army back to Oadsera. If he was cowed by this defeat it would give them time to plan how to bring their two realms together in peace. If peace were possible.

Fiadh, wanting to end the fighting in Dorcha Wood, suggested they split up when a group of Darragh's men burst through the trees, having finally joined the battle to finish off what was left of Rygeil's army. When they spied the elves, they rent the air with battle cries and charged. Gideon hesitated for only a moment as he saw faces he recognized, then let his training take over, the skills he had honed with his father and brother. As he swung his blade, he heard his father's firm voice telling him when to dodge and strike, heard his brother fighting beside him, and when Faraen yelled back-to-back, he did not falter. Pressed together they fended off Darragh's men, eventually disarming them, until there was nothing more to swing at.

It was over quickly, though each realized this was a lull as the forest still swarmed with soldiers. Not wishing to waste time, Gideon went from man to man, striking blows to their heads and watching them fall to the ground. He stopped when he got the last one, a young soldier who looked up at him with hate and fear.

"Where is Quinn and the rest of my men?"

He shook his head. "I don't speak to traitors."

Gideon sighed and crouched in front of the soldier. "These people you call your enemy have spared your life. Now, I ask you again, where is Quinn and my men?"

The soldier frowned, eyes darting to the elves and Cù-Sìth surrounding them. "At the keep. Donal sent them back to man the wall walk in case any elves attacked the castle."

Muttering a prayer of thanks, Gideon stood and swung the hilt of his sword, knocking the soldier out.

Krulan ordered two members of his pack to drag their unconscious forms from the woods. Gideon found Fiadh watching him, the look in her eyes making him stand a little taller. Krulan brushed by, almost knocking him off-balance, and went to his mistress.

She looked up into his yellow eyes. "I am well, just tired."

Low rumbling shook his chest as Gideon watched the exchange.

"You may be right, but I won't leave until the fighting stops."

Krulan snarled.

"That is the third time someone's called me a fool!" she snapped, glaring at the Cù-Sìth.

Gideon gave a startled laugh, and her eyes flashed at him.

Grumbling, Fiadh grasped the Cù-Sìth's shoulder and made her way to Meara, who stood tossing her head and stamping her hooves. When she was atop the unicorn, she raised her arms, lips moving, though Gideon heard no sound. The wind died down, rain turning to mist, then to nothing. Dropping her arms, she closed her eyes and listened.

Dorcha Wood echoed with the sounds of battle: the ring of metal, the screams of the dying, and the roars of fighting. She looked weary to Gideon's eyes, as if all the killing was draining her in some way, and as he studied her, he began to wonder if that was exactly what he was seeing. The Great

Mother was life itself. How could war not hurt her? And if Fiadh's connection was with the goddess, she must feel that death too, and it must hurt.

Krulan growled loudly.

"I will do no such thing, and you can stop asking," she said to him.

Gideon caught the roll of the Cù-Sìth's eye and the snarl that followed. "What's he saying?"

Fiadh mashed her lips. "He says I should return to Erabel. That I grow weak."

The Cù-Sìth huffed.

Looking at the massive animal, then back at Fiadh, Gideon said, "Perhaps, he's right. The toll all of this is taking is plain to see."

"As long as I have the strength, I will fight for Danu's children. All of them," she looked meaningfully at Gideon. "I owe her that much. We all do."

His mouth pressed into a thin line. "I see that you are still stubborn."

She lifted her chin.

"Could you call to Fionn?" Gideon asked. "I am honest enough to admit my legs are weary, and I'd prefer his strong back."

Fiadh smirked and called out to the buck who came silently among them minutes later.

Together, they made their way toward the thick of the fighting. Gideon swept his eyes around their band of fighters, marveling that he was among them. The ghosts of his family grew quiet as he gripped his sword and watched Fiadh, acknowledging that he'd follow her anywhere.

CHAPTER FORTY

*D*arragh watched what was left of the king's army pour out of the woods, strange beasts at their heels. His men scattered or were dragged from the forest by nightmarish creatures, left outside the border of that accursed place like refuse. He glared balefully at Dorcha Wood. It smoldered, yet breathed. Thousands of men had not been able to force that elven witch from its womb.

He would need the armies of every realm to bring it down, and the realization galled him. Barking an order to retreat, he swung onto his horse, yanking on the reins when he spotted a man-wolf hauling one of his soldiers out of the forest. The Faoladh fixed Darragh in his yellow gaze, smelling his fear and flashing a smile of pointed teeth before disappearing into the trees. Kicking the flanks of his mount, Darragh galloped for the safety of Felmore's walls.

From the trees, Fiadh and her party watched him go. He was not beaten, only wounded, and a wounded animal was more dangerous. But she refused to risk any lives to pursue him.

Turning Meara away from Darragh's retreating form, Fiadh came face-to-face with Rygeil. He melted from the forest, a dozen of his warriors at his sides. Scanning the faces around her, his gaze fell on Kaelari, Riani, and the two others who'd bent the knee to Fiadh.

Lip curling, he sneered, "You have traitors in your midst."

"You are the traitor," Fiadh said coldly.

"I?" Rygeil chuckled, the sound spasming into a cough. He looked unwell. "You do not see a child of man at my side, granddaughter."

Fiadh's eyes darted to Gideon.

"Have you seen into his heart? Felt the hate that hides there?"

She frowned. "Danu let him pass through our barrier while you cannot. That says all I need to know about his heart."

"The Great Mother is weak and has been fooled," he said, scowling. "Don't follow in her footsteps. Read his mind. I know you can. It is a gift passed down to you from me."

As Fiadh glared at him, she felt a soft fluttering in her mind, like the wings of a butterfly, only more sinister. Throwing up a mental shield, she spoke to Krulan. *He is using his power. Be ready.*

I am with you.

Pretending not to notice Rygeil's subtle attack on her senses, she said, "I would ask what's in *your* heart. I'd wager your hate burns brighter than his."

Rygeil looked at her coldly and lunged at her with his mind, battering hers as he called upon the earth and wind to rumble and howl. Meara reared, and Krulan leaped. All around her, the ring of steel filled the air, but she kept her eyes on her grandfather.

"You killed my brother!" she yelled. "For that, you should die, but I'm not going to kill you. I won't become what you are."

"You are weak. Had I known, I would have come for you long ago."

He muttered a spell and came at her. Fiadh sprang from Meara's back, landing on the balls of her feet. Bracing her legs, she whipped her hands in the air, creating a vortex of wind that she threw at him, watching as he was forced back. She saw his fingers mold tiny bolts of lightning, but his magic was weakening. The spell from Calum's blade when he'd pierced his side leaching into his body of power. Glancing at his face, Fiadh noticed a sheen of sweat on his brow and a waxen look in his cheeks. His energy was waning.

When the ball of electricity hurled toward her, she doused it with a shower of water. "Leave this place. Go back to Oadsera," she told him.

He faltered, struggling to call upon his depleted magic. *How has it come to this?* he thought frantically. *My army is defeated. Calum is dead.* In desperation, he grabbed his sword and charged, vowing to end his line—to kill Fiadh's vile wish of peace between men and elves.

She watched his glowing blade swinging toward her and felt Gideon. Time seemed to stop as her eyes swept to his and locked, just for a moment, before he broke the connection and threw himself in front of her. Deflecting Rygeil's blow, Gideon spun his blade and lashed out, a master of the weapons of mankind. Rygeil's sword fell to the ground.

He staggered back, but Gideon kept coming, leading him right into Riani. Metal stabbed through his neck, jutting grotesquely from his throat. She ripped it out and watched her king fall to the ground. The fighting stopped then, and an unnatural quiet enveloped the swath of forest in which they stood.

Fiadh made a strangled sound, hands fisting at her sides.

"I couldn't let him live," Riani whispered. "I couldn't."

Faraen put his arm around the elf's shoulders and drew her away.

Krulan brushed against Fiadh as she looked down at the cooling body of her grandfather.

I am sorry, young one.

"I am not your enemy," she whispered. "Neither is the whole of mankind." Rygeil's remaining fighters lowered their weapons. "You are free to leave," she said to them. "Return to Oadsera and tell our people that I do not seek a war with them. What I want is infinitely greater." She sighed. "So much killing. So much death. For what? Who won today?"

Fiadh looked up, marking those who had begun to grumble.

Meara bumped her gently, and she climbed onto her back, grateful for the aid Gideon gave as she struggled. "Peace is not a road easily traveled, but I welcome any who wish to walk it with me."

CHAPTER FORTY-ONE

Gideon found Fiadh at the graves of Calum and Rygeil. Bowing her head, she spoke to them of forgiveness and understanding, wishing things had been different. With a pass of her hand, she left their tombs and went to Veren's. Even from a distance, he heard her breath catch followed by a gentle sob. He watched as she placed a flower on Veren's grave, kneeling to press her cheek to the cool stone that cradled his body. She spoke softly, her words caught in the breeze and taken away. It was a private thing, but he couldn't leave just yet. Something in him was drawn to her, recognizing her grief as his own.

Reaching her arms around the head of the tomb, her body shook as she cried. Gideon looked away, heart aching to see her in pain, knowing he was not the one she would turn to as she sought to ease it. Krulan stepped silently to his side, the brush of his fur tickling his arm as the beast's yellow stare fixed on his mistress.

"She needs you," Gideon whispered.

Krulan dipped his head and rumbled low and quiet in his chest. He went to Fiadh, pressing the warmth of his body against hers. Gideon watched as she turned into her fierce protector, grabbing fistfuls of his fur as she wept. The Cù-Sìth glanced at him, then rested his muzzle on the top of her head, closing his eyes as they spoke to one another in their silent language. Gideon left and made his way to the courtyard outside the great hall.

The sky was clear again, the last of the lingering smoke from Dorcha Wood having finally dissipated. The castle had become a busy place, filled with more of Fiadh's people as those whose loyalty to Rygeil had begun to waver long before the battle, joined her. He'd even been allowed to bring Aridius into Erabel, having snuck onto Felmore's grounds in the wee hours of the morning following the battle to get him. Perhaps, one day Quinn and the others would be allowed to see this place. With Fiadh, all things seemed possible.

He paused and watched Fiadh enter the garden with Krulan. Her eyes looked red, but she was smiling warmly at something the Cù-Sìth said. He watched her hand run idly through Krulan's fur. Seeing the bond between the two of them reminded him of the life he'd helped to take. Krulan's mate. His children. The guilt of it weighed heavily.

Fiadh's face reflected a myriad of emotions when she spied Gideon. There was joy, but it was marred with grief and wariness. She kept her distance, and he respected that boundary, never pushing her too hard, only standing in the wings, ready when she needed him.

Krulan's yellow stare held him, and he watched the Cù-

Sìth walk past with a tilt of his head. He disappeared into the forest moments later, where another of his kind waited for him, the softer hues of her pelt blending with the trees.

Fiadh sat next to him. While Dasha, still weak from his injury, perched nearby, croaking softly. Bending down, Gideon plucked the long stem of a weedy flower and twined it around his fingers distractedly, gathering more that brushed his boots.

"Do you think it's over?" Fiadh asked quietly.

Gideon didn't need to ask what she meant. The drums of war had faded, but they weren't gone. "Not yet."

She nodded and looked into the trees. "So much has changed. Once again, I don't recognize my life."

"Nor do I."

His hands kept moving, and she listened to the soft whispers of his fingers. "You've changed."

"So have you." He paused and looked at her. "I cannot undo what I've done, but I can admit my wrongs. I have much to atone for."

"We all do."

For a while, there was only the sound of his hands fiddling with thin stalks of flowers. Fiadh reached out with her senses and touched the myriad of life that abounded in Erabel, then let her mind wander beyond her borders and into Dorcha Wood. Riona still lived there, her memory stamped into the forest itself as if she were part of it, and that is where Fiadh went to find her, to recall her voice and hear her words. She had always been the best of them, seeing goodness in everyone. Threa was there too, her strength was a part of Fiadh that she could now recognize.

Two mothers. Fiadh aspired to be like each of them. In that way, she embraced who she really was—the duality of her being. Danu, the mother of all things, would guide her.

Quiet fell like a blanket, and Fiadh turned toward Gideon, feeling him watching her. He smiled, the expression tinged with sadness and hope, and lifted his arms, placing a crown of flowers upon her head.

EPILOGUE

Zaeleria, the most powerful seer of the Aos Sí, stared into the still water of the cauldron at her feet, her mind fixed on events that had transpired as they had long been foretold. Calum. Fiadh. Rygeil. Such twisted lives. Intertwined, yet separate in their dreams for the future. There had been so much rage and sorrow in Threa's twins that her eyes stung as she watched tragic events unfold. Now, there was only one. Zaeleria hoped that Fiadh was ready to face a greater challenge when the time came.

Following the Great War, she had hied herself to the Scarlet Mountains, needing the solitude, reaching out to other seers rarely to share only those tidings which would give her people hope as they faced periods in their history, so dark and perilous, they would eclipse the horrors of the past. They had to have hope. Without it, the darkness that Rygeil had summoned would swallow the light of the Aos Sí. And when that light was extinguished, so Danu would be as well.

Turning away from that bleak possibility, Zaeleria shifted back to Fiadh. She was, even now, gaining strength, taught by those who knew the ways of war and would fight for her. Even the man who had wounded her when she was young and innocent, now stood at her side. She smiled as she watched the young female begin to understand the depth of the power that Danu had bestowed and what that power truly meant. The daughter of Erabel was stronger than she knew.

Scanning the castle beyond the borders of Dorcha Wood, she watched as a sinister ruler brooded and planned for his next move. It was power he craved, that much was obvious, but there was also a darkness that lingered around him like a shadow. His was a future she could not foresee, clouded in turmoil. The lives of man had always been unpredictable.

"Fickle beings," she muttered.

Drawing her sight to Fiadh, she watched as Kaelari passed along years of wisdom and skill, while Veren's touch and insight lived on in Fiadh and always would. His had been a warrior's heart, tempered by the purity of Danu's chosen. Fiadh would carry his loss for the rest of her days.

Hands, that had only recently begun to show the centuries of her life, gripped the edge, thumbs brushing the liquid and sending a slow ripple crawling across the surface. It was within the folds of the water that she caught a glimpse of a darker force, one that had lain hidden, waiting. Zaeleria sucked in a breath, her violet eyes growing wide.

"Dothur," she whispered, watching in horror as the vile being turned his head, freed from his iron prison, and stared back at her from the abyss, the shadowy figure of Crom Cruach by his side.

"You should not have looked this way, Zaeleria."

She sat, immobile, straining to rip herself from the evil that held her rigid and helpless. Dothur's power stabbed into her mind, flaying it open, shredding her will as he ruthlessly tore every thought and memory, every prophecy and warning. Blood ran from her nose, dripping into the water where it mixed with the lives reflected there.

Zaeleria whimpered, using the last of her strength to try and wrench free of the evil spawn of Carmun, but he had grown so powerful with his alliance with the old god. Too powerful.

With a grin of jagged teeth in his pale, alien face, he whispered, "Your prophecies die with you."

Her hands went slack as she slumped, striking her head on the ground. Mouth gaping open and closed, she summoned her familiar, a snowy owl who alighted on the ground at her face. Clacking its beak in distress, it preened Zaeleria's hair as she sent desperate thoughts into the bird's mind.

Fly. Fly to Erabel. Dothur... has been freed.

A faint sigh parted her lips, carrying her strength with it. She closed her eyes and let go. Danu cradled her prone form in her insubstantial arms, pressing it to her breast. The bird watched, seeing the Great Mother as his mistress had taught him. She smiled at the owl, passing along reassurances. With a soft hoot, he spread his wings and took to the sky, banking west toward Erabel. To Fiadh. To warn her of what was coming.

Fiadh's story concludes in Legion of Shadows

AFTERWORD

Unicorns are prevalent in mythologies worldwide, and Celtic culture is no exception. These creatures are known to be independent and challenging to capture. Most stories portray unicorns as white with spiral horns. I wanted to consider these beautiful animals as powerful elven warhorses. As such, my vision was one of incredible strength and loyalty.

Interestingly, the unicorn is Scotland's national animal. So yes, this is yet another example of why Scotland is amazing!

The Faoladh in Irish legends differ greatly from were-wolves in other cultures. Rather than bloodthirsty man-killers, the Faoladh were good and often referred to as protectors in Irish tales. Before medieval times, wolves were common in Ireland. Sadly, they were hunted to extinction by 1786. However, their history in Irish lore had already been established, and they remain in some form in many stories.

An each-uisce (ech-ishka), or water horse, is a dark creature from Irish lore. Much like a Kelpie, they lure people from the shore and drown them in the water. In some legends, it is said that they can shape-shift to better entice their victims.

Each book in the *Daughter of Erabel* series features unique Celtic knotwork. In *A Storm of Wrath & Ruin*, you see the Shield knot. The knot itself symbolizes protection and the warding off of evil spirits. Celts used shield knots in the form of amulets that were worn to protect the wearer. Another interpretation of the shield knot is that it is a symbol of eternal love and unity. Like many Celtic knots, it has no beginning and no end.

ACKNOWLEDGMENTS

A Storm of Wrath & Ruin began immediately following the completion of *Blood of the Lost Kingdom* and then quickly stalled. Weeks passed with little or no writing, and then NaNoWriMo came along! For those who are unfamiliar with this term. It is a month-long writing sprint during which participants strive to write fifty thousand words in November. It is a daunting task for someone like myself, who has a full-time job and family. But, I am a procrastinator at heart—I believe most writers share this trait—and the madness of NaNoWriMo kicked my butt into high gear. My wonderful husband and sons saw me planted in my writing chair for hours after work and every weekend. They left me alone when needed, cheered me on when I faltered and gave me the strength to finish what I'd started. For the first time, I met the goal of fifty thousand words in thirty days!

And thus, the first draft of A Storm of Wrath & Ruin was born!

As with any piece of writing, draft one is the starting point, and it takes a keen mind to read it and make it better. Cue my editor: David Taylor. I would never attempt to write a book without him!

And speaking of those who are essential in my author journey, I must give heartfelt thanks to my cover designer,

JD. He amazes me, and I am so blessed to have his keen artist's eye bringing my ideas to vibrant life!

And, to you, dear reader, I give my final thanks. You are part of my journey, and I'm so thankful to have you along for the ride!

ABOUT THE AUTHOR

Kristin Ward is an award-winning young adult author living in Connecticut. A science and math teacher for over twenty years, she infuses her geeky passions into stories that meld realism and fantasy. Kristin embraces her inner nerd regularly, often quoting 80s movies while expecting those around her to chime in with appropriate rejoinders. As a nature freak, she can be found wandering the woods or chilling in her yard with all manner of furry and feathered friends.

She is often referred to as a unicorn by colleagues who remain in awe of her ability to create or find various and sundry things in mere moments. In reality, the horn was removed years ago, leaving only a mild imprint that can be seen if she tilts her head just right. A lifelong lover of books and writing, she dreamed of becoming an author for thirty years before publishing her award-winning debut in 2018.

Her first novel, **After the Green Withered**, is one of many things you should probably read.

~www.kristinwardauthor.com~